Crackling Mountain
and Other Stories

Crackling Mountain
and Other Stories

by
Osamu Dazai

Translated by James O'Brien

Peter Owen · London

PETER OWEN PUBLISHERS
73 Kenway Road London SW5 0RE

First published in Great Britain 1990
English translation © 1989 by Charles E. Tuttle Co., Inc.

British Library Cataloguing in Publication Data
Dazai, Osamu, *1909–1948*
   Crackling Mountain and other stories
   I. Title
   895.634[F]

   ISBN 0–7206–0793–0

Printed in Great Britain by Billings of Worcester

Contents

Acknowledgments 7

Introduction 9

Memories 17

Undine 68

Monkey Island 80

Heed My Plea 91

Melos, Run! 110

On the Question of Apparel 127

A Poor Man's Got His Pride 147

The Monkey's Mound 164

The Sound of Hammering 179

Taking the Wen Away 199

Crackling Mountain 219

Notes 249

Acknowledgments

Before mentioning my debt to those who helped with the earlier translations, I must thank Wayne Lammers for his advice on several pressing questions. Those who did provide me with thoughtful comments and suggestions on the Cornell East Asia Papers edition of the translations include Marian Ury, J. Thomas Rimer, Royall Tyler, and Brett deBary. John Timothy Wixted and Wesley Palmer also contributed significantly to improving the three tales not included in the Cornell edition. I thank both the editors of the Cornell and Arizona State series for their interest in seeing that these translations reach the wide audience which Dazai's stories and sketches deserve.

The Japan Foundation has been instrumental in this process of translation and revision by awarding me a grant to work on the initial drafts and by providing a subsidy to assist the present publication. The Graduate School of the University of Wisconsin too has facilitated the work by supporting me for four months of research leave. Donald Keene and Howard Hibbett have also lent their much appreciated support. I must also thank Donald Richie for his enthusiastic review of my earlier translations, and for endorsing, along with Professors Keene and

Hibbett, the publication of the translations in this new format.

The revising of these translations has been greatly aided by my two editors. Ken Mori Wong encouraged me to rework earlier translations and made a number of pertinent criticisms, while Stephen Comee supervised the editorial process, especially in its latter stages.

Introduction

I

Osamu Dazai had tried to take his own life on a number of occasions, two of these attempts assuming the form of *jōshi*, the traditional Japanese suicide pact entered into by a pair of lovers. But when he disappeared with his mistress on a rainy night in mid-June of 1948, the signs that he was thoroughly prepared to die were unmistakable. Dazai and his companion, Tomie Yamazaki, left behind a series of farewell notes to friends and kin, the author conscientiously composing a last will and testament for his wife, Michiko. Photographs of Dazai and Tomie stood next to one another in Tomie's lodging in the Tokyo suburb of Mitaka, along with the traditional water offering to the deceased. Also nearby was a small pile of ashes, all that remained of the incense that the lovers had lit before departing.

After the police began an intensive search for the couple's whereabouts, they eventually found a suspicious-looking place along the Tamagawa Canal, midway between Dazai's own home and Tomie's residence. A strip of wet grass lay flattened from the top to the bottom of the bank, as if something heavy had slid down into the water. The ground nearby was strewn with several objects—a small bottle or two, a glass plate, a pair of scissors, and a compact. A little ways downstream, two pairs of wooden clogs were found against the lock of a dam. Despite these ominous signs, an intensive search along the canal failed to turn up anything more. It was almost a week later—on July 19, the author's thirty-ninth birthday—that a passer-by happened to notice two waterlogged corpses in the canal tied together with a red cord. This discovery occurred less than a mile from where the couple had evidently entered the water.

During this period of uncertainty, a few of Dazai's friends reportedly entertained hopes that he was merely in hiding. After all, they could remember those earlier occasions, including the two attempts at *jōshi*, when Dazai had gone away to commit double suicide only to return safe and sound. Perhaps, they reasoned, he would hesitate, or miscalculate, before again taking the fatal step—not merely to survive but, as usually happened, to write about his experience. In any event, given this history of abortive attempts upon his own life, it is only natural that certain friends might have held out hope even as they felt the deepest misgivings.

This life of desperation and tragedy seems wholly out of keeping with the favorable circumstances of Dazai's birth. His family had risen to a position of wealth and authority in the northern prefecture of Aomori through land acquisition and moneylending during the three generations preceding his own. By the time Dazai was born in 1909, his father owned the bank in the family village of Kanagi. Eventually Dazai's father would move into national politics, occupying a seat in each of the houses of the Japanese Diet at different times in his career.

Quite early in his life, however, Dazai began to see himself as a child of misfortune. The tenth of eleven children, he was more or less ignored by his frail mother. And the aunt and the nursemaid who did attend to him both went away while Dazai was still a child.

As the most intelligent of the family sons, Dazai did occupy the center of attention during most of his years of schooling. In the end, though, his intelligence proved to be detrimental, at least by his own estimation. Pressured to excel at school in order to uphold the family honor, Dazai came to hate his studies. After compiling an exemplary record in the local elementary school, he lapsed into mediocrity in the upper grades, and, shortly after enrolling at Tokyo University, he gave up altogether on his formal education. As schoolwork gradually became secondary, Dazai interested himself in the activities of radical students and worked at becoming a writer. His family became understandably upset by this turn of events, for its status and wealth were rooted in traditional social arrangements. One can readily imagine the family's indignation when Dazai published a tale evoking the cruelty and indifference of a landlord toward his tenant farmers, the landlord being a thinly disguised version of the author's father, already deceased at the time.

Even after Dazai left his home region in 1930 to enter university, he continued to plague his family. He insisted on marrying a low-class geisha, and he accepted a substantial monthly allowance from his family on the pretext that he was still attending the university and working toward his degree, a deception bound to have severe repercussions once it was discovered. Subsequently, Dazai was formally disowned by his oldest brother, who had succeeded his father as the head of the household. The emotional shock of this action was compounded a few years later when the allowance he had continued to receive was terminated, leaving him in desperate financial straits. Dazai had a taste for personal extravagance, and he was generous too in subsidizing his radical friends, many of whom lived in poverty. His early years in Tokyo were wild ones, with lots of drinking and, for a time, even drug addiction to contend with. Such a life could only exacerbate the propensity for tuberculosis that Dazai shared with certain other family members.

Having fallen on hard times, Dazai resolved to change his ways. Separated from his first wife, he made overtures toward a reconciliation with his family back in the Tsugaru region of Aomori. Eventually a second marriage was arranged for him through the good offices of the novelist Masuji Ibuse,[1] one that the family privately sanctioned. Following the wedding in January 1939, Dazai settled down to a stable life with his bride, Michiko Ishihara. Several months after the marriage, he took Michiko back to Tokyo from her home in Kōfu. A daughter was born in 1941, the first of three children.

During the years of World War II, Dazai gradually established his reputation as a leading writer of the time. He thereby achieved a degree of financial independence, and, just as important, he could now hope that the family might overlook his academic failure and even his youthful radicalism.

Dazai openly cultivated the good will of his family, returning to his Tsugaru birthplace several times during the war. When his house in Tokyo was severely damaged in a bombing raid, he went back home with his wife and children, and there he remained until November of 1946.

Returning to Tokyo, he soon became lionized as the writer who best expressed the desperation of a society in chaos. Exhausted by illness and besieged by everyone from opportunistic editors to maternalistic women, Dazai was simply unable to cope. It was almost inevitable that he would revert to his earlier life of dissipation. At the time of his death he was writing a comic novel about a bon vivant who tries to rid himself of a whole stable of mistresses. Critics of Dazai occasionally suggest that the author was expressing his own wish to rid himself of Tomie Yamazaki, whose insistent efforts to lure him into that final suicide pact are well documented.

II

The works translated in this book have, for the most part, been deliberately chosen as representative of writing by Dazai that is little known outside of Japan. Since his most significant postwar works, *The Setting Sun* and *No Longer Human*, are widely read in Donald Keene's translations, only one additional work has been selected from this period. This is "The Sound of Hammering," whose young protagonist exemplifies the mood of hopelessness evoked in the two novels.

"The Sound of Hammering" consists almost entirely of a letter written to an unnamed author. In fact, Dazai himself received a letter that provided him with the basic structure for his story. Strictly speaking, then, the story cannot be called auto-biographical. And yet, the desperate and somewhat confidential tone of the letter in "The Sound of Hammering" is quite similar to the manner of certain works by Dazai that qualify in some measure as autobiographical. One can hardly doubt that the actual letter struck a deeply sympathetic chord in Dazai.

Two works in this volume, "Memories" and "On the Question of Apparel," would certainly be regarded by most Japanese critics as primarily auto-biographical. "Memories" recounts the childhood and adolescence of a figure whose circumstances closely resemble those of the young Dazai, while "On the Question of Apparel" describes with deadpan humor a number of mishaps that occur to an author with Dazai's drinking habits. While the degree of personal revelation present in any Dazai work is difficult to gauge with precision, both of these compositions ask the reader to accept the narrator's word that the events actually happened to him. Like "The Sound of Hammering," "Memories" and "On the Question of Apparel" together suggest the range of Osamu Dazai when he writes in a mode of personal revelation.

The remaining eight stories in this book show Dazai as an inventive storyteller, rather than as a craftsman of reminiscence. With the exception of "Undine" and "Monkey Island," these works were all composed between the time of Dazai's marriage to Michiko in 1939 and the end of the war in 1945. As mentioned earlier, these years were relatively quiet ones for Dazai, a period when he worked to consolidate his writing skills, learning above all to diversify the autobiographical impulse by integrating his personal obsessions with fairly orthodox methods of storytelling. Dazai's own personal involvement in the tales will sometimes be obscure to the reader unfamiliar with his writings. It might be remarked here that, in order to provide some guidance on this and other matters, each of the tales in this volume has a prefatory note.

Though impelled to embody his personal concerns in these tales as well, Dazai was not bound by certain natural limitations of his semi-autobiographical mode. In these more fictional tales, he could evoke realms of fantasy, juxtaposing them in some instances with the real world. In addition, he was able to give his characters greater scope for individual initiative than he was willing to permit the autobiographical figures. Characters in these less realistic tales are often beset with difficulties, but they sometimes attempt to surmount them. Doubts and uncertainties in the latter group of stories come more from the author breaking into his narrative to voice an opinion than from the characters acting out the story. As the prefatory notes will make clear, a number of these non-realistic tales are based on such diverse sources as the New Testament and the medieval *Otogi Zōshi* tales. Perhaps Dazai used these sources as offering scope for action which his own experience would not validate.

Dazai frequently ends a tale on an inconclusive note—most obviously when he has a narrator confess to bewilderment concerning the significance of the very tale he has just told. Although this might be regarded as a technical feature—the author's way of prompting the reader to dwell on the work—it seems more likely that Dazai was giving vent to his own sense of things. How fitting for an author who flirted so with suicide to hesitate in writing "Finis" to end a story as well.

III

It remains only to remark that the translations that follow try to convey, in some measure, the highly idiosyncratic flavor of Osamu Dazai. In pursuing this goal, I have generally followed the author's practice of frequently omitting quotation marks for what appear to be direct quotations. Though violating standard English practice, such a procedure helps, in my judgment, to preserve something of the author's idiosyncratic quality.

Memories
Omoide

Beginning in 1912 with the death of Emperor Meiji, this account is closely tied to the circumstances of the author's own life. Just three years old at the time of his earliest memory, the narrator goes on to relate episodes from his childhood and adolescence in a fashion both piecemeal and informative. The memories come to his mind with apparent spontaneity, evoked by free association and unrelated to any design other than that of a loose chronology. By the time "Memories" is over, a decade and a half has elapsed and the narrator is about to enter college.

In his abrupt style of recollection, even those people intimately involved in the narrator's early life come and go with alacrity. An aunt occupies the center of attention for several paragraphs, only to be succeeded by a nursemaid. A few characters from the earlier sections of the narrative are recalled later, but most of them never return. Those that remain in the reader's mind do so by virtue of a striking detail or vivid turn of phrase from their moment in the narrative. Dazai typically subordinates his cast of secondary characters to his autobiographical self; in "Memories" the lesser characters serve mainly as agents of the narrator's upbringing.

In the final stage of this account, references to a

curious affair of the heart coalesce into an ongoing episode. Smitten in mid-adolescence, the hero is bedeviled by two problems. His love, a mere maid in the household, would hardly make a welcome match in the eyes of his prestigious family. And, to complicate matters, his younger brother also seems taken with the same girl.

Readers might wonder why the author, after recounting so many fragmentary recollections, ends his narration with this more sustained episode. In the story, the affair emerges quite naturally; and, in retrospect, it seems to confirm the portrait of the narrator suggested by earlier events. From almost the very beginning, many of the narrator's important gestures occur only in his imagination. The affair in question is no exception, and thus one might argue that it ends in self-delusion rather than in thwarted love.

The final scene of "Memories" shows Dazai using a photograph for symbolic effect, a tactic more widely employed in his novel No Longer Human. *By this stage of the game the loss of the maid Miyo should have taught the narrator a lesson about himself. In the company of his brother and putative rival, however, he seems still imprisoned by the inward nature of his outlook. Dazai concludes on a characteristic note of uncertainty: Will his narrator, that figure who represents in some measure his own youthful self, break free of his confining introspection? Or will he, as the graveyard scene and fortune-telling episode early in the narrative portend, stay trapped in his habit of self-dramatization and in his belief that he is a victim of fate?*

I

I was standing by our front gate as twilight fell. My aunt was there too in a quilted wrap, the kind a nursemaid often wears when carrying an infant strapped on her back. The road before our house had grown dim and everything was hushed. I have never forgotten that moment.

She was speaking of the emperor, and I can still remember bits and snatches of what she said—*His Majesty . . . gone into seclusion . . . a true living god*. Filled with wonder, I repeated certain words—*A . . . true . . . god . . .*

Then I must have said the wrong thing. *No*, my aunt scolded, *you should say, Gone into seclusion*. I knew exactly where the emperor had gone, but I asked about it anyway. I still remember how she laughed at that.

Emperor Meiji had been on the throne forty-two years when I was born. When he passed away, I was only three years old.

I guess it was about then that my aunt took me to visit some relatives. Their village was about five miles away, near a broad waterfall in the mountains. I remember how white the water looked against the green moss as it cascaded down the cliff. I didn't know the man who held me on his shoulders to watch. When he showed me the votive pictures in the shrine below the falls, I became very lonely. Eventually I broke into tears and called out, "Auntie! Auntie!"

In a hollow some distance off, my relatives and my aunt had spread rugs on the ground. They were making lots of noise when I cried out, but my aunt heard and jumped up immediately. She must have slipped just then, however, for she stumbled as though making a bow. The others couldn't resist teasing her. "Look!" they cried, "she's already drunk." As I watched these things occurring far down in the hollow, I felt so ashamed that I finally began screaming at the top of my lungs.

While still a child, I dreamed one evening that my aunt was going away and leaving me behind. I saw her standing in our front entranceway, totally occupying it with her bulk. Her breasts seemed large and red, and perspiration trickled down her skin. *I can't stand you*, she hissed, prompting me to run over and press my cheek to her breasts. No, I begged, please don't leave. Sobbing, I pleaded with her again and again. When my aunt shook me awake, I hugged her right there in bed and kept on crying. Even after I was fully aware, I wept quietly for a long time. Afterward I didn't tell anyone of my dream, not even my aunt. I remember plenty of things about my aunt from those early days. But I don't remember anyone else, even though there were surely many people in the house besides my father and mother. That's because our family included my great-grandmother and grandmother, my three older brothers and four older sisters, and my younger brother too. Then there was my aunt and her four daughters. Except for my aunt, however, I was hardly aware of anyone. Not, at least, until I was four or five years old.

We must have had five or six tall apple trees in our big garden out back. I remember a cloudy day when some girls were climbing about in those trees. The garden had a chrysanthemum patch as well, and I vaguely recall a crowd of girls gazing at the flowers in full bloom. They were standing in the rain with umbrellas. I suppose they were sisters and cousins of mine.

From the time I was five or six years old my memories become quite definite. Around that time a maid named Také taught me how to read. She really wanted me to learn, and we read all kinds of books together. Since I was a sickly child, I often read in bed. When we ran out of books, Také would bring back an armful from places like the village Sunday school and have me read them. I learned to read silently too. That's why I could finish one book after another without getting tired.

Také also taught me about right and wrong. Often we went to a temple where she would show me Buddhist hell paintings and explain the punishments they depicted. Sinners condemned to hell for arson carried flaming red baskets upon their backs, while those who had kept mistresses writhed in the grip of a green snake with two heads. The paintings depicted a lake of blood and a mountain of spikes, as well as a bottomless pit called "The Abyss" that gave off white smoke. Thin, pale wretches, wailing through barely opened mouths, were strewn over all these regions. Tell a lie, Také said, and you'd end up the same way—a sinner in hell with your tongue plucked out by devils. Hearing this, I screamed in terror.

The temple graveyard was on a small hill out back, with requiem posts[1] clustered along the hedge-rose border. Besides the usual prayers in brush writing, each of the posts carried a dark, metal wheel. Fastened in a slot high on the post, each wheel seemed to me then about the size of the full moon. Spin the wheel once, Také explained, and if it clattered round and round and came to a stop without turning back, then you would go to heaven. But, she warned, if the wheel started back, you'd end up in hell.

Také would give a push and the wheel would spin smoothly until it slowed to a complete stop. When I tried, however, the wheel sometimes turned back. I think it was in the autumn that I went alone to the temple to test my luck. The wheels seemed to be in league with one another, for they all turned back regardless of which one I pushed. Though tired and angry, I kept myself under control and stubbornly pushed them time after time. As dusk fell, I finally gave up and left the graveyard in despair.

My parents must have been living in Tokyo about that time, and I was taken by my aunt for a visit. I'm told we were there a long while, but I don't remember much about my stay. I do remember an old lady who came to the house every so often. I couldn't stand her and cried each time she showed up. Once she brought along a toy postal truck painted red, but it merely bored me.

Then I started going to the village grade school, and that left me with different memories altogether. Suddenly Také was no longer around. I learned that she had gone off to marry someone from a fishing village. She left without telling me this, apparently out of fear that I might follow her. It must have been the next year that Také came to visit us during the Festival of the Dead.[2] She seemed rather cold toward me, however, and when she asked how I was doing at school, I didn't answer. I suppose someone else told her. She didn't really compliment me. She just said, Don't get too big for your britches.

At about the same time certain events led to my

aunt's departure as well. Having no son to carry on the family name, my aunt decided that her oldest daughter would marry a dentist who would be adopted to continue the family line. Her second daughter got married and left, while the third died while still young. Taking along her oldest daughter and the new husband, as well as her fourth daughter, my aunt established a separate branch of the family in a distant town. The move occurred in the winter, and I was to go along. As the time to leave drew near, I crouched in a corner of the sleigh next to my aunt. That's when my next older brother came up and slapped my rump right where it pressed against the lower end of the hood. "Hey there, little bridegroom!" he sneered, thumping me time and again. Gritting my teeth, I put up with his insolence. Indeed I thought my aunt was adopting me as well as the dentist. But when school began once again, I was sent back to my village.

I ceased being a child soon after entering grade school. It was then that my younger brother's nurse taught me something that took my breath away. It was a beautiful summer day, and the grass by the vacant house out back had grown tall and dense. I must have been about seven, and my brother's nurse could not have been more than thirteen or fourteen. My brother was three years younger than I, and the nurse shooed him off. She said, "Go get some leaf-grass"—that's our word for clover back home. Then she added, "And make sure it's got four leaves too." After he left, she put her arms around me, and we started rolling around in the tall grass.

Thereafter we would play our secret little game in the storehouse or in one of the closets. My younger brother was always in our way. He even started howling one day when we left him outside the closet, an event that put my next older brother on to us. Having found out from my little brother what the trouble was, my older brother opened the closet door. The nurse did not get upset; she merely said that we were looking for a lost coin.

I was always telling fibs too. On the Girls' Festival[3] day of my second or third year in grade school, I told the teacher that my family wanted me home early to help arrange the doll display. Having lied my way out of class, I went home during the first period and told everyone school was out for the Peach Festival. My assistance wasn't needed, but I got the dolls from their boxes all the same.

I had lots of fun collecting bird eggs too. There were always plenty of sparrow eggs right under the tiles of our storehouse roof. But starlings and crows didn't nest there, and I had to turn to my classmates for these eggs. (The crow eggs were green and seemed to glow, while the starling eggs were covered with strange speckles.) In return for the eggs, I would hand over a bunch of my books. Wrapped in cotton, the eggs in my collection eventually filled an entire drawer of my desk.

My next older brother must have suspected something. One evening he asked to borrow two books, a volume of Western fairy tales and a work whose title I've forgotten. My brother did this from spite, and I hated him for it. The books were gone, for I had traded them both for eggs. If I admitted this, my brother would have gone to reclaim them. So I told him the books were around somewhere and I would look for them. Lamp in hand, I searched my own room and then went all over the house. My brother laughed as he followed me about. He kept saying, They're not here, are they? And I kept insisting, They are too. I even climbed up to the highest kitchen shelf for a look. Finally my brother told me to forget it.

The compositions I wrote for school were mostly hokum. I tried to portray myself as a model boy, for I believed people would applaud me for that. I even plagiarized. The essay entitled "My Younger Brother's Silhouette" was a masterpiece according to my teacher, but I actually lifted it word for word from a selection of prize stories in a magazine for youngsters. The teacher had me make a clean copy with a brush and enter the work in a contest. When a bookish classmate found out what I had done, I prayed that he would die.

"Autumn Evening," composed about the same time, was also praised by my teacher. I began this sketch by mentioning a headache I got from studying, and then went on to describe how I went out on the veranda and looked at the garden. I gazed entranced upon the quiet scene, the moon shining brightly, the goldfish and the carp swimming about in the pond. When a burst of laughter came from a nearby room where my mother and some other people were gathered, I snapped out of the reverie and my headache was suddenly gone—that's how the sketch ended.

There wasn't a word of truth to this. I took the description of the garden from my older sister's composition notebook. Above all, I don't remember studying enough to get a headache. I hated school and never read a textbook. I only read entertaining books. My family thought I was studying as long as I was reading something or other.

But when I put down the truth, things always went wrong. When I wrote that Father and Mother didn't love me, the assistant disciplinarian called me into the teachers' room for a scolding. Assigned the topic, "What If a War Breaks Out?" I wrote how frightening war could be—worse even than an earthquake, lightning, fire, or one's own father.[4] That's why I said that I would flee to the hills, at the same time urging my teacher to join me. After all, my teacher was only human, and war would scare him just like it would me.

This time the assistant disciplinarian and the school principal both questioned me. When asked what prompted these words, I took a gamble and said I was only joking. The assistant disciplinarian made a note in his book—*Full of mischief!* Then a brief battle of wits ensued between the two of us. Did I believe, he asked, that all men were equal? After all, the assistant disciplinarian went on, I had written that my teacher was only human too. I hesitated before replying that, Yes, I thought so. Really, I was slow with my tongue.

If, the assistant disciplinarian continued, he himself was equal to the principal, why didn't they get the same salary? I thought about that awhile and said, Isn't it because your work is different?

His thin face set off by the wire frames of his spectacles, the assistant disciplinarian immediately recorded my answer in his book. And then this man whom I had long admired asked whether or not he and I were equal to my own father. That one I just couldn't answer.

A busy man, my father was seldom at home. Even
when he was, he usually didn't bother about his
children. I once wanted a fountain pen like his, but
was too afraid to ask for one. After wrestling with
the problem, I fell back on pretending to talk in my
sleep. Lying in bed one evening, I kept murmuring,
Fountain pen . . . fountain pen . . . Father was talking with a guest in the next room, and my words
were meant for him. Needless to say, they never
reached his ear, let alone his heart.

Once my younger brother and I were playing in
the large family storehouse piled high with sacks of
rice when Father planted himself in the doorway and
shouted, Get out of here! Get out, you monkeys!
With the sunlight at his back, father loomed there
like a dark shadow. My stomach turns even yet when
I recall how frightened I was.

I didn't feel close to Mother, either. I was first
raised by a nursemaid, then by my aunt. Until the
second or third year of grade school, I didn't really
get to know my mother. Some years later, as she lay
in her bedding next to mine, Mother noticed how my
blanket was moving about. What was I up to? she
asked suspiciously. Well, two of the manservants
had taught me something, and Mother's question put
me on the spot. I managed to say that my hip was
sore, however, and that I was rubbing it. You needn't
be so rough about it, Mother replied. Her voice
sounded drowsy. I massaged my hip awhile, without
saying anything.

My memories of Mother are mostly dismal ones.
There was the time I got my older brother's suit from
the storehouse and put it on. Then, strolling among
the flower beds in the garden out back, I hummed a

mournful tune that I had made up and then shed a few tears besides. Suddenly I felt that, while wearing this particular outfit, I might try fooling around with the student who did our household accounts. So I sent a maid to call him. He didn't come, though, even though I waited a long time. In my anxiety I ran the tip of my shoe along the bamboo fence. Finally my patience gave way and, with both fists thrust into my pockets, I let out a wail. When Mother found me, she got me out of that suit and, for some reason or other, gave me a good spanking. I felt utterly ashamed.

Even as a child I wanted to be well dressed. My shirts had to be made of white flannel, and I wouldn't even wear one unless it had buttons on the cuffs. My undershirt collar must be white too, for I let it show an inch or two above my shirt collar. During the Full Moon Festival[5] the students in the village all dressed up in their Sunday best for school. I always chose my flannel kimono with the wide brown stripes for this occasion. Arriving at school, I would glide along the corridor with tiny steps, just like a girl. I made sure no one was around, since I didn't want people knowing what a fop I was.

Everyone kept saying that I was the ugliest boy in the family. And if they had known how fussy I was about clothes, they would surely have had a good laugh at my expense. I pretended not to care about my appearance, and this seemed to do the trick. I gave the impression of being dull and uncouth, no doubt about it. At mealtime my brothers and I sat on the floor, a tray before each of us. Grandmother and Mother were also present. It was awful hearing them remark over and over how ugly I was.

Actually I was quite proud of myself. I'd go down

to the maids' quarters and ask offhandedly who was the best boy in the family. The girls usually said that my oldest brother was. Then they added that Shūcha—that's me—was second best. I resented being second, but blushed to hear it all the same. Indeed, I wanted them to say I was better than my oldest brother.

It wasn't just my looks that displeased Grandmother. I was clumsy as well. At every meal she cautioned me about holding my chopsticks properly. She even said that the way I bowed made my rump stick out indecently. I had to sit properly in front of her and make one bow after another. No matter how often I tried, she never once complimented me.

Grandmother was a headache for me in other ways too. When a theater troupe came from Tokyo to celebrate the opening of our village playhouse, I went to every performance without fail. My father had built the playhouse, so I always had a good seat for nothing. Each day when I got home from school, I hurriedly changed into a soft kimono. Then I ran off to the playhouse, a narrow chain dangling from my sash with a pencil attached to the end. That's how I first got to know about Kabuki. While watching the performances, I would shed one tear after another.

Even before this time I had been something of a performer myself. I really enjoyed calling the manservants and maids together and telling old stories or else showing films and slides. After the Tokyo troupe had left, I rounded up my younger brother and my cousins to put on my own show. I arranged three Kyogen pieces for the program—*Yamanaka Shikanosuke*, *The House of the Dove*, and a comic dance known as *Kappore*. The first had a teahouse scene set in a valley, during which Shikanosuke gains a follower named Hayakawa Ayunosuke. Adapting the scene from a text in a young peoples' magazine, I took infinite pains to cast the words in Kabuki rhythms: "Your humble servant/A man known to the world as/Shikanosuke." From *The House of the Dove*, a long novel that I had read over and over (and never without crying), I selected an especially pathetic section to render as a two-act play. Since the Tokyo troupe always ended its program with the entire cast performing *Kappore*, I decided to include the dance as well.

With five or six days of rehearsing over, we scheduled our first performance for that evening. We had set up the stage on the wide veranda before the library-storehouse, with a small curtain suspended in front. It was still broad daylight when Grandmother came by, but she didn't notice the wire. When her jaw got caught on it, she cried out, You pack of river bums![6] Stop it! That wire could've killed me.

Despite this incident, we gathered ten or so manservants and maids for the evening performance. The memory of Grandmother's words weighed heavily upon me. While performing the title role in *Yamanaka Shikanosuke* and that of the boy in *The House of the Dove*, and even while dancing *Kappore*, I felt isolated and completely listless. Eventually I put on such plays as *The Rustler*, *The House of the Broken Plate*, and *Shuntoku Maru*, but Grandmother always looked disgusted.

Though I didn't much care for Grandmother, I was grateful to her on sleepless nights all the same. From the third or fourth year of grade school, I had suffered from insomnia. Midnight would be long past, and I would still be lying awake in bed. Since I cried so often at night, the family tried to come up with remedies for my insomnia. Lick sugar before bed, I was told, or else count the ticking of the clock. I tried other suggestions, like cooling my feet in a pan of water or placing a leaf from the "sleeping tree" under my pillow. But nothing seemed to work. A bundle of nerves, I would anxiously turn over one thing after another in my mind. This only made falling asleep more difficult. I had a succession of bad nights after secretly playing with Father's pince-nez and cracking the lens.

The notions shop two doors away handled several kinds of books and magazines. One day I was looking at the illustrations inside the front cover of a ladies journal, one of them a watercolor of a yellow mermaid. I wanted this illustration so badly that I decided to steal it. I had quietly torn the page out when the young manager sharply called out my boyhood name, Osako! Osako! I flung the magazine to the floor and rushed home. Blunders such as this one kept me awake for nights on end.

Sometimes I'd lie in bed needlessly worrying that a fire might break out. I wondered, What if the house burned down? and after that I couldn't sleep at all.

One evening I was heading for the toilet just before bedtime. The room where the family accounts were kept was right across the hallway from my destination. The room was dark, and the student who kept the accounts was running a movie projector. The picture on the sliding door hardly seemed bigger than a matchbox, but I could make out a polar bear about to plunge off an ice floe into the sea. Observing this, I sensed something unbearably sad about the student. Back in bed, I thought about the movie scene and reflected as well on the life of this student, my heart pounding all the while. What would I do if the film caught fire? I wondered. Beset by these worries, I couldn't get to sleep until almost dawn. On nights such as this, I would feel especially grateful to my grandmother.

Around eight o'clock in the evening, a maid would come to my room and lie next to me until I fell asleep. Since I felt sorry for her, I would lie still with my eyes closed. As soon as she left, I'd start praying that I could fall asleep. I would toss and turn until almost ten o'clock, then break into a whimper and get up. By that time the whole family other than Grandmother would be in bed.

Grandmother would still be in the kitchen by the large hearth, sitting across from the night watchman. Ensconced between them in my quilted pajamas, I would dejectedly listen to their inevitable gossip about people in the village. Late one night, as I leaned over to hear, the beat of a great drum echoed from afar. People were still up, celebrating the Insect-Expulsion Festival,[7] an occasion when farmers try various means of ridding their fields of harmful pests. I have not forgotten how reassuring it was to know that others were still awake.

That far-off drumbeat brings other memories to mind. My oldest brother was at a university in Tokyo around then, and whenever he came back for a summer vacation, he brought word of the latest trends in music and literature. My brother studied drama, and he even published a one-act play in a local magazine. Called *The Struggle*, it was much discussed by the young people hereabouts. Along with my other brothers and sisters, I had listened to him recite the play just after he had finished the manuscript. Everyone had complained that it didn't make sense. I alone understood, even down to the poetic curtain line, "Ah, how dark the night is!" However, I did think the title should be *The Thistle* rather than *The Struggle*. And in tiny letters I wrote this opinion in a corner of some used manuscript paper. Perhaps my brother didn't notice, for he published the play without changing the title.

My brother's large collection of phonograph records had both Japanese and Western melodies. I already knew the Japanese melodies because of the geishas who came to our house. Whenever he gave a party, my father would send word to a city some distance away to request their services. I remember being hugged by these geishas from the age of four or five. I recall watching them dance too, and listening to their songs, "Once Upon a Time" and "The Tangerine Boat from Ki Province."

As I lay in bed one night, a fine melody filtered out of my brother's room. I lifted my head from the pillow, listening closely. The next morning I got up early and went over. I selected one record after another and played every one on my brother's phonograph. At last I found the melody that had so excited me last night, a samisen ballad about the ill-fated drummer Ranchō.[8]

Nevertheless, I felt much closer to my second oldest brother. After graduating with honors from a Tokyo business school, he had come back to work in the family bank. This brother was treated callously, just like I was. Mother and Father said he was the worst boy in the family (after me, of course), so I figured looks were the problem with him too. He would sometimes say to me, I don't need anything now—but if only I'd been born good-looking. Then, turning to me, he would ask teasingly, What do you think of that, Shū?

Despite such bantering, I never thought my brother so ill-favored. I regarded him as one of the smarter boys in the family, too. He seemed to drink every day and then quarrel with Grandmother. Each time this happened, I felt a secret hatred for her.

With my third brother, the one just older than me, I was always feuding. He knew many of my secrets, and that made me uneasy. He looked quite a bit like my little brother, and everyone remarked how handsome he was. I was, so to speak, being squeezed from above and below, and I could hardly bear it. When this older brother went off to high school in Tokyo, I breathed a sigh of relief.

My little brother was the family baby. He had a gentle look as well, and this endeared him to Father and Mother. I was always jealous and would hit him now and then. Mother would scold me, and then I'd resent her too. I must have been about nine or ten when the problem with the lice occurred. They were all over me, scattered like sesame seeds on the seams of my underwear and my shirt. When my brother grinned about this, I just knocked him down—I really did. His head began swelling in several places, and that worried me. I got hold of some ointment labeled "For External Use Only" and applied it to his bruises.

I had four older sisters, all of them fond of me. The oldest one died, however, and the next one left to get married. The two youngest sisters went off to school, each to a different town. Whenever their vacation came to an end, the two of them had to go seven or eight miles from our village to reach the nearest train station. During the summer they could take our horse-drawn carriage. When the hail was blowing about in the fall, however, or the snow melting in the spring, they had no choice except to walk. They might have gone by sleigh during the winter, but the sleigh happened to make them both sick. That's why they ended up walking then too. Whenever they were due back in the winter, I'd go out to the edge of our village where the lumber was piled up. Even after the sun went down, the road remained bright in the snow. When the flickering lamps that my sisters carried finally emerged from the woods of the next village, I would throw up my arms and let out a whoop.

The school of the older sister happened to be in a smaller town. Because of that, the souvenirs she brought back could not compare with the younger sister's. Once she took from her basket five or six packets of incense-sparklers and handed them to me. I'm so sorry, she said, a blush upon her cheeks. At that moment I felt my breast constrict. According to my family, this sister too was homely.

She had lived in a separate room with my great-grandmother until she went away to school, so how could I avoid thinking of her as the old lady's daughter? Then, about the time I was finishing grade school, my great-grandmother passed away. I caught a glimpse of the small, rigid body dressed in a white kimono as it was being placed in the coffin. I fretted about what to do if this scene kept haunting me.

I graduated from grade school in due course, but I was too frail for high school. My family decided to send me to a special intermediate school for one year to see if I got stronger. If I did, Father would send me to high school here in the province. My older brothers had all studied in Tokyo, but that would be bad for my health. I didn't care much about going to high school, anyhow. But I did get some sympathy from my teachers by writing about how frail I was.

The intermediate school belonged to the county, a new unit of government back then. Five or six villages and towns had gotten together and put up the building in a pine grove more than a mile from my home. Many bright students from grade schools throughout the area were enrolled, and I had to maintain the honor of my own school against this competition. I had to strive to be the best, even though I would often be absent because of my health.

Nonetheless, I didn't study there either. To one headed for high school, the place seemed dirty and unpleasant. I spent most of every class drawing a cartoon serial. During recess I would explain the characters to my classmates and even give impersonations of them. I filled four or five notebooks with such cartoons.

With my elbow braced on the desk and my chin resting in my palm, I would gaze outside for a whole hour. My seat was near the window where a fly had been crushed against the pane. Glimpsed from the side, the fly astonished me time and again. It almost seemed to be a large pheasant or a mountain dove.

I would play hookey with five or six friends and together we would head for the marsh just beyond the pine grove. While loitering at the edge of the water, we'd gossip about the girls in our class, then roll up our kimono skirts to stare at each other's fuzz. It was great fun to compare how we were all doing.

I kept my distance from every girl at school, though. I was so easily aroused that I had to watch myself. Two or three of the girls had a crush on me, but I was a coward and pretended not to notice.

I would go into Father's library and take down the volume of paintings from the Imperial Art Exhibition. As I gazed at a nude painting buried somewhere among the pages, my cheeks would begin to glow. Another thing I would do is put my pair of pet rabbits in the same cage, my heart pounding as the male climbed on and hunched its back. By doing these things I kept my own urge from getting out of hand.

I was really a prig and didn't tell anyone about the massaging. When I read how harmful it was, I decided to stop. But nothing seemed to work.

Since I walked all the way to school and back each day, my body grew stronger. At the same time little pimples came out on my forehead like millet grains, much to my embarrassment. I would paint them with a red ointment.

That same year my oldest brother got married. On the evening of the wedding my younger brother and I tiptoed up to the bride's room and peeked in. She was having her hair done, with her back to the door. I caught a glimpse of the pale, white face in the mirror, then fled with my younger brother in tow.

"What's so great about her?" I swaggered. Ashamed of my forehead and the red ointment, I reacted all the more violently.

As winter drew near I had to start studying for the

entrance exam to high school. I looked over the book ads in the magazines, then ordered various reference works from Tokyo. I arranged them on my shelves, but didn't do any reading. The high school of my choice, located in the province's largest city, would attract two or three times more applicants than it could admit. Now and then I was overcome with fear; I must get down to studying or else I would fail the exam. A week of hard work would restore my confidence. During these bouts of study I would stay up until midnight and usually get up at four the next morning. A maid named Tami stayed by me. I'd have her keep the charcoal fire going and make the tea. No matter how late she stayed up, Tami always came to wake me at four o'clock the next morning. While I puzzled over an arithmetic problem involving a mouse and the numbers of her offspring, Tami sat quietly nearby reading a novel. Presently she was replaced by a fat, elderly maid. When I heard that Mother was behind this change and thought of what her motive might be, I could only frown.

Early the following spring, while the snow was still deep, my father coughed up blood in a Tokyo hospital and died. The local paper published his obituary in a special edition, an event that affected me more than the death itself. My own name appeared in the paper too, on a list of people from the gentry.

Father's body was brought home in a great coffin mounted upon a sleigh. I went along with a large crowd to meet the hearse near the next village. Eventually a long procession of sleighs glided from the woods. The hood of each vehicle reflected the moonlight, creating a lovely scene.

The next day our family gathered in the shrine room where the coffin rested. When the lid was opened, everyone burst into tears. Father seemed to be asleep, his prominent nose looking very straight and pale. Enticed by the weeping, I too shed some tears.

For the next month the house was in such chaos that one might have thought a fire had occurred. I forgot about my studies altogether. And, when the time for the final exam arrived, I could only give haphazard answers. The examiner knew about my family, though, and I was graded third highest among the group. I suspected that my memory was starting to weaken. For the first time ever, I felt I could not handle an exam without preparing for it.

II

Although my scores were low, I passed the exam for high school that spring. The school was in a small town on the coast and, when the time came, I had to leave my own village. I dressed quite stylishly for the trip—new *hakama*,[9] dark stockings, laced boots. In place of the blanket I had been using, I threw a woolen cloak over my shoulders and deliberately left it unbuttoned. When I reached my destination, a dry-goods store with an old tattered *noren* curtain hanging in the front entrance, I took off this outfit. The shop was run by distant relatives to whom I became deeply indebted over time.

There are people who get suddenly worked up over anything whatever, and I'm one of them. Now that I was in high school, I'd put on my student cap and new *hakama* just to go to the public bathhouse. Catching my reflection in the shop windows along the way, I'd even nod my head and smile.

I couldn't get excited about school, however. Not that the place wasn't nice enough. The building was situated at the edge of town, with a park behind extending to the Tsugaru Strait. It was painted white outside, and inside there were wide hallways and classrooms with high ceilings. During class one could hear the hiss of the waves and the sough of the pines.

But the teachers in that school were always persecuting me. As early as orientation day the gymnastics instructor called me a smart aleck and started hitting me. That really hurt, since he was the very person who had been so gentle with me on the oral examination. Knowing that my father had passed away, he had understood why I wasn't prepared for the entrance exam. When he had mentioned this, I had hung my head for his benefit.

Then the other instructors started hitting me. They gave all sorts of reasons for dishing out such punishment. I was yawning, grinning, or whatever. My unrestrained yawning apparently became a subject of conversation in the teachers' room. It amused me to think what dumb things they talked about there.

One day a student from my own village called me over to the sand dune in the schoolyard. You're bound to flunk, he warned, as long as they keep hitting you like that. And, he added, you really do act like a smart aleck. I was dumbfounded. That afternoon after class, I hurriedly set out for home along the beach. With no one else around, I sighed as the waves licked against my shoes. I raised my arm, wiping the sweat from my brow with my shirt sleeve. A gray sail, astonishingly large, wavered past my very eyes.

I was a petal quivering in the slightest breeze, about to fall any moment. Even the slightest insult made me think of dying. Believing I would amount to something before long, I stood up for my honor so firmly that I could not allow even an adult to make light of me. That's why failing at school would have been a disaster. From that time on I became tense in the classroom, so anxious was I to pay attention. During every lesson I believed myself in a room with a hundred invisible foes. I could not let my guard down in the least. Every morning before setting out for school, I turned up a playing card on the desk in search of my daily fortune. A heart was lucky, a diamond promising; a club was foreboding, while a spade meant certain disaster. At this time of my life, spades turned up day after day.

With an exam coming soon, I memorized every word of my natural history, geography, and ethics textbooks. I was finicky, and for me the exam was a matter of do or die. But my method turned out to be faulty. Inexorably I felt hemmed in and unable to adapt to the exam. Certain questions I answered almost to perfection. In other cases, however, I tripped over the words and phrases in my confusion and ended up soiling the test booklet with mere gibberish.

Nonetheless, my marks that first term were the third highest in the class. Even in deportment I received an A. I seized my report card in one hand and, holding my shoes in the other, dashed out to the beach. Having been tormented by the prospect of failing, now I was absolutely elated.

With the term over, I made preparations to go home for my first vacation from high school. My younger brother and his friends would hear of my brief experience in glowing terms. I stuffed everything I had acquired into the trunk, going so far as to include even the sitting cushions.

Tossed about in the carriage, I came out of the woods of the neighboring village. The rich green of the rice paddies spread out like the sea, and the familiar roof of my own home, with its red tiles, rose conspicuously in the distance. I gazed toward home as though I had been away for ten years.

Never have I been so elated as during the month of that vacation. To my younger brother I boasted of the school as something one might dream of. In my telling, even the small coastal town seemed part of a vision.

I was supposed to paint five watercolors and collect ten rare insects for my homework. I spent the whole month wandering through the fields and the river valleys, sketching the landscape and looking for insects. I took my younger brother along for help. He could hold the collector's kit, with the tweezers and jar of poison, while I carried the net on my shoulder. I chased after locusts and cabbage butterflies all day long. When night fell, I would get a crackling fire going in the park and, as the insects flew by, flail away at them with a net or a broom.

My next older brother was enrolled in the sculpture division at art school. He was making a bust of my next older sister, who had just graduated from a girls' school. While he fiddled with clay beneath the chestnut tree in the garden, I stood nearby sketching her portrait time and again.

She may have taken her posing quite seriously, but my brother and I merely poked fun at each other's work. My sister was usually more impressed with my work, yet my brother only ridiculed my talent. When you're young, he claimed, everyone says you're gifted. He dismissed my writing too, calling it grade-schoolish. In return I was openly contemptuous of his abilities.

One evening this brother came over to where I slept and whispered, "Osa! I've got a bug for you!" Squatting on the floor, he slid a tissue wrapping beneath the edge of the mosquito net. He knew I was collecting rare insects. And when I heard the scratching noise inside the tissue as the insect struggled to get out, I realized what kinship meant. I undid the paper roughly, and my brother gasped, "He'll get away! Look! Look!" I could see it was only a stag beetle, but I put it down as "sheathed and winged," one of my ten types, and handed it in.

I was depressed to see the vacation end. Returning all alone to my second-floor room at the dry-goods store, I opened my trunk and almost burst into tears. At such times I always sought refuge in a bookstore. There was one close by, and I hurried there now. Just to see all the books lining the shelves would lighten my mood as if by magic. This particular store had one corner containing a half dozen volumes that I couldn't buy even though I wanted to. Now and then I would linger there and peek inside the covers. I would try to act casual, but my knees would be shaking. Of course, I didn't go to bookstores just to read articles on anatomy. I went because any book gave me comfort and solace at the time.

My schoolwork, however, became more and more

boring. Nothing was worse than coloring in the mountain ranges, harbors, and rivers on an outline map. I was a stickler about things, so I would spend three or four hours at this. In history and certain other classes the teachers told us to take notes on the main points of the lectures. Listening to a lecture was like reading a textbook, so the students merely copied sentences straight from the book. Being attached to grades, I worked away at such tasks day after day.

In the fall there were various athletic events for the high-school students in town. Out in the countryside we had never played baseball, so I only knew such terms as "center field," "deep short," and "bases loaded" from books. Eventually I learned how to watch a game, but I didn't get worked up about it. Whenever my own school competed in tennis, judo, or even baseball, I had to join the cheering section. This made me dislike high school all the more.

Our head cheerleader would look purposely shabby as he climbed the knoll in the schoolyard corner and, holding a fan with the rising sun insignia, give us a pep talk. Reacting to him, the students would cry out with glee, "Slob! You slob!" When a match took place, this cheerleader leaped up during every break in the action and started waving his fan. "ALL STAND UP!" he'd shout in his funny English. And we would get up, our tiny purple banners flapping in unison, and sing the fight song: "Our Foe is Worthy, But . . ." It was quite embarrassing. When I spied an opportunity, I'd slip away from the cheering section and go home.

Not that I myself never played sports. My complexion had a faint darkness, which I blamed on the

massaging. I became flustered when people mentioned my face, for they seemed to be indicating this
secret vice of mine. Somehow or other I felt I must improve my color. That's why I took up sports.

I had long fretted about my complexion. As early
as my fourth or fifth year of elementary school, my
next older brother had already spoken to me of
democratic ideas.[10] Then I heard certain complaints,
even from Mother. She once told visitors to our
home that democracy had meant much higher taxes
and that most of the family harvest now went to the
government. I was quite confused by the various
things I heard. At the same, I tried to be democratic
toward our family's servants. In the summer I lent a
hand to the men mowing the lawn, and in the winter
I helped shovel snow from the roof. Eventually I
discovered that my help wasn't welcome. It even
seems the men had to redo the part of the lawn that I
had tried to mow. To tell the truth, I was actually trying to improve my color. But even hard work didn't
do any good.

During high school I got into sports because of my
complexion. On the way home from school in the
summer, I always took a dip in the ocean. I liked to
use the breast stroke, keeping my legs wide apart,
just as a frog might. With my head sticking straight
out of the water, I could observe various things even
as I swam—the delicate shading of the waves, the
fresh leaves on shore, the drifting clouds. I kept my
head stretched out like a turtle. If I could bring my
face even a bit closer to the sun, I'd get a tan that
much quicker.

There was a large graveyard behind the house
where I lived. I laid out a hundred-meter course for

myself and took up sprinting in earnest. Since the graveyard was surrounded by a dense row of tall poplars, I could loiter within the grounds and examine one requiem post after another whenever I got tired. I read some unforgettable phrases— "Moonlight Penetrates the Pool Bottom," for example, or "Three Worlds, One Purpose."

One day, on a dark, moist gravestone covered with liverwort, I made out some writing that said, "The Deceased, Jakushō Seiryō." Ascribed to the dead man in accord with Buddhist practice, the name evoked the solitude and quiet of the grave. Disturbed by this discovery, I made up several lines of verse and wrote them down on the white paper that had recently been folded like a lotus leaf and left before the grave. Intended to suggest a certain French poet, the lines read: I am in the ground now, together with the maggots. With my index finger I traced the words in mud as delicately as a ghost might have done.

The next evening I went to the grave before I did my sprinting. The words of the ghost had washed away in the rain that morning, so none of the bereaved kin would have been offended by seeing them on a visit to the grave. The white lotus leaves had torn in places.

Even as I fooled around like this, I got better at running. My leg muscles began to bulge too, but my complexion remained the same as ever. Beneath the deep tan on my face a pale, dirty color still lingered. It was quite unsavory.

I was very intrigued by my face. When weary of reading, I would take out a hand mirror and gaze at myself. Smiling, frowning, looking contemplative with my cheek resting on my palm, I never got bored. I mastered certain expressions guaranteed to make people laugh. Wrinkling my nose, pursing my mouth, and squinting, I would turn myself into a charming bear cub. I chose that particular look when puzzled or dissatisfied.

Around this time my next older sister was in the local hospital because of an illness. If I showed her my bear-cub face, she would roll about in bed laughing hard and holding her stomach. My sister had a middle-aged maid from home for company, but she was still lonely. That's why my visits meant a lot to her. My slow footsteps in the hospital corridor echoed louder than those of other people, so my sister could hear me approaching her room. By the time I got there, she would be elated.

If I didn't visit her for a week, my sister would send the maid to fetch me. With a solemn look the maid would say, You'd better come or your sister's temperature will go up. She'll be worse off then.

I was now fourteen or fifteen, and veins had become faintly visible on the back of my hand. I felt something strange and momentous taking place within me. I was secretly in love with a classmate, a short fellow with dark skin. We always walked home together after school, blushing when our little fingers merely grazed one another. Once, as we were heading along the back road after school, my friend noticed a lizard swimming right in a ditch where parsley and chickweed grew wild. Without a word he scooped up the lizard and gave it to me. I couldn't stand such creatures, but I pretended to be overjoyed as I wrapped this one in my handkerchief. Back home, I released the lizard in the garden pool where it swam around, its tiny head wavering. I looked in the pool the next morning, but the lizard was gone.

Stuck on myself, I never considered telling my companion how I felt. I usually didn't say much to him, anyway. With the skinny girl from next door, it was even worse. She was a student too, and I was quite aware of her. Even when I came toward her on the street, though, I quickly looked away as if in contempt.

One night in autumn a fire broke out near our house. Along with the others I got up to watch the flames shooting from the darkness of the neighborhood shrine and the sparks scattering all around. A grove of dark cedars loomed above the flames, and small birds darted through the air like innumerable fluttering leaves. I knew perfectly well that the girl was standing in her white pajamas by the gate next door and looking at me. I kept gazing toward the fire, though, with the side of my face toward her. I figured the glare of the flames would make my profile glitter and look splendid.

Being this way, I couldn't initiate anything on my own, neither with this classmate nor with the girl next door. When alone, though, I would act bold. I'd close one eye and laugh at myself in the mirror, or carve a thin mouth in the desktop with a knife and press my lips to it. When I colored it with red ink afterwards, the mouth turned so dark and ugly I gouged it out with my knife.

One spring morning as I was heading for my third-year class in high school, I stopped on a bridge and leaned against the vermilion-painted railing. A wide stream flowed below, just like the Sumida River, and I drifted into a reverie the like of which I had never known. I felt as though someone else was behind me, and that I myself was always assuming some pose or other. I would comment on my every gesture, no matter how slight, as if I were standing beside my own self. Now he's perplexed and is just looking at his palm—that's what I would say. Or maybe—He muttered something now while scratching behind his ear. Because of this habit, I could no longer act on the spur of the moment, as one less aware of himself would. When I came out of that reverie on the bridge, I trembled in my loneliness. And, while still in this mood, I thought of my past and my future. I went on across the bridge, various memories coming to mind, my footgear clattering on the floorboards. Again, I fell to dreaming. And I finally let out a sigh. Could I really become someone?

That's when I started getting fretful. Since I couldn't be satisfied with anything, I kept writhing about in vain. Masks in one layer after another—as many as ten or twenty—had fastened themselves upon me, and I could no longer tell how sad any one of them really was. In the end I found a dreary way out of my dilemma—I would be a writer. There were many others who were subject to this same sort of incomprehensible agitation, and all of them would be my confederates.

My younger brother had started high school by then, and the two of us shared a room. After talking over the matter, we got together with five or six friends and began a little magazine. A large printing shop stood just down the street on the other side, and I easily arranged to have our magazine produced there. I had the shop use a pretty lithograph for the front cover too. When everything was ready, we distributed copies to our classmates.

Thereafter I published something in each monthly issue. At first I wrote philosophic stories on ethical questions. I proved adept at composing a few lines in the style of the fragmentary essay. We kept the magazine going for about a year, but I got into trouble with my oldest brother about it.

Anxious about this mania for writing, my brother sent me a long letter from home. Chemistry uses equations, he wrote, while geometry depends on theorems. With literature, however, there wasn't anything equivalent to these equations or theorems that helped clarify matters. That's why genuine understanding of literature came only with age and the right circumstances.

My brother had written in a formal and stiff manner, and I agreed with what he said. In fact, he had set down my very qualifications. Responding immediately, I wrote that I was truly fortunate to have such a splendid older brother. His letter was right on the mark. However, I had to point out that my interest in literature didn't hamper my studies. Indeed, I worked all the harder because of it. I let my brother know exactly where I stood, mixing in some exaggerated feeling here and there.

More than anything, I felt I had to stand out from the crowd. The very thought kept me at my books, and, from the third year of high school, I was always at the head of the class. For someone who doesn't want to be thought a drudge, that's quite an accomplishment. Instead of my classmates jeering at me, I actually brought *them* to heel, including the judo champ we had nicknamed Octopus. In one corner of the room there was a large jar for wastepaper. Sometimes I would point to it and wonder out loud if an octopus could fit inside. The champ would stick his head in the jar and let out a strange, reverberating laugh.

The good-looking fellows in class were devoted to me as well. Even when I cut out triangular, hexagonal, and flower-shaped plasters and pasted them over my pimples, no one joked about it.

The pimples were distressing all the same, especially when they kept on spreading. Each morning when I awoke, I would run my hand over my face to see how things were. I bought all sorts of ointments, but nothing seemed to work. Before going to the drugstore, I'd write down the name of the ointment. Do you have any of this? I would ask, showing the scrap of paper with the writing. I had to make it seem I was doing someone else a favor.

I was horny—that's what the pimples really showed. The mere thought made me dizzy with shame. Actually, I'd be better off dead. My face attained its greatest notoriety within my family just about then. My oldest sister, who had gone to live with her husband's household, supposedly said that no woman would come to our own house as my bride. Informed of this, I applied even more ointment.

My younger brother worried about my pimples too. Time after time he went to buy medicine in my stead. As children my brother and I had never gotten along; when he took the entrance exam for high school, I prayed that he would fail. After we began living together away from home, though, I gradually came to appreciate my brother's even temper. As he grew up, he turned quiet and shy. Occasionally he submitted an essay to the magazine, but his writing was flat. His grades didn't look good next to mine either, and this troubled him. I would be sympathetic, and then he'd get even more discouraged. His hair came down in a widow's peak over his forehead, something he detested as effeminate. He sincerely believed that his narrow forehead had made him a dunce.

When I was with someone during this period of my life, I would either reveal everything about myself or else conceal it. To be honest, the only one I really confided in was this brother of mine. He told me everything about himself and I did the same.

One dark night in early autumn we went out to the harbor wharf. A breeze was blowing in from the strait as we talked about the red string my Japanese-language teacher had once described. The teacher had said that each boy in the class had such a string tied to the baby toe of his right foot, but no one could see it. The other end was always attached to a girl's baby toe. The string was very long, and it wouldn't break even when the boy and girl were far apart. It wouldn't tangle either, even if the two of them met right on the street. And, our teacher said, this string meant that the boy and girl were destined to marry each other.

When I first heard this story, I was so excited that I rushed home to tell my younger brother. And that evening on the wharf, listening to the waves and the cry of the sea gulls, we spoke of the red string once again.

What's your wife-to-be doing right now? I asked.

My brother shook the wharf railing two or three times with both hands. Then, somewhat awkwardly, he said, She's walking in a garden.

That was just like my brother. Yes, a young girl in large wooden clogs, walking in a garden with her fan and gazing at the primroses—how perfect for him.

Now it was my turn. Gazing out at the dark sea, I said, Mine's wearing a red sash. And then I closed my mouth tight. A ferry boat heading across the strait seemed to roll on the horizon, its windows entirely lit up as though the boat were actually a large inn.

One thing I had kept from my brother. When I came back for the vacation that summer, a new maid was working in the house. Wearing a red sash over her *yukata*, this petite girl had been very abrupt in helping me out of my shirt and trousers. Her name, I had learned, was Miyo.

Whenever I went to bed, I would secretly light up a cigarette and think of various ways to begin a story. At some point Miyo must have detected this habit. One evening, after laying out the bedding, she placed a tobacco tray right beside my pillow. When she came in the next morning to straighten up, I told her that I smoked on the sly and she should not bring me the tray. All right, she said, a sullen look on her face.

When a troupe of storytellers and musicians came to our village that summer, the household servants were allowed to see a performance. You go too, my brother and I were told. But at that period of our lives, we only made fun of such provincial amusements. Instead of the theater, we headed for the rice paddies to catch fireflies. We had gone almost as far as the woods of the neighboring village, but the dew was so heavy we came back with only twenty or so fireflies in our cage.

Presently the servants came wandering in from the theater. I had Miyo spread the bedding and hang up the mosquito net. Then my brother and I turned out the light and released the fireflies inside the net. As they glided back and forth, Miyo stood outside the net watching. I sprawled out on the bedding alongside my brother, more aware of Miyo's dim figure than of the faint glowing of the fireflies.

"Was the performance interesting?" I asked, a little awkwardly. Until then, I had never talked to a maid about anything other than her household chores.

"No," Miyo answered softly.

I burst out laughing. But my younger brother remained silent as he waved his fan at a firefly caught on the edge of the net. Somehow or other I felt very odd.

After that, I became quite conscious of Miyo. Whenever the red string was mentioned, it was her image that came to mind.

III

I was in the fourth year of high school now, and several classmates came over to visit almost every day. I would serve cuttlefish and wine, then tell them all sorts of nonsense. A book's just come out, I once said. It tells how to light charcoal. Another time I showed them my copy of The Brute Machine, a novel by an up-and-coming writer. I had smeared oil over the cover, so that I could exclaim, Here's how they're selling things nowadays. A queer binding job, isn't it? I astonished them again with a work entitled My Lovely Friend. I had cut out certain parts and arranged for a printer I knew to insert some outrageous paragraphs of my own. This book, I told my friends, was truly a rare specimen.

Miyo began to fade from memory. Anyway, I had this odd feeling of guilt over two people falling in love in the same household. Besides, I never had anything good to say about girls. I'd think of Miyo for only a moment, but still I'd get angry with myself. So I didn't say anything about her to my friends, let alone to my brother.

Then I read a well-known novel[11] by a Russian author that gave me pause. The work tells of a woman who gets sent to prison. Her downfall begins when her employer's nephew, a university student from the nobility, manages to seduce her. I lost track of the general sense of the novel, but I did put a bookmark of pressed leaves at the page where they kiss for the first time beneath a wildly blooming lilac. For me, a great novel wasn't about other people; I couldn't avoid seeing myself and Miyo in this couple. If only I were bolder, I'd act like that student. Just thinking about these things plunged me into despair. Timid and provincial, I had led a totally dull life. I would prefer instead to be a glorious martyr.

I told my younger brother these thoughts one evening after we went to bed. I had meant to be serious, but the pose I assumed got in the way. I ended up acting flippant—patting my neck, rubbing my hands together, and speaking without any elegance whatever. How pathetic that habit forced me to act this way.

My younger brother listened in bed, his tongue flicking across his thin lower lip. He did not turn toward me.

Will you marry her? he asked. It seemed a difficult question to ask.

For some reason or other I was taken aback. Who knows, I shrugged, if that's even possible? I tried to sound disheartened.

My brother suggested that such a marriage wasn't very likely. He sounded surprisingly circumspect and grown-up.

Listening to him, I realized how I truly felt. I was offended and angry. Sitting up on the bedding, I lowered my voice and insisted, That's why I'm going to carry on this fight.

My younger brother twisted about under his calico blanket, as if he were going to say something. He glanced at me and smiled slightly. I too broke out laughing and said, Well then, since I'll be leaving . . . Then I extended my hand toward him.

My brother stuck his right hand out from the blanket. I shook his limp fingers several times, laughing softly.

It was easier to convince my friends. They pretended to rack their brains as they heard me out, but that was merely for effect, as I well knew. They would accept my plan in the end. And that's exactly what did happen.

During the summer vacation of that fourth year, I virtually dragged two of these friends home with me, insisting that the three of us prepare for our college entrance exam together. I also wanted to show off Miyo to them, but this I kept to myself. I prayed that neither of my friends would seem disreputable in the eyes of my family. The friends of my older brothers were all from well-known families in the region and wore jackets complete with all the buttons. My friends had every button but two missing.

At that time a large chicken coop stood near the vacant house out back. There was also a caretaker's shed where the three of us could spend the morning studying. The outside of this shed was painted green and white, while the inside had a wood floor about four tatami mats[12] large and a new table and chairs, the furniture varnished and arranged in an orderly manner. There were two wide doors, one to the north and the other to the east, along with a casement window facing south. When someone opened the window and doors, the wind always blew in and riffled the pages of our books. Outside a flock of yellow chicks ran in and out of the grass that grew as thickly as ever around the shed.

The three of us would look forward to lunchtime, eagerly trying to guess which of the maids would come to fetch us. If it was someone other than Miyo, we would make a fuss by pounding on the table and clicking our tongues. When Miyo came, we would fall silent, only to burst out laughing when she left. One fine morning my younger brother joined us to study. As noon approached, we began our usual guessing game. My brother kept to himself, however, pacing back and forth near the window as he memorized his English vocabulary cards. The rest of us made all sorts of jokes; we threw books at one another and stomped on the floor. I also went so far as to get personal with my brother. Anxious to draw him into the fun, I said, You're pretty damned quiet today. What's the matter with you? Then, chewing lightly on my own lip, I glared at him.

Shut up! he yelled. His right arm whirled about, and several vocabulary cards flew from his hand. I turned away in amazement. And suddenly I made an unpleasant decision. From now on, I'd give up on Miyo. Within a few minutes I was doubling over with laughter, as though nothing had happened.

Luckily someone other than Miyo came to announce lunch. We went back in single file to the main house, taking the narrow path that ran through the bean field. I lingered behind, whooping it up as I tore off one round leaf after another.

From the very beginning I had never thought I'd be the victim. At the moment I was merely disgusted, nothing more. My clusters of white lilacs had been soiled with mud. And I was all the more disgusted when the prankster turned out to be my own flesh and blood.

For two or three days thereafter I fretted over all sorts of things. Wouldn't Miyo herself have walked in the garden? My brother had been almost embarrassed when shaking my hand. In brief, hadn't I been taken in? For me, nothing was more humiliating than that.

During this period one misfortune followed another. My friends, my brother, and I were all seated at the table one day as Miyo served lunch. Even while doing this, she crisply waved a round fan with a monkey's face painted in red. I would watch her carefully, to see which one of us she fanned the most. When I realized that she favored my brother, I gave way to despair and let my fork clatter onto the plate.

Everyone was banding together to torment me. I rashly suspected my friends of knowing all along. I'd better just forget about Miyo—that's what I told myself.

Several days thereafter I went out to the shed in the morning while neglecting to remove the package with five or six cigarettes by my pillow. Later, realizing my mistake, I rushed back only to find the room made up and the cigarettes gone. Now I was in for it. I called Miyo and asked reproachfully, What happened to the cigarettes? Did someone find out?

She looked gravely at me and shook her head. The next moment she stood on her tiptoes, reached behind the upper wall panel, and brought out the small green package with its sketch of two flying golden bats.

This episode restored my courage a hundredfold and revived my earlier determination. All the same I felt disheartened over my brother's role in the affair. I was uncomfortable with him because of this; and, in the company of my friends too, I stopped making a fuss about Miyo. From now on I wouldn't try to entice her. Instead, I would wait for her to make the next move. I was able to give her lots of opportunities too. I often summoned her to my room and told her to do useless chores. Whenever she came in, I somehow managed to assume a relaxed and carefree pose.

In order to attract Miyo, I paid close attention to my face. The pimples had now disappeared, but I maintained the treatments out of habit. Among my possessions was a compact, a beautiful silvery thing with a lid carved entirely in the pattern of a long, twisting vine. I gave myself an occasional facial, putting a little of my heart in the task each time.

I figured it was now up to Miyo—except that the right moment didn't come. Every so often I would slip out of the shed where we were studying and go back to the main house. Catching a glimpse of her flailing away with her broom, I would bite my lip.

The summer vacation finally came to an end, obliging me to leave home along with my younger brother and my friends. If only I could instill a small memory in Miyo, something to remember me by until the next vacation. But nothing ever happened.

When the day came to leave, we all piled into the family carriage with its dark hood. Miyo was at the front door for the leavetaking, along with the other members of the household. She kept her eyes on the ground without looking at my brother or me. The light green cord that usually held up the sleeves of her kimono was untied; she kept fumbling it like a rosary, even as the carriage pulled away. I left home on that occasion filled with regret.

In the autumn I went with my younger brother to a hot-spring village on the coast, a trip that took about thirty minutes by train from the school town. Our youngest sister had been ill and she had come to this village to take the waters. I lived there awhile, in a house Mother was renting, just to prepare for my college entrance exam. Since there was no escaping my reputation as a bright student, I had to demonstrate that I could graduate from high school and go on to college. I came to hate school more and more, but something drove me to study with all my might.

I would stay overnight with my mother and sister at the rented house, commuting back and forth to school each day by train. My friends came to the village every Sunday for a visit. By then, Miyo was only a distant memory to all of us. We would go out for a picnic, selecting a large flat rock by the sea upon which to have our beef stew and wine. My brother had a beautiful voice and knew lots of new songs. He would teach us some of them, and we'd sing together. When we finally got tired of this, we would lie down on the rock and take a nap. By the time we awoke, the tide would be in, cutting off the rock from the shore. For a moment we seemed to be dreaming yet.

I saw these friends during the week too. I'd get depressed if even a day went by without them.

One autumn day when a brisk wind was blowing, one of my teachers struck me on both cheeks in class. It was an arbitrary punishment for some gallant deed of mine, and my friends were livid. After school, the entire fourth-year class gathered in the natural history room and talked about getting the teacher fired. There were even students who clamored, Strike! A strike! I was quite upset by all this. If you're going on strike just for my sake, please stop it, I begged. I don't hate the teacher. It's not important, not really. I went among them making this plea.

Coward! Egotist!—that's what my friends called me. Gasping for breath, I hurried from the room and went all the way back to our rented house. When I arrived, I headed straight for the bathhouse. There was a plantain tree in a corner of the garden just outside the window. The wind had stripped it bare, except for a few leaves that remained to cast a greenish shadow onto the bath water. I sat on the edge of the pool, sinking into a reverie like someone already half-dead.

When haunted by a shameful memory, I would try to get rid of it by going off alone and mumbling, Oh well . . . I pictured myself wandering among the students and murmuring, It's not important, not really. I scooped water from the pool and let it trickle back over and over. And I kept repeating the words, Oh well . . . Oh well . . .

The next day the teacher apologized to the class. The strike never occurred, then, and things were patched up between the students and me. Nonetheless, the mishap cast a pall over my life. Miyo was often in my thoughts after that. Without her, I might well go to pieces.

My sister's treatment had ended, and she was supposed to depart with Mother on Saturday. I decided to go along, on the pretext of seeing them safely home. I kept the trip secret from my friends, and I didn't tell my brother why I was really going home. I thought he would know anyhow.

I set out from the village with my mother, sister, and brother, the latter accompanying us only as far as the school town. There we all paid a courtesy visit to the people at the dry-goods store who were helping my brother and me, then headed for the station and the trip home. As the train for home was about to pull out of the station, my brother stood on the platform and pressed his pale forehead with its widow's peak to the window. Don't give up!—that's all he said. Not on your life, I blithely replied. I was certainly in a good humor.

Yet by the time we had passed the last village and the family carriage was drawing close to home, I was very much on edge. The sun had gone down, and both the sky and surrounding hills were pitch dark. Listening to the rice fields rustle in the autumn wind, I was suddenly terror-stricken. I kept my eyes on the darkness outside the window, my head jerking back in surprise whenever a pale clump of Japanese pampas grass loomed up from the roadside.

Virtually the entire household was crowded under the dim entry lamp to greet us. As the carriage halted, Miyo herself came bustling out, her shoulders hunched against the cold.

That evening, lying in bed in a second-floor room, I thought of something depressing. I was tormented by the idea of mediocrity. Hadn't I been a fool in this affair? Anyone could fall for a woman. And yet, I told myself, with me it was different. I couldn't put it in a word. There simply wasn't anything vulgar involved, that's all. I mean vulgar in every sense too. But wouldn't any man in love make the same claim? Still, I mused, sticking to my guns even as I choked on my cigarette smoke, in my case there's a philosophy at stake.

During the night, while pondering the family quarrel that would surely erupt over my marriage plans, I attained an almost chilling sort of courage. I would never do anything mediocre—of that I was convinced. And I would definitely make my mark in the world. Thinking over these things, I became quite lonely—without knowing why, either. I couldn't get to sleep, so I gave myself a massage. During that time I put Miyo out of my mind. I would not defile her along with myself.

When I awoke early the next morning, the sky was bright and clear—perfect autumn weather. I got up immediately in order to gather some grapes in our arbor. I had Miyo come too, with a large bamboo basket. In giving her instructions, I tried my best to sound nonchalant, so that no one would get suspicious.

The arbor, which was in the southeast part of the field across from our home, covered an area roughly equal to twenty tatami mats. As the grapes ripened, a reed screen was normally set up about the arbor. We opened the little wicket gate in one corner and went into the enclosure. A few yellow bees were buzzing about in the warm enveloping air. Sunlight filtered through the screen and the grape leaves, casting Miyo in a pale green light.

On the way over I had devised one plan after another, my mouth twisting in a villainous smile. It felt so awkward to be alone with her, however, that I almost got irritated. Upon entering the enclosure, I had purposely left the wicket gate open.

Since I was tall, I didn't need a stool to reach the grapes. I began snipping off the clusters with my garden shears and handing them to Miyo one by one. She would quickly wipe the dew with her clean apron and put each cluster into the basket below. For what seemed a long time neither of us spoke. I was getting quite resentful when Miyo, reaching for the last cluster, quickly drew back her hand.

I shoved the grapes at her and shouted, What're you doing! My tongue clicked in disapproval.

Groaning, Miyo seized her right wrist with her left hand.

You got stung? I asked.

Yes, she replied, her eyes squinting as if dazzled by something.

Fool! I scolded.

She smiled and didn't say anything.

I couldn't remain there any longer. I'll get some ointment for it, I said, and hurried toward the gate.

Having taken her back to the main house, I looked for the ammonia in our medicine cabinet. When I spotted the purple tinted glass, I seized the bottle and shoved it toward her as roughly as possible. I wouldn't treat the sting myself.

A bus with a gray tarpaulin for a roof had just started running to our village and back. Tossed about in this humble vehicle, I departed that very afternoon. Everyone urged me to take the family carriage, but I felt that its shimmering black finish and its coat-of-arms were far too aristocratic for me. Holding in my lap the basket of grapes that Miyo and I had gathered, I gazed with profound feeling upon the fallen leaves that covered the country road. Having done my best to instill a small memory, I was at peace with myself. Miyo was mine now. I could relax.

The vacation that winter was my last as a high-school student. As the day drew near for going home, my younger brother and I felt a certain awkwardness toward one another.

Arriving at home, we went over to the kitchen hearth and sat down. We were on the floor, directly across from one another, with our legs crossed. As we glanced around anxiously, our eyes met two or three times. Miyo was nowhere about.

After dinner, my second oldest brother invited us to his room. We sat around the charcoal brazier to play cards, but every card in the deck seemed blank to me. While conversing with my older brother, I seized an opportunity to ask, Isn't one of the maids missing? I tried to sound casual, keeping my face hidden behind the five or six cards in my hand as though truly absorbed in the game. It was fortunate that my younger brother was present. If pressed by my older brother, I'd make a clean breast of everything.

My older brother cocked his head this way and that. While deciding which card to play next, he mumbled, You mean Miyo? She had a quarrel with Granny and went home. An obstinate bitch, if ever there was one.

He threw down a card. I played one of mine, and my younger brother, without a word, played his.

Four or five days later I went out to the caretaker's shed by the chicken coop. The young caretaker, who liked to read novels, filled me in on what had really occurred. Miyo had been defiled by a manservant. It had happened only once; but when the other maids found out, she could not bear to stay on. The manservant had done other mischief too and had already been sent away. But the caretaker had to spill the entire story, including the manservant's boast of how Miyo had murmured, but only after the deed, Stop! Stop it now!

With New Year's Day past and the winter vacation nearly gone, my younger brother and I went into the family library to look at various book collections and scroll paintings. As the snow fluttered down on the skylight, I gazed around eagerly. Since Father's death, my oldest brother had been making changes as the new head of the family. I could see something different each time I visited—from the selection of books and paintings to the newly decorated rooms. I unrolled a painting that my oldest brother must have sought out quite recently—a depiction of yellow roses scattering on water.

My younger brother brought over a large box of photographs and started going through the collection quickly, warming his fingertips now and then with his white breath. After a time he showed me a newly mounted print. Miyo must have gone to my aunt's house with Mother, for the print showed all three women. Mother sat by herself on a low couch while Miyo and my aunt, who were the same height, stood behind. The garden was in the background, with roses blooming in abundance.

My brother and I sat next to one another and gazed momentarily upon this print. In my own heart I had long ago made peace with my brother. I had hesitated to tell him of this other business concerning Miyo, and so he still didn't know about it. I could now look at the photo with a show of equanimity. Miyo must have moved slightly, blurring the outline of her head and shoulders. My aunt, her hands folded upon her sash, was squinting. They even look like one another, I thought.

Undine
Gyofukuki

The literal title of this tale, "An Account of Taking on the Guise of a Fish," has been altered to "Undine" in the interests of euphony. Undine figures in Western mythology as a female water spirit who can become human by marrying a man and bearing a child. This title has been chosen for want of a better one, and in the hope that it will prove memorable with readers.

According to some critics Dazai's story calls to mind a famous Japanese tale by the eighteenth-century exponent of the ghostly and macabre, Ueda Akinari. Akinari's tale, "The Carp That Came into My Dream," features a Buddhist priest named Kōgi, possibly an actual person from early in the Heian period (794–1185). In the tale, Kōgi practices compassion by purchasing the entire catch of certain fishermen, then releasing the fish and painting them as they swim away.

With a setting of almost idyllic beauty, "Undine" might impress one initially for its simplicity and charm. Both of the main characters—a charcoal-maker and his daughter, Suwa—are simple people who seem quite at home in their surroundings. They need not speak to each other often. The rural argot they do employ in their occasional exchanges (an *argot that I have not attempted to convey in the translation) only underlines how rooted they are in their own environment.*

As the tale unfolds, Suwa comes to regard her idyllic existence as merely a pointless routine. This change in her outlook eventually leads to the final climactic scene, which takes place after the girl hurries to the waterfall on sheer instinct. Her end might well be understood with reference to several earlier scenes that, though seemingly fortuitous at the time, take on meaning as the function of water as a unifying symbol becomes apparent. In one of these scenes a student perishes at the waterfall, while in another the brothers Saburō and Hachirō are separated at a stream. The story concludes with Suwa attempting to escape her father and to join up with a friend, impulses that have come to her by way of the tale of the serpent and the death by drowning of the young student.

The peaceful tenor of life early in "Undine" is disturbed by specific actions as well as by Suwa's state of mind. The greatest disruption—and the one most cryptically described—occurs when her father returns to the hut late at night. What he attempts in this brief scene confirms that he is drunk and also deeply frustrated over his daughter's alienation from him. However, a second symbolic network in the tale, even more obscure than the one related to Suwa's fate, gives a different complexion to this drunken attempt at violence. Suwa, it will be noted, arranges her hair before awaiting her father's return. Here, she seems to be her usual innocent self, and perhaps she is. However, a curious gesture of hers from earlier in the story—the placing of her father's finger into her mouth after she hears his tale of Saburō and Hachirō—becomes quite ominous in retrospect and makes one wonder, for a moment at least, whether Dazai doesn't see her as a temptress, though perhaps an unwitting one.

"Undine" portrays a girl who eventually undergoes the stresses of puberty while living alone with her stolid father. Having rejected him, she instinctively heads toward the waterfall and the pool, the milieu that has come to represent for her the possibility of companionship and consolation. Like the student, she ends up being pulled into the depths—whether to be destroyed or fulfilled the author does not say.

I

In the far north of Honshu there's a row of low hills known as the Bonju Range. Only three or four hundred meters high at best, these hills don't appear on an ordinary map.

Long ago the entire area was apparently under the sea, and people in the region still say that the hero Yoshitsune once came here by boat. It happened after he had gone into hiding and was fleeing northward toward the shores of faraway Ezo. His boat ran aground—there's a square patch of red soil some ten meters across on a low tree-covered hill midway along the range that shows where he landed.

They call this particular place Bald Horse Hill. That's because, from the village below, the patch of red soil is supposed to resemble a galloping horse. In fact it's more like an old man's profile.

Bald Horse Hill is also famous hereabouts for its scenery. A stream emerges from behind the hill and flows past the village and its twenty or thirty homes. Several miles up this stream a waterfall descends from a cliff. The waterfall is one hundred feet high and looks very white.

The trees covering this hill begin to change color at the end of summer. The leaves are beautiful in the autumn, and people come from the provincial towns to view them, enlivening even this remote place for a time. At the foot of the falls there is a small tea stand to serve them.

Just as the season was getting underway this year, a death occurred at the falls—an accidental death, though, and not a suicide. The victim was a student from the city with a pale complexion. He had come, as others occasionally do, to collect some of the rare ferns that grow here.

The pool below the falls is surrounded almost entirely by high cliffs. A narrow gap opens to the west, and here the water rushes against the rocks and pours out into the stream. The ferns grow in patches down the cliffs, moistened by the constant spray and quivering in the roar of the waters.

The student had been scaling one of the cliffs. It was afternoon, and the early autumn sun still shone overhead. When he was halfway up, a rock the size of a man's head suddenly gave way beneath his foot, and he fell as though he had been torn away from the cliff. On the way down he got snared by the branch of an aging tree. But the branch snapped, and he was sent plummeting into the pool below with a horrible splash.

Several people nearby witnessed the fall. The girl

who looked after the tea stand—she was going on fourteen—saw it best.

She watched him sink far into the pool and then float up until his body rose halfway above the surface. At that moment his eyes were shut, his mouth was slightly open. His blue shirt was torn in places while the collector's box still hung from his shoulder.

The next moment he was again sucked down—all the way to the bottom.

II

On clear days from late spring until well into fall, columns of white smoke can be seen even from faraway rising over Bald Horse Hill. The sap runs abundantly then, and the trees are just right for producing charcoal. So the charcoal-makers work hard at their kilns during this period.

There are ten or so huts on Bald Horse Hill, each with a kiln. One of the kilns is located near the waterfall, off by itself. The other charcoal-makers are from this area, while the man working this kiln comes from a distant part of the country. The girl who runs the tea stand is the man's daughter. Named Suwa, she lives alone with her father throughout the year.

Two years ago, when Suwa was twelve, her father set up the little stand with logs and a reed screen. He also arranged a number of things on the shelves for her to sell—lemonade and crackers, rice jelly, and all sorts of sweet candies.

With summer approaching once again and people beginning to come around, Suwa's father would assemble the stand. He would then carry the provisions there every morning in a basket, his daughter skipping along behind him in her bare feet. Upon reaching the site, he would soon go back to the hut and his own kiln, leaving Suwa there all alone.

If she caught even a glimpse of any sightseers, Suwa would call out the greeting her father had taught her—"Hello! Please stop in for a while." But the roaring falls drowned out her sweet voice, and she could seldom catch anyone's attention. In a whole day she could not even take in fifty sen.

Her father would return at dusk, his entire body black as charcoal.

"How much did you get?" he'd ask.

"Nothing."

"Too bad," he would mutter, as if it didn't much matter. After looking up at the falls, he would place the sweets back in the basket. And then they would go back to the hut.

It went on like this day after day until the frost came.

Suwa's father could leave her alone at the tea stand without having to worry. Since she had grown up among these hills, she wasn't going to lose her footing on a rock and plunge into the waterfall pool. In fact, when the weather was good, she would take off her clothes, dive into the pool, and swim up close to the falls. If she noticed someone while she was swimming, she would toss her short brown hair from her forehead with one hand and then cry out, "Hello! Please stop in for a while."

When it rained, Suwa would crawl under a straw mat in the corner and take a nap. A large oak grew out over the tea stand, its abundant leaves providing shelter from the rain.

Suwa would gaze up at the thundering falls and imagine that the water would eventually run out. She also wondered why the waterfall always took the same shape.

Lately her thoughts had deepened.

She could now tell that the waterfall didn't always keep the same shape. In fact the varying width and the changing pattern of the spray made one dizzy. Finally the billowing at the crest made her realize that the falls was more clouds of mist than streams of water. Besides, she knew that water itself could never be so white.

One day Suwa lingered dreamily beside the falls. As the sky became overcast and the early autumn wind reddened her cheeks and made them smart, she remembered the tale her father had told her some time ago. He had held her in his lap then, while keeping an eye on the kiln.

The story concerned two brothers, Saburō and Hachirō, both of whom worked as woodcutters. Hachirō, the younger brother, had caught some trout in a mountain stream and had brought them back home. Before Saburō returned from the mountains, Hachirō grilled one of the trout and ate it. The fish tasted good, so he ate two or three more of them. After that, he couldn't stop until he had eaten the entire catch. He was thirsty now—so thirsty that he drank all the water in the well. Then he ran to the river at the edge of the village and kept on drinking. Scales suddenly spread out over his body. By the time his brother came running back, Hachirō had become a great serpent and was swimming in the river.

"Hachirō! What is it?" Saburō called out.

Shedding tears, the serpent called back from out in the river. "Ah, Saburō!"

Weeping and wailing, the two brothers called back and forth, one from the bank and the other from the river—"Ah, Hachirō!" "Ah, Saburō!" Unfortunately there was nothing that could be done.

This tale had so moved Suwa that she had put her father's charcoal-blackened finger into her small mouth and wept.

Coming out of her reverie, she gazed at the falls in wonder. The water seemed to murmur—"Ah, Hachirō! Ah, Saburō! Ah, Hachirō!"

Her father, pushing the leaves aside, emerged from the red ivy that hung along the cliff.

"How much did you sell, Suwa?"

Her nose glistened with spray from the falls. She rubbed it without making any reply. Silently her father gathered up the things.

They headed home, pushing through the bamboo grass that overgrew the mountain road. Before they had covered the quarter mile back, Suwa's father said, "Maybe you should quit now." He shifted the basket from his right hand to his left, the lemonade bottles clinking against one another. "It's getting cold," he went on, "and no one's coming any more."

As the sunlight faded, the only sound was that of the wind. Once in a while the leaves falling from the oak or fir trees would strike against the father and daughter like sharp hailstones.

"Papa," Suwa called out from behind, "what are you living for?"

The huge shoulders merely shrugged. Then Suwa's father looked closely into his daughter's determined face and muttered, "Nothing, I guess."

Suwa bit off part of the long grass leaf she was holding.

"You're better off dead, then."

His hand flew up—he would teach her some respect! Then, hesitantly, he lowered it. His daughter had been on edge for some time now. He realized that she was getting to be a woman and he must leave her be.

"All right," he conceded, "all right."

Stupid! That's what this listless reply was—stupid! Suwa spat out bits of the leaf. "Fool!" she screamed. "You're a fool!"

III

The Festival of the Dead[1] was over, and the tea stand had been taken down for the winter. For Suwa this was the worst time of the year.

Every fourth day or so her father would hoist a bag of charcoal onto his shoulders and set off for the market. There were men for hire who did this sort of work, but he could not afford the fifteen or twenty sen they would charge. Leaving Suwa all alone, he would carry the load himself to the village below the hill.

When the weather was good, Suwa would hunt mushrooms while her father was gone. After all, the charcoal would not bring in enough for them to live on, even when it sold for five or six sen a bag. So Suwa had to pick mushrooms for her father to sell as well.

The moist, pea-shaped *nameko* would fetch a good price. They grew in clusters on decaying logs among clumps of fern. Each time Suwa saw moss on the logs, she thought of the only friend she had ever had. She liked to sprinkle the moss on top of her mushroom-filled basket and head for home.

Whenever her father sold the charcoal or mushrooms for a good price, he would return with saké on his breath. Once in a while he would bring back a paper purse or some other gift for Suwa.

One day a raging wind blew about the hill from early morning, causing the straw mats that served as curtains to swing back and forth within the hut. Suwa's father had gone down to the village at dawn.

She decided to stay inside today and arrange her hair, an unusual thing for her to do. When she had finished tying up her curls in a paper ribbon patterned with waves, a present that her father had given her, Suwa stoked the fire and sat down to await his return. Now and then the call of a wild animal could be heard, along with the rustling of leaves.

After the sun went down, Suwa prepared her supper. It was fried bean paste over brown rice, and she ate it all alone.

As the night deepened, the wind died down and the weather turned cold. An unearthly quiet settled upon the hill, the kind of quiet in which wondrous events are bound to happen. Suwa heard all sorts of things—*tengu* demons[2] toppling the forest trees, someone right outside the hut swishing adzuki beans[3] in fresh water. She even caught the clear echo of a hermit's laughter in the distance.

Tired of waiting for her father, Suwa wrapped herself in a straw quilt and lay down by the hearth.

As she dozed, a creature occasionally lifted the straw mat hanging in the doorway and peeked in. Thinking that this was a hermit from the mountains, Suwa pretended to be fast asleep.

In the glow of the dying fire, something else could just be made out fluttering through the entrance onto the dirt floor. Snow—the first of the season! Suwa was elated, even as she appeared to dream.

Pain. The heavy body almost numbed her. Then she smelled the reeking breath.

"Fool!" she screamed. Blindly she fled outside.

Snow! Whirling this way and that, it struck her right in the face. She sat down, her hair and dress already covered with flakes. Then she got up and trudged ahead, her shoulders heaving as she gasped for breath. She walked on and on, her clothes whipping about in the gale.

The sound of the falls grew steadily louder. On she marched, wiping her nose over and over with the palm of her hand. Now the roar of the falls was almost at her feet.

There was a narrow gap among the wintry, moaning trees. She leapt through it, murmuring one word.

"Papa."

IV

When she came to, it was dim and shadowy all over. She sensed the rumbling of the waterfall far above. Her body, vibrating with the sound, felt chilled to the bone.

Ah, the bottom of the waterfall pool. With that realization she felt refreshed and clean.

She stretched her legs, sliding ahead without a sound. Her nose nearly bumped against the edge of a rock.

Serpent!

Yes, she had turned into a serpent. How fortunate that she could never again go back to the hut. Telling herself these things, she tried moving her chin whiskers in a circle.

In fact, she was only a small carp. Her tiny mouth nibbled at the water while the wart on her nose wiggled back and forth.

The carp then swam about in the pool, near the deep basin beneath the waterfall. Moving her pectoral fins, she rose close to the surface, then suddenly dove, her tail thrashing hard.

She chased after tiny shrimp in the water, hid in the reeds along the bank, and tugged at the moss growing upon a rock's edge.

Then the carp lay still. Once in a while the pectoral fins twitched ever so slightly. It remained this way for a time, as if in contemplation.

Then, with a twisting motion, the carp headed straight toward the waterfall basin. In an instant the waters were swirling about, sucking it down like a leaf.

Monkey Island

Sarugashima

Two of the eleven works in this volume have animals as the principal characters—and another has a pet animal of human inclinations playing a crucial role. Though hardly a persistent motif in Dazai, the use of animals as real characters is striking, especially when it is the human psyche under duress that so monopolizes the attention in the author's best-known novels and stories.

For a brief tale, "Monkey Island" has more than its share of color and suspense. Dazai carefully draws the proper physical perspective for the characters he creates and the place they inhabit. Still, the illusion that real people are involved does persist, helped along by the lively dialogue and by the totally natural reaction of the characters to their changing circumstances.

The two principal characters have been sent across an ocean from Japan to some other island. In certain descriptive passages this island appears to be England, an identification confirmed in the coda of the story. The date 1896, also mentioned in the coda, was likely chosen after some deliberation. At this point, over midway through the Meiji Period, Japan was beginning to extricate itself from the unequal treaties by which the principal Western maritime *powers, England included, had imposed such restrictions as extraterritoriality upon the country.*

The allusions to history, though marked, are somewhat incidental to the story, the focus of which remains on the contrast between the two principal characters. One of them, a recent arrival on the island, displays considerable pluck and bravado, while his companion, a longer occupant of the island, is more settled and conservative in his outlook. While gradually learning the truth about the unfamiliar surroundings, the new arrival comes into conflict with his somewhat reluctant tutor. He is prepared to take a chance, even if this means rejecting a life of security and ease; his cohort would prefer to adapt to circumstances, relinquishing much of his freedom but avoiding any risk to his present status.

The issues involved, then, are serious ones. Dazai, however, treats them quite casually, as if he were more intent on offering the reader a bit of diversion than a moral lesson.

Imagine how bleak those early moments were. I had come all the way across the sea, and the island was shrouded in mist. Was it night? Or day? I couldn't even tell which as I blinked my eyes and tried to look the place over. Finally I made out some large, bare rocks heaped upon one another to form a steep slope. Here and there, among the rocks, the dark mouth of a cave loomed. Could this really be a mountain? Without even one blade of grass?

I tottered along the beach at the foot of the slope.

A strange cry reached my ears now and then—and not from far off, either. Was it a wolf? Or maybe a bear? I was exhausted after the long voyage, but that only stiffened my will. Ignoring the cries, I followed the path that ran along the beach.

I was amazed at the monotony of the place. No matter how far I walked, the path went on and on. The mountain was on my right, with a vertical wall of rough, pebbly stones on the left. Between them ran the path, six feet wide and utterly bare.

As long as it continued, I would keep on going. I was too tired and confused for words, but that made me absolutely fearless.

I must have come about a mile when I found myself back where I had started. Only then did I realize that the path merely went around the foot of the mountain. But hadn't I passed by this very spot even after I started out? Of course. I must have gone around twice without realizing it. So the island was smaller than I had first imagined.

The mist was gradually lifting, and the mountain-top now seemed to press directly upon my brow. Irregular in shape, the mountain had three different ridges. The middle one was a mound, maybe thirty or forty feet high. This mound sloped gently on one side toward a ridge below; on the opposite side, it dropped off sharply until, about halfway down, it bulged out into another ridge. In the gap between the cliff and this ridge, a waterfall descended straight down. The rocks on this misty island were dark with moisture, especially those that were by the waterfall. There was a tree at the crest of the falls, apparently an evergreen oak. Another tree stood on top of the bulging ridge, but I had never seen anything like it before. Both of the trees were bare.

For a time I gazed at this desolate scene in utter amazement. The mist kept lifting until sunlight fell upon the high middle ridge, its surface wet and glistening. This was the morning sun, no doubt about it. I can tell morning from evening because of the difference in fragrance. Had the dawn finally arrived then?

Somewhat revived, I started to scramble up the mountain. The slope had looked steep from the bottom, but it was easy to climb. I found one foothold after another and soon reached the crest of the falls.

Here the morning sun came directly down, and a gentle breeze played upon my cheek. I went over to the tree that had seemed an evergreen oak and sat down. Was it really an evergreen oak? Or a Japanese oak instead? Maybe it was a fir? I looked all the way to the tip. Thin, dead branches stood out against the sky all along the trunk, with most of the lower ones roughly broken off. Should I climb up?

> *The blowing snow*
> *Is calling me.*

That sound was probably the wind. I found myself shinnying up the trunk.

> *Calling me*
> *From captivity.*

One hears all kinds of singing when exhausted. Reaching the tip, I swung back and forth on a withered-looking branch.

> *Calling me*
> *From a wretched life.*

Suddenly the branch snapped. Grabbing the trunk, I slid down recklessly.

"You busted it! Damn you!"

I definitely heard this, from somewhere above. Clinging to the tree trunk, I stood up and gazed in the direction of the voice. Instantly a shiver ran down my spine. From the gleaming, sunlit cliff a lone monkey was nimbly making his way down. At that moment the rage that I had kept down suddenly flared up.

"C'mon," I bellowed, "all the way down too! I broke it. If you want a fight, I'm ready."

He had reached the bottom of the cliff. "That's my tree," he said, coming toward the waterfall. I stood my ground, but he merely wrinkled his forehead. While gazing at me, he seemed dazzled by the sun. Finally he broke into a broad grin and laughed aloud. The laugh irked me.

"What's so funny?"

"You," he replied. "I'll bet you came here from across the sea, didn't you?"

"Yep," I remarked, nodding. My gaze remained on the crest of the falls where the water kept billowing wave upon wave. I was thinking of the long voyage by sea in the small wooden crate.

"I mean the wide sea, whatever it's called."

"Yep." I nodded once more.

"Just like me, then."

After uttering these words, he scooped some water from the falls and drank it. In a few moments we were sitting side by side.

"We're from the same neck of the woods. One look and you can tell. It's the glossy ears. All the fellows from there have them."

He seized my ear and pinched it hard. Angrily I knocked his hand away. Then we looked at one another and broke out laughing. For some reason I felt relaxed.

Suddenly a shriek went up nearby. Startled, I looked around. A flock of hairy, thick-tailed monkeys were standing guard atop a mound and screaming at us. I leapt up.

"Hey, calm down! They're not looking for a fight. We call them howlers. They face the sun and howl like that every morning."

I kept standing, dumbfounded. Monkeys had gathered on each ridge, bending down to bask in the sun.

"Are they all monkeys?" I asked. I might have been dreaming.

"That's right. Not the same as us, though. They're from a different woods."

I looked closely at the monkeys, one by one: a mother nursing a baby, her fluffy, white hair riffling in the wind; a crooner humming a tune, his large, red nose lifted toward the sky; a lover mounting his mate in the sun, his gorgeously striped tail wagging; a frowning malcontent busily striding about.

"Where could this be?" I whispered.

His eyes filled with compassion as he said, "I don't know, either. It doesn't seem like Japan, though."

"H'mm," I wondered, letting out a sigh. "But look at this tree—it's like the Kiso oak."

He turned around and rapped the trunk of the withered tree. Then he looked all the way to the tip.

"No, it doesn't. The branches are different. And, the bark on this one doesn't reflect the sun, does it? Of course, we can't really tell until the buds come out."

I leaned against the withered tree even as I stood there. Then I asked, "Why aren't there any buds?"

"It's been withered all spring, ever since I got here. Let's see, April, May, June—that's three months now. It just gets more and more shriveled. Maybe it's a cutting; there certainly aren't any roots. The tree beyond is even worse—it's covered all over with their dung."

He pointed at the howlers as he said this. They had ceased their howling, and the island had become quiet.

"Why don't you sit down. Let's talk this over."

I sat down right next to him.

"It's not a bad spot—the best on this island, at least. Plenty of sunshine here, and the tree too. And there's the sound of water, besides."

He glanced contentedly toward the cascade at his feet and went on talking. "I'm from northern Japan, near the Tsugaru Strait. From my birthplace you can just hear the waves breaking in the night. Waves— ah, there's a sound that really grows on you. It's just unforgettable."

I wanted to speak about my home. "I was born in the mountains, right in the middle of Japan. For me, it's the woods rather than the sound of waves. I'll take the smell of fresh leaves anytime."

"That's right! We all yearn for the woods. That's why every fellow on this island wants to settle down near a tree—just one will do."

As he spoke, he divided the hair in his crotch, revealing a number of large, dark-red scars.

"It took some doing to make this place mine."

I thought I'd better be off. "Sorry, I didn't realize it was yours . . ."

"That's all right. I don't mind. You see, I'm all alone here. There's room for you, though. Just make sure you don't break any more branches, okay?"

The mist had disappeared entirely, and a fantastic scene lay before us. Fresh leaves—that's the first thing I noticed. I realized this was exactly the season when the oak leaves back home were at their peak. Nodding with pleasure, I gazed ecstatically upon a row of trees with their fresh leaves. But not for long. Another amazing sight opened up below the branches. There, on a gravel path sprinkled with fresh water, human beings were streaming past. They had blue eyes and were dressed in white. The women wore gaudy feathers in their bonnets while the men waved their heavy snakeskin canes and smiled hither and thither.

I was already trembling when my partner gave me a reassuring hug and quickly whispered, "Easy, now. It's like this every day."

"What's going to happen? They're all looking for us."

I remembered the whole ordeal—from my capture in the mountains to when I arrived on this island. I bit my underlip.

"They're putting on a show," he quickly remarked. "Just for us. Quiet down, now, and we'll have fun."

Once again he slipped his arm about me. Then, waving his other arm toward this person or that, he spoke to me in a whisper. That one's a wife, he began, and she knows only two ways to live—either she's the husband's boss or else his toy. I've heard this strange word belly-button, and I often wonder if people use it with someone like her in mind. There's a scholar, he went on, a creature who earns his bread by footnoting a dead genius or sniping at a living one. Just looking at the likes of him will make you drowsy. He pointed to an actress next, calling her an old hag. He told me how she played her own life more dramatically than any stage role. He groaned with exaggeration then, and he said, Oh, how this back tooth of mine hurts! And there, he continued, goes a landlord, a coward who always grumbles about how hard he works. Whenever you see him, you feel as though lice were crawling along the bridge of your nose. And over there, sitting on that bench and wearing white gloves—he's the worst one of all. Look at him! All I can say is, when he shows up, the air seems to smell like yellow shit.[1]

I listened to his chatter half-heartedly, for something else had caught my attention. For some time now, two children had been peeping at the island, their faces just above the pebbly wall. They had a greedy look about them, and their clear blue eyes seemed on fire. Both must have been boys, with short blond hair that riffled in the breeze. One had a nose with dark freckles, while the other had cheeks fresh as peach blossoms.

Presently the boys cocked their heads, as if thinking something over. Then the freckled one pursed his lips and whispered excitedly into the ear of his friend. I seized my companion and shrieked, "What's he saying? Tell me! What're those kids talking about?"

The monkey seemed to be stunned. He stopped jabbering right away, then looked back and forth between the boys and me. Lost in thought, he twisted his mouth about and muttered, giving me the impression that he was greatly troubled. Even after the boys sputtered some words or other and disappeared behind the wall, he remained hesitant, his hand touching his forehead one moment and scratching his rump the next. At last, the corner of his mouth twisted in a cynical grin. "Those boys," he slowly drawled, "were grumbling how everything's the same whenever they come."

Finally, I caught on—everything's the same. My suspicions, which I had kept to myself until now, were right on target. If they were complaining, then we were putting on the show.

"I see. You lied to me before, didn't you." I could have thrashed him on the spot.

His arm tightened about my waist and he replied, "The truth is cruel."

I sprang upon his enormous breast, disgusted at his concern for me. I was even more ashamed of my own stupidity.

"Stop your whimpering. It won't do any good." Then, gently patting my back, he went on in a weary voice. "There's a long, narrow signboard over there. You see it, sticking above the stone wall? The back side is facing this way—just a piece of weather-beaten wood. But the other side's got something written on it. Maybe it says, 'The Japanese Monkey, known by its glossy ears.' Or else, something even more humiliating."

I didn't want to hear any more. I let go of him and raced over to the withered tree. Scrambling all the way up the trunk, I caught hold of a branch and looked out over the entire island. The sun was already high, and patches of haze were forming here and there. Beneath the blue sky, at least a hundred monkeys basked peacefully in the sun. He remained crouched near the waterfall, but I shouted down to him anyway, "None of them realize?"

Without looking up, he replied, "Them? Probably just you and me."

"Can't we make a run for it?"

"You want out?"

"I'm going," I insisted. The green leaves, the gravel path, and the stream of people rushed before my eyes.

"You're not scared?"

He shouldn't have said that. I shut my eyes tight, trying to block out his words.

In the breeze caressing my ears, there echoed a low, melodic voice. Was he singing? My eyes grew warm. It was the very song that had brought me down from the tree before. I closed my eyes and listened.

"No, no. Come down. It's lovely here. There's sunshine and trees. You can hear the sound of water. Best of all, there's no worry about where your next meal's coming from."

I heard his voice as if from afar. And also the low laugh that followed.

Ah, how tempting it was. And close to the truth as well. Maybe it was the truth. Something almost collapsed within me. And yet, the stirring—the stirring of my mountain blood—would not be quelled.

I wouldn't stay!

A bulletin from the London Zoo was issued in mid-June, 1896. A break had occurred at Monkey Island. Two Japanese monkeys, not merely one, had escaped. Both of them, the bulletin concluded, remain at large.

Heed
My Plea
Kakekomi uttae

The first of several tales in this collection based extensively on other texts, "Heed My Plea" amply demonstrates the author's familiarity with the New Testament and his intense interest in the figure of Christ. Dazai calls up his biblical quotations and references so freely as to startle the reader accustomed to seeing the scriptural passages in their usual context. Since the author employs a lively style to recast the biblical episodes, it seemed preferable to depend on a contemporary translation for the quoted passages rather than one of the more stately, older translations. The New English Bible: New Testament, *published by Oxford University Press, was judged most suitable for this purpose.*

Scholars have shown that Dazai began to study the Bible during the mid-1930s, applying himself to the task with special intensity in the autumn of 1936 while spending a month in a hospital for psychiatric observation. Although his interest appears to have diminished after his marriage to Ishihara Michiko in 1939, there is documentation showing that he subscribed from 1941 through 1946 to a Japanese periodical entitled Biblical Knowledge.

Dazai's wife has revealed that her husband dictated "Heed My Plea" to her orally at one sitting ear-

ly in their marriage—without pausing to choose his words, either. Her testimony is occasionally cited as evidence that the author was expressing ideas and feelings very close to him—indeed, that he had personally experienced an internal conflict acted out in the tale between Christ and Judas. Be that as it may, the tale is wholly in the form of a dramatic monologue by Judas, his breathless tone being crucial to the narrative but difficult to convey in translation.

Although Judas addresses his plea to one or more officials, some Japanese critics, mindful of the above testimony, contend that Dazai is simply using Judas as a means of venting his own cri du coeur upon the reader. Although the author presumably prepared himself carefully before sitting down with Michiko, the heightened rhetoric and the sudden transitions of the monologue do convey an impression of spontaneous composition.

However, the degree of authorial deliberation behind the tale becomes evident when one takes note of the irony in a host of passages. Such irony is especially evident in those passages where Judas abruptly changes his mind—and he often does, nowhere more egregiously than at the end of his monologue, where he seems to deny his entire protest. Furthermore, the original title of the tale, "The Direct Appeal," possibly evokes less immediate sympathy for Judas than the freely rendered English title.

In any event some readers will possibly dismiss Judas as a totally unreliable narrator because of his sudden changes of mind; others will possibly take this very phenomenon as a sign that the witness is being forthright. Dazai himself seems to render an adverse judgment by having Judas finally admit to a mercenary motive. Although the passage where this occurs seems conclusive in the telling, it does not come across as the culmination to which the tale has been leading. The sense of an arbitrary ending could signify that the author might not have resolved the precise nature of Judas' quarrel with Christ.

Listen to me! Listen! I'm telling you, master, the man's horrible. Just horrible. He's obnoxious. And wicked. Ah, I can't bear it! Away with him!

Yes, yes, I'll be calm. But you must put an end to him—he's against the people. Yes, I'll tell everything—the whole story from beginning to end. And I know where he is, so I'll take you there right away. Put him to the sword then, and don't show any mercy. It's true that he's my teacher and lord, but I'm thirty-three years old too; I was born just two months after him, so there's really not much difference between us. The arrogance of the man, the contempt . . . Imagine, ordering me about like that! Oh, I've had enough. I can't take it anymore—better to be dead than to hold in one's wrath. How many times have I covered up for him? But no one realizes that—not even him. I take that back, he does realize it. He's fully aware of it, and that makes him all the more contemptuous of me. He's proud too, so he resents any help I give him. He's so conceited that he ends up making a fool of himself. He's convinced that taking help from someone like me makes him look weak. That's because he's desperate to have others believe him omnipotent. Pure stupidity! The

world's not like that. You've got to bow before someone to get on. That's the only way—struggle ahead
one step at a time while keeping the others back.
What can he do, really? Not a thing. He's like a lamb
that's lost in the woods. Without me he'd have died
long ago in some abandoned meadow, together with
his good-for-nothing disciples. "Foxes have their
holes, the birds their roosts, but the Son of Man has
nowhere to lay his head." There's the evidence! You
see it, don't you?

And what good does Peter do? Or James, John, Andrew, and Thomas? Fools, the whole bunch of them!
They only follow at his heels uttering their unctious,
spine-chilling compliments. They're completely
taken in by this mad notion of a heaven, and every
one of them will want to be some sort of royal
minister as the day of the kingdom draws near. The
fools can't even earn their daily bread here in this
world. Wasn't it I who kept them from starving? I
who had him preach his sermons and then coaxed a
donation from the crowd? I who got the wealthy
villagers to contribute as well? Besides that, I did our
everyday shopping and looked after our lodging too.
I did everything and didn't complain either. But not a
word of gratitude did I get, either from him or from
those foolish disciples. Day after day I slaved on my
own, but instead of thanking me, he would pretend
not to know. And always there were those impossible commands: "Feed the multitude!" he insisted,
when all we had were five loaves and two fishes. I
had to struggle behind the scenes then and fill the
order. Oh yes, I admit that I helped him time and
again with all those miracles and sleight-of-hand
tricks.

Considering the sort of things I did, I might seem a stingy person. I'm a man of taste, though, and not stingy at all. I saw him as a lovely, innocent person without the slightest greed. That's why even though I scrimp and save to buy the daily bread, I don't hate him for squandering our every penny. He's a beautiful man of the spirit, and I appreciate him even though I'm only a poor merchant. I don't even mind when he wastes every pittance I've scraped together. But if he only had a kind word for me now and then . . . instead of all this hostility.

He was kind to me just once. We were all strolling along the shore one spring when he suddenly called out to me and said, "I realize that you, so helpful to me always, feel pangs of loneliness. But you mustn't keep looking so depressed. It's the hypocrite, wishing others to know of his melancholy, who lets his feelings show. You may be lonely, but you can wash your face, smooth your hair with pomade, and smile as if nothing is wrong. That's the way of the true believer. You don't quite understand? Let me put it this way, then. We may not be able to see our True Father, but He can see even into our hearts. Isn't that enough for you? No? It isn't? But everyone gets lonely."

At these words I felt like crying out, "I don't care whether the Heavenly Father knows about me or not. Or people too, for that matter. I'm satisfied so long as you know. I love you. The other disciples may love you, but not the way I do. I love you more than anyone else does. Peter and the two Jameses merely follow you in hopes of getting something, but I alone understand. And yet I know that nothing will come of following you, and that makes me wonder why I can't leave. Well, without you, I would simply perish. I could not go on living. Here's an idea that I've kept to myself until now. Why don't you just abandon those useless disciples and give up preaching the Heavenly Father's creed. Be an ordinary man and live the rest of your life with your mother Mary and with me. I still own a small house in my native village. The large peach orchard is still there, and so are my aging parents. In the spring, just about now, the blossoms are splendid. You could spend your entire life there in comfort. And I would always be near, anxious to help. Find a good woman and take her as your wife."

After I had spoken, he smiled wanly and murmured as if to himself, "Peter and Simon are fishermen. They have no fine orchard. James and John are also poor fishermen. They have no land on which to spend their lives in comfort."

He resumed his quiet stroll along the beach, and thereafter we never spoke intimately to one another again. He simply would not confide in me.

I love him. If he dies, I shall die with him. He is mine—mine alone, and I will slay him rather than hand him over. I forsook my father, my mother, and my land. I followed him until now. But I don't believe in heaven or in God, and I don't believe he will rise from the dead either. *Him* the King of Israel? Those foolish disciples believe he's the Son of God, and that's why they leap about each time he speaks the Good News of God's Kingdom. They'll be disappointed soon—I'm certain of that. The man even says that he who exalts himself shall be humbled and he who humbles himself shall be exalted. Does anyone in the real world get away with such cajolery? Deceiver! One thing after another—nonsense from beginning to end. Oh, I don't believe a word he says, but I do believe in his beauty. Such beauty is not of this world, and I love him for that—not for any reward. I'm not one of your minions who believes the Heavenly Kingdom is at hand and cries out, "Hurrah! Now I'll be a minister of some branch or other!" I simply don't want to leave him, that's all. I'm content to be near him, to hear his voice and to gaze upon his person. If only he would cease preaching and live a long life together with me. Ah, if only that were possible, how happy I'd be. I only believe in happiness in *this* world. I'm not afraid of any judgment hereafter.

Why doesn't he accept this pure and unselfish love of mine? Ah, slay him for me! I know where he is, master, and I'll take you there. He hates me, despises me. Scorned—that's what I am. But he and his disciples would have starved without me. How could he mistreat me when I kept all of them fed and clothed?

Listen to this! Six days ago a woman from the village stole into the room where he was dining at Simon of Bethany's house. It was Mary, the younger sister of Martha, and she was carrying an alabaster jar filled with Oil of Nard. Without a word she poured the oil over him from head to toe—and didn't beg his pardon afterward either. No, she merely crouched there, quite calm, and began gently wiping his feet with her own hair.

The whole thing appeared very strange as the room became filled with fragrance. Then I shouted angrily at the girl—she shouldn't be so rude! Look! I went on, Wasn't his garment soaked through? And spilling such expensive oil—wasn't that almost a crime? What a foolish woman! Didn't she realize that such oil cost three hundred denarii? How pleased the poor would be if the oil were sold and the money given to them. Where waste occurs, want will follow.

After I had scolded her, he looked straight at me and said, "Why must you make trouble for the woman? It is a fine thing she has done for me. You have the poor among you always; but you will not always have me. When she poured this oil on my body it was her way of preparing me for burial. I tell you this: wherever in the world this gospel is proclaimed, what she has done will be told as her memorial." By the time he finished, his pale cheeks were slightly flushed.

I usually don't believe what he says, and I could easily have ignored this as more puffery on his part. But there was something different, a strangeness in the voice and in the look too, that had never been there before. For a moment I was taken aback; but then I looked again at the slightly flushed cheeks and faintly brimming eyes, and suddenly I knew. Oh, how horrible! How disgraceful even to mention it. A wretched farmgirl—and him in love with . . . No, not quite *that*—surely not that. And yet, it was something perilously close to it. Wasn't that how he felt? How humiliating for him to be moved even slightly by an ignorant farmgirl. A scandal beyond repair.

All my life I've had this vulgar, detestable ability to sniff out a shameful emotion. One look and I can spot a weakness. It might have been slight, but there was something special in his feeling for her. That's the truth, no question about it. My eyes cannot err.

No, it just couldn't be so! This was intolerable! He was caught in a trap. Never had he seemed so ridiculous. No matter how much a woman had loved him, he had always remained beautiful—and calm as the very waters. Never had he been the least bit ruffled. And then he gave in, like any slouch. He's still young, so perhaps this was natural. But I was born just two months after him, so we're almost the same age. We're young, both of us, but I'm the one who's held out. I gave my heart to him alone and refused to love any woman.

Martha the older sister has a sturdy build; indeed, she's big as a cow, and has a violent temper too. She works furiously at her chores—that's her one virtue. Otherwise she's just another farmgirl. But Mary the younger sister is different. She has delicate limbs and almost transparent skin. Her hands and feet are tiny but plump, and her large eyes are deep and clear as a lake. There's a distant dreaminess about them too, and that's partly why the villagers all marvel at her gracefulness. Even I was so astonished that I thought of buying her something, maybe even some white silk, while I was in town. Oh, now I'm getting off the track. Let's see, what was I saying . . . Oh yes, I was bitter. It just didn't make sense. I could have stamped my feet in resentment. If he's young, well so am I. I've got talent too, and I'm a fine man with a house and orchard besides. I gave up everything for him only to realize that I'd been taken in. I discovered that he was a fraud.

Master, he took my woman. No! That's not it! She stole him from me. Ah, that's wrong too. I'm just blurting things out—don't believe a word. I'm confused, and you must pardon me. There's not a word of truth to my babbling. Mere ranting and raving— nothing more. But I was ashamed, so ashamed that I wanted to rend my breast. I couldn't understand why he felt this way. Ah, jealousy is such an unbearable vice, but my longing for him was so great that I continued to renounce my own life and kept following him till now. But instead of consoling me with a kind word, he favored this wretched farmgirl, blushing in her company even. Well, he's a slouch and he's done for. There's no hope for him. He's mediocre—a nobody. So what if he dies. Perhaps the devil had possessed me, but here I suddenly had a frightening thought. He was going to be slain anyway, I reasoned, so why shouldn't I do it? He sometimes acted as though he wanted someone to slay him. I'd do it with my own hand, then, because I don't want anyone else to. I'd slay him, then die myself. Master, I'm ashamed of these tears. Yes, all right, I won't weep anymore. Yes, yes, I'll speak calmly.

The next day we set out for Jerusalem, the city of our dreams. As we drew near the temple, a large crowd of both young and old followed after him. Presently he took note of a lone, decrepit ass standing by the road, and, mounting the animal with a smile, he looked grandly at his disciples and spoke of fulfilling the prophecy, "Tell the daughters of Zion, 'Here is your King, who comes to you in gentleness, riding on an ass.' " I alone was depressed by the incident. What a pathetic figure. Was *this* how the Son of David was to ride into the Temple of Jerusalem for the long-awaited Passover? This the debut for which he had always yearned? Making a spectacle of himself astride this decrepit, tottering ass? I could only pity him for taking part in this pathetic farce. Ah, the man was done for. If he lived another day even, he would only humiliate himself further. A flower doesn't survive if it's wilting—better to cut it in bloom. I love him best, and I don't care how much the others despise me. I resolved ever more firmly to slay him right away.

The crowd swelled moment by moment, and garments of red, blue, and yellow were flung down all along the route. The people welcomed him with their cries and lined the way with palm branches. Before and behind him, from the left and the right, the crowd swirled about like a great wave, jostling the man and the ass he was riding, while everyone sang, "Hosanna to the Son of David. Blessings on him who comes in the name of the Lord. Hosanna in the Heavens."

Peter, John, Bartholomew, and the other disciples—fools to the man—embraced one another ecstatically and exchanged tearful kisses, as if they had been following a triumphant general or seen the Kingdom of Heaven with their own eyes. The stubborn Peter held onto John and broke into joyful weeping. As I watched, I recalled the days of poverty and hardship when we traveled about preaching the gospel. In fact, warm tears welled in my own eyes.

And so he entered the temple and descended from the ass. Who knows what it was that possessed him then, but he picked up a rope and began brandishing it, both driving out all the cattle and sheep that had been on sale, and knocking over the tables of the money-changers and the seats of the pigeon sellers. "My house shall be called a house of prayer," he thundered, "but you are making it a robber's cave."

Was he daft? How, I wondered, could this gentle man carry on like a drunkard? The astonished multitude asked what he was talking about, and, gasping for breath, he replied: "Destroy this temple, and in three days I will raise it again." Even those simple disciples, unable to accept this claim, could only stare.

But I saw what he was up to—he was showing off like a child might. Since he was constantly saying that all things were possible through faith in him, here was his chance to show his mettle. But flailing a rope about and chasing away helpless merchants? What a niggardly way to prove something! I almost smiled at him from pity. If defiance meant no more than kicking over the seats of the pigeon sellers, then he was finished. His self-respect was gone, he simply didn't care anymore. He knew that he had reached his limit. And so he would be seized during Passover and take leave of the world, before his weakness became too evident. When I realized what he was up to, I gave him up for good. How amusing to think that I had once loved this conceited pup so blindly.

Presently he faced the crowd gathered at the temple and spewed forth the most insolent abuse yet. I was right—surely the man was desperate. To my eye he even looked slightly bedraggled. He was just itching to be slain.

"Alas for you, lawyers and Pharisees, hypocrites! You clean the outside of your cup and dish, which you have filled inside by robbery and self-indulgence! Blind Pharisees! Clean the inside of the cup first; then the outside will be clean also.

"Alas for you, lawyers and Pharisees, hypocrites! You are like tombs covered with whitewash; they look well from outside, but inside they are full of dead men's bones and all kinds of filth. So it is with you: outside you look like honest men, but inside you are brimful of hypocrisy and crime.

"You snakes, you vipers' brood, how can you escape being condemned to hell?

"O Jerusalem, Jerusalem, the city that murders the prophets and stones the messengers sent to her! How often have I longed to gather your children as a hen gathers her brood under her wings; but you would not let me."

Silly and stupid—that's what I thought. It turns my stomach just to repeat his words here. Why, the man who says such things has got to be deranged. He's carried on about other nonsense too—famines, earthquakes, stars falling from the sky, the moon not giving its light, vultures gathering to peck the carcasses that fill the land, the weeping and the gnashing of teeth. He speaks in such a reckless manner, as if he's stuck on himself. It's madness—the man doesn't know his place. But he won't get away with it. It's the cross for him—that's for certain.

Yesterday I heard from a pedlar in town how the elders and priests had met secretly in the latter's court and decided to execute him. I also learned they were fearful the people would rise up if he were seized in public, so thirty pieces of silver would be given to anyone who reported when he would be alone with his disciples. He was going to die then, so there was no time to lose. I had better hand him over, I thought, rather than let someone else do it. It was my duty to betray him, a last sign of my enduring love. But this would place me in a trap too—will anyone, I wondered, recognize the devotion behind this deed?

It makes no difference, though, because mine is a pure love that doesn't seek recognition. And even if people despise me forever and I end up suffering in eternal hellfire, it will be like nothing alongside of my unquenchable love for him. So determined was I to fulfill my mission that a shudder ran over me as I thought the matter over. I quietly watched for an opportunity, and finally, on the day of the Feast, it came.

We had rented a second-floor room in an old eating place upon the hill. All thirteen of us, both Master and disciples, were seated in the dim chamber about to begin the supper when suddenly he rose and removed his tunic without a word. What could he be up to? we wondered. We watched as he took the pitcher from the table and carried it to a corner. There he emptied the water into a small basin. Then, having tied a clean, white towel about his waist, he began to wash our feet. While he was washing the feet of one disciple, the others would idle about in total bewilderment. I alone sensed what was lurking in the Master's mind.

He was lonely—and so frightened that he would now cling to these ignorant bigots. What a pity. He must have realized what fate held in store for him. Even as I watched, I felt a cry rising in my throat until suddenly I wanted to embrace him and weep. Oh, how sad. Who could ever accuse you? You were always kind and just, ever a friend to the poor, and always shimmering with beauty. I know that you are truly the Son of God. Please forgive me, for I have watched these two or three days for a chance to betray you. But not any more. How criminal to think of betraying you! Rest assured that, even if five hundred officials or a thousand soldiers should come, they won't lay a finger on you. But they are watching, so let's be wary. And let's be on our way too. Come, Peter. And you too, James. Come, John. Everyone, come! Let's live the rest of our lives protecting this gentle Master of ours.

I felt a profound love for him, but I couldn't express it. There was something sublime about it that I had never known before. The tears of contrition that flowed down my cheeks felt quite agreeable. Finally he washed my feet—ever so quietly and gently, and then he wiped them dry with the towel at his waist. Oh, how he touched me! Ah, at that moment I seemed to be in paradise.

Thereafter he washed the feet of Philip and Andrew. Peter was next, but the simple man could not hide his misgivings. Pursing his lips, he petulantly asked, "Master, why do you wash my feet?"

"Ah, you do not understand what I am doing, but one day you will," the master gently admonished, crouching next to Peter. But Peter grew yet more stubborn. "No! Never! You must never wash my feet, for I am unworthy of it," he said, then drew back his feet.

Raising his voice ever so slightly, the Master gave notice: "If I do not wash you, you are not in fellowship with me." The startled Peter bowed low and implored, "Ah, forgive me. Not only my feet, Lord, wash my hands and head as well."

I couldn't help laughing. The other disciples grinned, and the whole room seemed to brighten up. He smiled too and then said to Peter, "A man who has bathed needs no further washing; he is altogether clean. And not only you. But James and John too.

All of you are clean and without sin. All except . . ."
Here he paused and sat up straight. For an instant his
eyes took on a look of unbearable suffering. Then
they shut tightly and did not open. "Except . . . if
only all of you were clean . . ."

I instantly thought—Me! That's who he meant! He
had seen through my melancholy a moment ago and
knew that I planned to betray him. But things were
different now—I had changed completely. I was
cleansed and my heart transformed. Ah, but he
didn't realize it. He hadn't noticed. No! You're
mistaken! I wanted to cry out, but the words lodged
in my throat and I cravenly swallowed them like spit.
For some reason I couldn't speak. I just couldn't.

After he had finished speaking, something
perverse sprang up within me. Meekly I gave in to
the feeling, whereupon the cowardly suspicion that
perhaps I was unclean expanded into a dark, ugly
cloud that swirled within my gut and exploded into a
righteous indignation. What! Damned? Me damned?
He despised me from the bottom of his heart. Betray
him! I told myself. Yes, betray him! I would slay
him—and myself too. My earlier determination revived, and I became an utter demon of vengeance.
Seemingly unaware of how turbulent my feelings had
become, he presently took up his tunic, carefully put
it on, and sat down at the table. By the time he
spoke, his face was pale.

"Do you understand what I have done for you?"
he asked. "You call me 'Master' and 'Lord,' and
rightly so, for that is what I am. Then if I, your Lord
and Master, have washed your feet, you also ought
to wash one another's feet. I shall probably not be
always with you, and thus I have set an example for

you to follow. In very truth I tell you, a servant is not greater than his master, nor messenger than the one who sent him. If you know this, happy are you if you act upon it." Wearily he spoke these words, then began to eat in silence. Bowing his head, he spoke once more: "In truth, in very truth I tell you, one of you is going to betray me." There was a deep sorrow in his voice, as if he were both weeping and moaning.

The disciples nearly recoiled in shock. They stood up, knocking the chairs over, and gathered about him. "Is it I, Lord? Master, can you mean me?" they cried. Like one already condemned, he barely moved his head. "It is the man to whom I give this piece of bread when I have dipped it in the dish. Alas for that man by whom the Son of Man is betrayed. It would be better for that man if he had never been born." For him, these were unusually specific words. After he had spoken them, he took a piece of bread and, stretching forth his hand, placed it unerringly in my mouth.

Instead of shame, I now felt hatred. My courage immediately came back, and I hated him for turning malicious once again—he was his old self, humiliating me before the others. He and I were like fire and water; we would always be separate. To place a piece of bread in my mouth as though feeding his dog or cat—was this all he could do in revenge? Ha! The fool! Master, he then told me to do the deed quickly, and so I ran from the place and fled along the dark road as fast as I could. I arrived here only moments ago, and I've made my plea in haste. You must punish him—punish him as you see fit. You can seize him and beat him with a rod, strip and crucify him even. I've had enough of him; he's terrible . . .

obnoxious . . . Tormenting me even yet . . . Ah, damn him! He'll be in the Garden of Gethsemane, by the River Kidron. The meal is over, and it's the hour for prayer, so he'll be there with the disciples. No one else will be around. If you go right away, you can capture him easily. Oh, those birds are making such a ruckus, aren't they? I wonder why I hear them singing tonight? I remember how the birds were chirping even as I ran through the wood. It's an unusual bird that sings in the night. My childlike curiosity got the better of me, and I wanted a glimpse of the bird. So I stopped and, tilting my head, looked up at the trees . . . ah, forgive me, I'm boring you. Master, is everything ready? Ah, the sweetness—it makes me feel splendid. It's also the final night for me, isn't it? Master, you'll be so good as to observe both of us standing side by side after tonight. I'll show you the two of us, Master, standing side by side this evening. I don't fear him. We're the same age, and I won't lower myself. I'm a young man of quality, just like him. Ah, those birds are still making a ruckus. How annoying! Why do songbirds chirp here and there? What's all the noise about? Oh yes, the money! You're handing it over? Thirty pieces of silver—for me? Ah yes, but I really don't want it. So take it back before I hit you. I didn't make this plea for money. Take it back! No, wait, I didn't mean that. Please forgive me. I accept your offer. Yes, I'm a merchant. That's why that lovely man always scorned me. But I am a merchant, so I'll take it. I'll betray him fully, just for the lucre. That'll be my best revenge. Betrayed for thirty pieces of silver—just what he deserves! And I won't shed a tear since I don't love him anyway. I never loved him at all. Master, everything I said was false; there's no question that I followed him around for the money. When I realized this evening that he wouldn't let me earn a penny, I quickly changed sides, like any merchant would. Money—that's the only thing. Thirty pieces of silver. Oh, how splendid! I accept. I'm just a penny-pinching merchant, and I can't help being greedy. Yes, thank you. Yes, yes, I forgot to mention it, but I'm Judas the Merchant. Yes, that's Judas Iscariot.

Melos, Run!

Hashire Merosu

Based partly on the classic tale of Damon and Phintias, but following in the main the retelling of this
legend by the German poet Friedrich Schiller in "The
Hostage," "Run, Melos!" could possibly be the most
widely read work by Dazai in his own country. Simple in style. and highly moralistic in substance, the
tale has found its way into many school anthologies
and into popular editions of Dazai as well.

Insofar as the Schiller poem will be unfamiliar to
many, a brief summary is in order. Much shorter
than Dazai's retelling, the poem contains just twenty
stanzas of seven lines each. In the first stanza Damon
the hero is seized by the guards of Dionysius, the
tyrannical king of Sicily. Thereafter Damon persuades the king to release him, so that he can arrange
his sister's wedding. The king agrees, on the condition that Damon return to face execution within
three days, leaving his friend (named Philostratus in
Schiller's poem) as a hostage. The wedding is described in several lines, with the remainder of the
poem taken up mostly with the obstacles Damon
encounters on his return journey to Syracuse—the
flood, brigands, enervating heat—and the ominous
news that Philostratus has likely been executed.
However, Damon reaches the execution ground just

in time, his effort wringing from the tyrant-king the admission that fidelity is not the empty illusion he had thought it to be.

Dazai both expands episodes in Schiller and adds some of his own invention. Nowhere does he add more blatantly than in the anticlimactic paragraphs depicting Melos as foolishly unaware of his own nakedness, a stroke that certainly deviates from the heavy didacticism of the tale. (This passage, it should be mentioned, has usually been excised from the school anthologies.) Particularly when read alongside of Schiller's poem, "Melos, Run!" can almost seem to be a mock-heroic tale, the passages that Dazai added to Schiller's work often portraying Melos as a somewhat proud simpleton. It must be admitted, however, that many critics do accept the hero's self-assessment at face value, and thus see him as embodying ideals of trust, fidelity, and friendship.

Quivering with rage, Melos decided that he must rid the land of this wicked and ruthless king.

He was only a village shepherd who tended his flock and played upon his flute. Yet, though ignorant of politics, he was more sensitive to evil than most other people.

He had left his village early that morning and traveled the ten leagues to Syracuse over mountains and fields. His younger sister was a shy girl of fifteen who had become engaged to an honest shepherd. Since Melos had neither father nor mother nor wife, he must select the bride's gown and order food for the wedding feast himself. It was to perform these tasks that he had come to Syracuse.

Having taken care of this business, Melos strolled down the main street looking for Selinunteus, a boyhood friend of his who worked in the city as a stonemason. They had not seen each other for quite some time, and Melos looked forward to the meeting. As he walked along, however, he began to sense that something was wrong. Since dusk had fallen, it was only natural that the city was quiet. Despite that, the place seemed so desolate that even the carefree Melos began to feel uneasy.

He stopped a youngster and asked if anything had happened. On a trip here two years ago, he had found the place lively, with people singing even at night. The boy merely shrugged and didn't say anything. Melos next questioned an old man, more insistently than he had the boy. The man didn't reply either until, seizing and shaking him with both hands, Melos again asked what the trouble was. In a whisper that couldn't be overheard, the old man replied: "The king's executing people."

"Why is that?"

"He says we're evil, but it's not true."

"Has he executed many?"

"Yes. First it was his own brother-in-law. And then his very son and heir. His sister and her children were next. And then the queen. The wise councilor Arekisus was . . ."

"That's terrible," Melos interrupted. "Is the king mad?"

"No, he's not mad. He says he can't trust people. Recently his own vassals have come under suspicion. If one of them lives a little too grandly, the king demands a hostage. And if the vassal refuses, why then he's condemned to death. The king had six of them crucified today."

Melos quivered with rage as he listened. "That's terrible," he exclaimed. "The king has got to be stopped."

Melos, being a simple man, marched straight into the castle still carrying his purchases. When the guards seized him, they found a dagger inside his cloak. An uproar ensued, and Melos was dragged before King Dionysius. His face pale and his brow carved with wrinkles, the tyrant questioned Melos in a quiet but authoritative voice.

"What were you going to do with this dagger? Speak up!"

Without flinching, Melos responded, "Free this town from its wicked king."

"You . . . ?" The king's smile was condescending. "Impossible fool! How could someone like you realize how alone I am."

"Hold your tongue!" Filled with indignation, Melos came right back at the king. "There's nothing worse than suspicion. And you suspect your own subjects."

"They made me suspicious. They're selfish and unreliable, and I can't trust them." The tyrant spoke these words calmly and then he sighed, "After all, I too want peace and quiet."

"What for," Melos sneered, "except to keep your power? Killing innocent people—that's peace for you."

Instantly the king looked up and retorted, "Silence, you wretch! You can prattle on about innocence, but I've got to see into people. I'll have you begging for mercy on the cross soon, but don't expect me to listen."

"Ah, the king is wise. Go ahead, flatter yourself. I've decided to die, anyway. I won't beg for mercy. Only . . ." Melos hesitated, his eyes lowered. "If you pity me at all, delay the execution for three days while I see to my sister's wedding. I'll return from my village once the ceremony's over. I'll be here within three days, I promise that."

"Ridiculous!" The tyrant laughed softly, his voice hoarse. "Are you trying to tell me a captured bird will return after it's been let free? What a joke."

"I'll be back," Melos insisted. "I don't break my word. Give me three days. My sister's expecting me. If you don't trust me . . . All right then, there's a stonemason named Selinunteus in this city. He's my best friend, and he'll be my hostage. If I'm not back by sunset, have him strangled. Give me a chance; I'll prove I can keep my word."

At these words the coldhearted tyrant grinned. He could tell that Melos was bluffing and that he would never return. He would play along, though, pretending to be taken in and letting Melos go free. It would be fun to have the hostage executed three days later. And as the execution was being carried out, he himself would wear a melancholy look to show how much he regretted that people could not be trusted. Yes, he would teach these so-called honest fools a thing or two.

"I grant your request. You may summon the hostage. But come back," he cautioned, "in three days. And by sunset. If you're late, I shall execute him. Well, on second thought, you might come back a bit late. I'll see that you're acquitted for good."

"What was that?" Melos declared. "I don't see what you're getting at."

"Oh, come now, anyone can see that you don't want to die. If it suits you, be late. I can tell what you're up to."

Melos stamped the ground in anger. He wouldn't utter another word.

Late that night Selinunteus was brought to the castle, and the friends met in the presence of the king. Though two years had passed since their last meeting, Melos had only to explain the situation to Selinunteus who nodded and firmly embraced his friend. Nothing more was required between them. After Selinunteus was bound with a rope, Melos set off under an early summer sky filled with stars.

He hurried along the road, never pausing to rest. By the time he reached home, the sun was high and the villagers were busy in the fields. His sister was there too, tending the flock. Seeing her weary brother approach with faltering steps, she began to ply him with questions.

"No," Melos replied, "nothing's wrong." Forcing a smile, he went on. "I've still got something to do in town, so I must go back soon. The wedding will take place tomorrow—the earlier the better."

His sister blushed.

"Are you pleased? Look, I bought a nice dress for you. Now go tell the villagers the ceremony will be tomorrow."

After tottering on home, Melos barely managed to decorate the family altar and arrange the banquet chairs before collapsing to the floor. There he slept the entire day, hardly seeming to breathe. When he awoke, he went to see the bridegroom. There was a

problem, he said, and the wedding would take place
tomorrow.

That was impossible, the amazed shepherd replied.
He hadn't been able to prepare anything yet, and so
he asked that the wedding wait until the grapes were
harvested.

It couldn't wait, Melos insisted. The groom would
simply have to arrange the wedding for tomorrow.

But the shepherd was stubborn, just like Melos,
and he would not agree to the idea. They continued
the dispute through the night until finally, after much
soothing and cajoling, Melos prevailed. By then, it
was already dawn.

At noon the bride and groom took their marital
vows before the gods. Yet, even as the ceremony was
taking place, dark clouds began to cover the sky. At
first, just a few drops fell, but then the rain started
coming down in torrents. The guests at the banquet
felt something ominous, but they roused themselves
and began clapping their hands and singing lively
songs in spite of the warm, stifling air. For the time
being, Melos could smile with delight, his promise to
the king forgotten.

The banquet grew even livelier as dusk fell and the
guests stopped worrying about the rain. They were
good company, and Melos wished he could stay. But
he was bound by a pledge and could not do as he
wished. Although he must leave the banquet, he
could still have a nap before setting out. It was a long
time until sunset tomorrow, and it would be best to
leave only after the rain had let up. Even a hero such
as Melos feels attached to his home, and that's why
he would linger there as long as possible.

Melos went up to the bride, who seemed almost

dazed with happiness, and offered his congratulations. "I'm very tired," he went on, "and so I'll sleep awhile and then leave for town to take care of that business I mentioned to you. You're married to a fine man, so you won't miss me when I'm gone. You know the two things I hate most, don't you? Being suspicious of someone and telling lies. All I have to say is that I hope you'll be honest with your husband. And be proud of your brother, too, for he may well achieve something."

After the bride nodded to him as if she were dreaming, Melos went up to the groom and clapped him on the shoulder. "The wedding had to be performed all of a sudden," he explained, "and neither one of us could do anything about this. I've got only two things of value—my sister and the sheep. I don't have anything else to give you. There's just one more thing to say," he went on. "We're brothers now, and I want you to be proud of that."

Melos smiled as the embarrassed groom rubbed his palms. Then he bade farewell to the villagers too and left the banquet. When he reached his own sheep-pen, Melos crawled inside and fell sound asleep.

He awoke in the pale light of dawn. Oh God, he thought, springing to his feet, have I overslept? No, there was still time. If he left at once, he could reach Syracuse by sunset. He would show the king that men kept their word. And then he would laugh as they fastened him to the cross.

The rain seemed to slacken as Melos calmly prepared for the journey. When he was ready to leave, he swung his arms in a circle and dashed out into the drizzle like a flying arrow.

Tonight I shall die, he told himself. I will be put to

death for having run. But I will rescue my hostage friend and defeat the wicked king as well. I must run—run that I may be put to death. Melos, be faithful even in your youth. Farewell, my native village.

It was heartrending to leave, and young Melos almost halted several times. But each time he rebuked himself, crying "Faster! Faster!" until his village receded behind and he found himself cutting through fields and woods. By the time he reached the next village, the rain had stopped and the sun was well up in the sky. Clenching his hand, Melos wiped the sweat from his brow.

Having come this far, he no longer yearned for home. The wedding had taken place, so he needn't worry any longer about his sister. He need only go straight to the castle—and, since there was plenty of time before sunset, he could walk the rest of the way. Lapsing into his usual nonchalant manner, Melos strolled along chanting his favorite ballads.

He covered two more leagues, then a third. When he was halfway to Syracuse, disaster suddenly confronted him. Melos stopped dead in his tracks. What a sight! The river before him had flooded from yesterday's downpour in the mountains. The muddy torrent had gathered strength and knocked the bridge out; now it roared past, smashing the fallen girders to pieces. Melos stood in amazement before looking around and calling for help as loud as he could. But the boats had been swept from their moorings without a trace, and there was no longer even a ferryman present.

The river kept rising until it spread out like the sea. Melos could only crouch on the bank and weep like a child in spite of his years. Lifting his arms, he prayed to Zeus: "I beseech you, hold back this surging current. Time is going by, and the sun is high already. If I cannot reach the castle before dusk, my faithful friend will die."

As if to mock his plea, the muddy torrent rose even further. Wave engulfed wave, whirling and spreading out as the moments slipped by. Melos decided there was only one way across, and that was to swim. Calling on the gods to witness that the love and fidelity within him were stronger than this swift current, Melos plunged in. It was a desperate struggle, for the churning waves coiled about him like a mass of serpents. But Melos plowed ahead, putting all of his strength into each stroke. What matter if the swirling waves pounded him and pulled at his body? Perhaps the Powers That Be helped the fiercely struggling youth out of pity. In any event he was being swept away when—bravo!—he grasped a tree trunk on the opposite bank and held on.

Praise be the gods! Melos shook the water from his body like a horse emerging from a stream. With the sun already going down, he could not waste a moment. And so he set off running again. Gasping for breath, he climbed a mountain pass. Having reached the top, he let out a sigh of relief only to have a gang of thieves leap forth and cry, "Don't move!"

"What's the meaning of this?" Melos responded. "Get away! I've got to reach the king's castle before sunset."

"Leave your goods. Then be off."

"All I've got is my life. And I'm taking that to the king."

"We'll take it to him for you."

"So the king sent you to ambush me, then?"

Without a word the thieves began swinging their clubs. Melos ducked quickly, then flew at the nearest assailant and wrenched away his weapon.

"Sorry," he declared, "I wouldn't do this if my honor weren't at stake." A ferocious assault sent three of them sprawling. As the others cringed, Melos raced down the pass without even pausing for breath.

As he ran on, however, the sun beat down on him and he felt exhausted. One bout of dizziness succeeded another, but he would not give in. With each attack he summoned his strength and stumbled ahead a few steps. But finally his knees buckled, and he lay helpless. Gazing at the heavens, he wept in despair.

Ah, Melos, you swam a muddy torrent and knocked down three thieves. A mighty effort had brought him this far; he had run like Skanda himself, the Indian god who caught up with the fleeing culprit who made off with the ashes of the Buddha. But now he was exhausted and could not go on. How tragic that a dear friend would die for trusting him. The king had been right: Melos would be known as a notorious traitor.

Melos reproached himself, but his sagging body could not even maintain a snail's pace. He rolled into the grass by the roadside. When the flesh is weary, the spirit too gives up; and somewhere within the body a sense of indifference takes root. In this extremity, Melos simply gave up.

He had already struggled valiantly, never questioning his pledge, and the gods knew he had done his best. He had run until he could no longer move. He wasn't a traitor. Oh, if only he could rend his breast and reveal the heart within. Then Selinunteus would see that love and loyalty were in his very blood. But at this crucial moment his strength was gone, leaving him utterly wretched. Surely he would be mocked and his family name besmirched. He had deceived his friend. Better if he had not set out at all than to collapse along the way. But fate had taken over and he no longer cared what happened.

Forgive me, Selinunteus. You always trusted me, and I have been loyal. Our friendship has never once been darkened by clouds of suspicion. Even now you await me, confident of my arrival. I am so grateful for that, Selinunteus. Trust between friends is the world's finest treasure, and I can hardly endure what has happened. I ran, Selinunteus; I never intended to deceive you. Believe me! I ran faster and faster. I swam a muddy torrent and escaped a pack of thieves. I raced down the mountain pass in one breath. I did it because that's the sort of person I am. But don't expect anything more. Let me be. I don't care any longer. I've lost. I'm a good-for-nothing. Oh, go ahead and laugh at me.

The king whispered that I should return a little late. The hostage would be dead by then and I could go free, he promised. I hated the king for being so deceitful, but things are turning out his way. I'll probably be late, and he'll just assume he was right. He'll have a good laugh and then let me go. And that will be worse than death. I'll always be a traitor, the lowest of creatures. Selinunteus, I too shall die. Let me die with you. You alone trust me, that's certain.

(Or, Melos suddenly wondered, am I merely taking you for granted too?)

Ah, perhaps I should just be a scoundrel. I've got a home in the village and the sheep too. If I live, my sister and her husband will surely welcome me back. Justice, love, fidelity—they're really worthless when you think about it. We kill others to save our own skin—that's the way of the world, isn't it? Oh, nonsense! I'm just a disgraceful traitor. It's all over for you, Melos, you're finished. Go ahead and do as you please.

Stretching his limbs, the hero dozed off.

Melos awoke to the sound of trickling water. Holding his breath, he slowly raised his head. The sound seemed to come from just beyond his outstretched legs. Struggling to his feet, Melos saw clear water bubbling from a rock. He bent over the spring as if drawn down into it. Then he scooped a handful of water and swallowed it. Melos breathed deeply, as though awakening from a dream. He could walk.

He must be off. Perhaps he could still fulfill his pledge and die with honor. The rays of the setting sun still shone on the branches and leaves of the trees. Dusk had not yet fallen, and his friend must be waiting—quietly, trustfully. Compared with that trust, Melos' life meant nothing. He could take his own life to make up for his suspicion, but that would be too simple. He must live up to his friend's trust—that alone mattered. Thereupon he cried out, Melos, run!

Someone trusted him. The evil dream of moments before was a delusion and he must forget it. When exhausted, anyone might have such a dream. Melos' honor was still intact, and he was brave as ever. He figured that if he started running now, he could still arrive on time. How fortunate! He could die honorably, then. But he realized that the sun was going down fast, and soon it would be gone. Oh Zeus, he pleaded, please don't hurry things so much. I grew up loyal, so don't let me die a traitor.

He fled like the very wind, shoving aside or knocking down wayfarers in his path. There was group of revelers picnicking in a meadow too, and Melos ran right through them, leaving everyone bewildered.

He kicked away a dog and hurdled a stream, his pace far exceeding that of the sun. Racing by another group of travelers, he caught an ominous remark— "The fellow should be hanging from the cross about now." Ah, this was the friend for whom Melos ran, the friend who must not die. Hurry, Melos. You mustn't be late. Reveal the power of love and fidelity. Don't worry about your appearance.

Melos was almost naked. He could hardly breathe, and blood spurted now and again from his mouth. Then he saw it—the Tower of Syracuse. Small and far off, the tower glittered in the setting sun.

Then a voice seemed to groan in the wind, "Ah, Melos."

"Who is it?" Melos called even as he ran.

"Philostratus, apprentice to your good friend Selinunteus," cried the youth even as he hurried after Melos. "Stop, it's too late. He can't be saved."

"But the sun's not down yet."

"They're putting him to death this very moment. You're too late. What a shame. If you had only been a little faster . . ."

"But the sun's still up," cried Melos, his heart

nearly bursting as he stared at the huge, red orb. He knew that he must persevere.

"Stop, please. Don't run any farther. Your life's at stake now. Selinunteus believed in you. He was calm when they led him to the gallows. Even as the king mocked him, he remained faithful. He simply replied, 'Melos will return.' "

"That's why I run," Melos retorted, "because he trusts me. It doesn't make any difference whether I'm on time. I'm running for more than a life. Follow me, Philostratus."

"Ah, you must have lost your senses," exclaimed Philostratus. Then he gave in and said, "Well, maybe you won't be late. So keep on running."

This was well said. The sun had not yet disappeared, and Melos ran with his last ounce of strength. His mind was blank; he didn't think of anything. Impelled by a mysterious force, he merely ran. Finally, as the quivering sun dipped beneath the horizon and the twilight began to fade, Melos raced like the wind onto the execution grounds. He was in time.

He tried to cry out, "Wait! Don't execute him! Melos has returned. Here I am, just as I promised." But with his throat so raw, he could barely whisper, and no one heard him. The cross had been raised, and Selinunteus, a rope wound about his body, was being slowly hoisted. Melos plunged into the crowd, struggling forward with all his remaining strength just as he had when he had swum the muddy torrent.

"Hangman, it's me." Though hoarse, Melos cried out as best he could. "I'm the condemned one— Melos. I left Selinunteus as a hostage. Now I'm back."

Finally Melos climbed the platform and caught hold of his friend's ascending feet.

A stir ran through the crowd and everyone cried out together, "Hurrah! Let him down."

Selinunteus was freed of his bonds.

With tears in his eyes, Melos addressed his friend. "Strike me, Selinunteus. Strike me with all your might. I had an evil dream on the way back. If you don't strike me, I shall not be worthy to embrace you. Strike me."

Selinunteus nodded as though he understood everything. Then he slapped Melos forcefully on the right cheek, the blow resounding throughout the grounds. Thereupon Selinunteus smiled gently and said, "Strike me, Melos. Strike me on the cheek just as hard. Once during the three days you were away, I lost my trust in you—for the first time ever. If you don't strike me, I won't be able to embrace you."

His hand whizzing through the air, Melos slapped his friend on the cheek.

"Thank you, friend," they both said at the same time. Then they embraced each other firmly and wept with joy. In the crowd too weeping could be heard.

The tyrant Dionysius, who had been gazing from the rear, silently approached the two friends with a look of shame on his face.

"You have won me over, and your hopes are fulfilled. Loyalty isn't just a hollow word," he said. "Will you both accept me as a friend? Please listen to this request. I wish to be your friend."

A cheer went up from the crowd. "Long live the King! Long live the King!"

A girl came forward, holding a scarlet cloak.

Melos was confused, so his friend stepped in and said, "Melos, don't you realize you're utterly naked? Hurry up and put the cloak on. This pretty girl doesn't want everyone here seeing you like that."

The hero blushed deeply.

(From a traditional legend and the Schiller poem)

On the Question of Apparel

Fukusō ni tsuite

The narrator of "Memories," it will be recalled, had a secret yearning to dress in style. This interest in clothes crops up regularly in Dazai's writings. Dazai wrote one story entitled "The Dandy" and began another with a sketch giving the narrator's thoughts on suicide and dress. Having received some fabric for a summer kimono, the narrator postpones committing suicide until he can wear the new garment.

The present tale is a comic tour-de-force, the author portraying himself as one who gets into trouble even in trying to escape the hold of fashion. Here the emphasis on dress and appearance becomes a means whereby the author can create and manipulate his own self-image. Several incidents are described in turn, each of them more complicated than the previous one. The author-figure involved in these incidents is jaunty and sociable enough. But his companions—whether his drinking buddies or his wife—are kept more or less in the background, and his jauntiness readily lapses into a kind of mordant humor. In a more thorough way than his counterpart in "Memories," this narrator is playful and self-mocking. The mood of pathos and humor that he creates out of these attributes is one quite common in Dazai's anecdotal reminiscences.

The sketch ends with the most striking incident of all, the argument at the Asagaya tavern. Here Dazai uses the approaching wartime environment of Japan as background. ("On the Question of Apparel," it should be noted, was published in February 1941, when the Japanese were being urged to avoid extravagance by, among other things, wearing drab khaki clothing. In fact, the author refers to this very phenomenon by playfully confronting his readers with a "homework assignment" at the end of his narrative.) Dazai's narrator engages in the argument mindful of a celebrated incident at Ataka Barrier[1] involving Yoshitsune and his bodyguard Benkei, two of the most romanticized figures in Japanese history. Yoshitsune, mentioned briefly in "Undine" and the heroic general of the Genpei War (1180–85), was trying to escape capture and death at the order of his older brother Yoritomo, the de facto ruler of Japan at the time, owing to Yoshitsune's vanquishing of the Heike forces. In order to gain passage for Yoshitsune past Yoritomo's suspicious guards at the barrier, Benkei boldly struck his master. Convinced that a subordinate would never commit such an outrage, the guards were deceived into believing that Yoshitsune was in fact an underling, and they accordingly allowed him to pass through.

I was fascinated for only a short time—fascinated with apparel. While a freshman at Hirosaki High, I would wear a stiff sash over my striped kimono—whether I was heading for the house of a certain lady for lessons in ballad chanting or merely out for a stroll. This caper lasted just one year. When it was over, I threw away my stylish clothes in disgust.

Not on principle, mind you, not at all. But something happened that freshman year that made me change my ways. Having come to Tokyo for the winter recess, I flung aside the entrance curtain to an *odenya* bar[2] one evening and walked in dressed to the hilt. With the nonchalant assurance of a man-about-town, I told the waitress, Make it a hot flagon. Mind you, make it hot, now.

It was hot all right, but I still managed to swallow the saké. Then, having gotten my tongue untied, I let go with every bit of bluster I had memorized for the occasion. And when I had uttered my final sentence—something like, What the hell're you talking about?—the waitress smiled brightly and asked in total innocence, So you're from Tōhoku?

She probably meant it as a compliment, but this reminder of my provincial speech quite sobered me. I'm not an utter fool. In disgust I gave up on stylish clothes right then, and thereafter I tried my best to wear ordinary things. But I'm tall for a Japanese and I stand out even when walking down the street. (I've been measured at five feet, seven inches, but I don't believe it. I'm actually five-six and a half.)

Even when I got to the university, I tried to dress normally. But my friends kept up their warnings, claiming that high rubber boots were out of place—and that was that. But I found them convenient. You don't need any socks; you simply wear the boots over your bare feet or *tabi*,[3] and no one ever knows the difference. Generally, I wore mine without socks, and they kept my feet plenty warm. When you leave the house, there's no need to squat at the front door and fiddle around forever tying up the laces. You shove one leg into a boot, then the other, and off you go. And when it's time to remove the boots, you needn't bother taking your hands from your pockets. Give a kick and your boot comes right off. While they're on, you can go through a puddle or along a muddy lane without a care. They're real treasures, these rubber boots of mine, so why shouldn't I walk about in them?

But, my solicitous friends replied, the boots were strange and I had better give them up. They claimed that wearing such boots in perfect weather seemed eccentric. So they must have thought that I wore the boots just to be stylish—a terrible mistake on their part. Ever since that freshman year when I learned to my sorrow that I wouldn't qualify as a man-about-town, I had cherished simplicity and economy in matters of food, dress, and shelter. But I was taller than most men, and my features—my nose, for example, or my entire face—were larger than average. Somehow this seemed to offend people. I would put on a sports cap in total innocence, only to hear all sorts of advice from my concerned friends. What! You've really come up with something there! . . . Hardly suits you . . . It's strange, so you'd better get rid of it.

So what was I to do? Evidently a man must discipline himself in proportion to his size. I would have gone quietly into hiding, but people would not permit it.

In desperation I considered growing a full beard in the manner of our prime minister a few years back, His Excellency Hayashi Senjūrō; but the sight of a big, bearded fellow prowling in and out of the three rooms of my small house would be strange indeed, so I had to give up the idea.

Once a friend of mine looked at me seriously and said, You know, if George Bernard Shaw had been born in Japan, he would not have made it as a writer. Equally serious myself, I pondered the extent of literary realism in Japan and then replied—Yes, you're right. Our approach to writing is quite different here. I was going to mention several more ideas when the friend laughed and said—No, that's not what I mean. Isn't Shaw seven feet tall? A writer like that couldn't manage in Japan.

He was quite offhand and took me in utterly. I couldn't really laugh off his innocent joke, either. Indeed, there was something quite chilling about it. If I had been just a foot taller . . . ! That was too close for comfort.

Having surmised in that freshman year how evanescent fashion could be, I gave up on choosing my garb. Instead, I put on whatever was at hand and acted as though I were dressed like any ordinary person. My friends kept finding something or other to criticize all the same. Unnerved by their remarks, I gradually began to worry about my appearance. Even so, I had been told time and again about my uncouthness and was sick of hearing about it. That's why I never felt any longer like wearing anything special or ordering a *haori*[4] jacket of antique cloth tailored just for me. No, the craving for style was gone now, and so I docilely put on whatever had been given to me.

I'm not sure why, but I'm very stingy about clothes and *geta*.[5] Spending money on such things cuts me to the quick—that's really how I feel about it. I'll set out to buy a new pair of *geta* with five yen in my pocket, only to pace back and forth in front of the shoe store. When I'm completely bewildered, I make a determined rush into the beer hall next door to spend every sen. I must be set against wasting my own money on clothes.

Until three or four years ago, Mother would send me clothes and other things from home for every season. But we hadn't seen one another for over ten years, and I could tell from her choice of gaudy patterns that she didn't realize I was now a man of taste who sported a moustache. A certain kimono in the flecked style, loose-fitting and unlined, made me seem like a sumo wrestler of low rank, while the nightshirt dyed all over with peach blossoms transformed me into a doddering actor of the modern stage. This simply wouldn't do. And yet, since it was my policy to meekly wear whatever was given to me, I did so regardless of how appalled I really was. Friends who dropped in could hardly keep from laughing when they saw me sitting gravely on folded legs in the middle of my room and puffing on a cigarette. I was hardly amused, however, so I eventually got up and took the offending clothes to a storehouse.

I can't even have Mother send me one kimono any more. Instead I must buy whatever clothes I need from my own income as a writer. I'm so stingy, though, that I've bought just two kimonos the last three or four years: an unlined, flecked garment in the Kurume style[6] and a white, summer kimono, also flecked. When I need something else, I withdraw one of Mother's selections from the storehouse. For summer wear I've another flecked kimono with a white background, and as autumn draws near, I alternate between two unlined kimonos—one of a patterned fabric, the other of silk. At home I always wear a *yukata*, right underneath my *tanzen*.[7]

When I walk about in the silk kimono, the hem of the skirt rustles pleasantly. Unfortunately it always rains if I go out in that garment, a warning perhaps from my dead father-in-law who once owned it. I've encountered veritable floods in that kimono, once in southern Izu and again at Fuji-Yoshida. The Izu incident occurred in the early part of July, when a rampaging stream almost swept away the tiny inn where I was staying. I was drawn into the incident at Fuji-Yoshida because of the Fire Festival in late August. When a friend from the area invited me for a visit, I replied, It's too hot now, but I'll come once the weather cools down. My friend's response to this was rather testy. The Fire Festival occurs just once a year, he wrote, and the weather's plenty cool already here in Yoshida. By next month it'll be too cold.

I hastily got ready to leave. As I left home, my wife found fault with my appearance. You'll run into a flood once again if you keep wearing that same kimono, she said. Her words gave me a sense of foreboding.

The weather was fine as far as Hachiōji. But from the moment I boarded the train at Ōtsuki for Yoshida, the rain came down in buckets. The passengers on their way for sightseeing or mountain-climbing were so packed in they could barely move. Hearing each and every one of them grumble about the rain, I was so overcome with guilt for having worn my late father-in-law's kimono that I couldn't even look up. Since the rain was even worse at

Yoshida, I scurried along with the friend who met me into a nearby restaurant. My friend seemed to feel sorry for me, but I was the one to really feel contrite, knowing as I did the real cause of the storm. I couldn't confess, though, for my sin was too terrible.

The Fire Festival was a shambles.

On the day Mount Fuji closes for the winter, each household in Yoshida heaps up kindling at the front gate, hoping to start a blaze greater than all the others. The spectacle was in honor of Kono-hanasakuya, the princess who subjected herself to an ordeal by fire in giving birth to her three children, thus proving to the human deity Ninigi that he was indeed their father.[8] I had never seen the festival and was anxious to be there. But the downpour had ruined the preparations, so my friend and I just stayed in the restaurant and drank as we waited for the rain to slacken. As the wind picked up in the evening, a waitress opened the shutter slightly and murmured, "Ah, there's a small fire out there."

My friend and I stood up and observed the glow in the southern sky. Even in the midst of this raging storm, at least one person had managed to light a beacon for the princess. But I couldn't help being depressed, knowing as I did that my own kimono had brought on this terrible storm. If I so much as hinted to the waitress that the man standing before her had come brazenly down here from Tokyo on no special errand and ruined one of the few annual pleasures to which both the young and old, the men and women citizens of Yoshida looked forward, I would probably end up getting thrashed by the townspeople. And so, ever a blackguard, I told neither the waitress nor my friend about this crime.

When the rain eased up late that evening, my friend and I left the restaurant to spend the night at a large inn near the lake. By the next morning the weather had cleared, so I said good-bye and boarded the bus that ran to Kōfu through Misaka Pass. The bus had gone by Lake Kawaguchi and must have been starting its climb up the pass some twenty minutes later when it came to a halt. Seeing the huge avalanche that blocked the road, we fifteen or so passengers got off, hitched up our kimono skirts, and started picking our way over the avalanche in groups of two or three. Finding the road again, we kept on walking, determined to get through the pass. No matter how far we went, though, the bus from Kōfu never appeared. Finally we gave up, returned to our own bus, and headed back to Yoshida.

All of this came about because of that cursed silk kimono of mine. The next time I hear even a rumor about a drought, I'll put on the kimono and set out for the affected area. I'll just take a stroll, and the rain will come down in torrents—an unexpected service from someone so generally incompetent.

In addition to the Rain-maker, I still own the first kimono I ever bought with a manuscript payment, an unlined garment in the Kurume style. I take good care of this article, wearing it only when I go out on special occasions. I consider it a first-class garment, yet other people don't give it much attention. Whatever business discussions I have while wearing this kimono turn out rather poorly. I'm treated offhandedly, and that means the kimono must seem like ordinary apparel in the eyes of others. Feeling defiant as I head for home, I hit upon the example of my fellow Tsugaru writer, Zenzō Kasai, a careless dresser if there ever was one. That's when I swear firmly never to give up my unlined kimono.

The period during which I change from unlined to lined clothing is a difficult one. For about ten days, from late September through early October, I'm totally alone with my miseries. I have two lined kimonos sent by Mother, one of a patterned fabric, the other of some kind of silk. The design of both is so delicate and the color so subdued that I keep them at home, without depositing them at a storehouse in some obscure corner of town. However, I'm not the sort to turn out in a silk kimono and felt sandals, twirling a cane as I stroll along. In fact I've worn the silk kimono only twice in the last year or so—to celebrate the New Year at my wife's home in Kōfu and to assist a friend at a meeting with a prospective bride. In both instances I had misgivings about the kimono, and a cane and felt sandals were simply out of the question. I dressed instead in *hakama* and a new pair of "single-block" *geta*.

I'm not trying to act barbarian by disliking sandals. After all, sandals look elegant and they don't make a racket like *geta* do. So you needn't leave them at the cloakroom when entering a quiet place like a theater or library. But when I tried wearing a pair of them, the soles of my feet seemed to be slipping on a straw mat. It was irritating and unbearable. I felt far more weary than when I wear *geta* and since then I've never put on a pair of felt sandals.

To walk about twirling a cane gives one a feeling of importance, and that's not bad at all. But I'm a bit taller than most people, and canes are always too short for me. I've got to bend somewhat to make sure the tip strikes the ground. I must seem an old lady on her way to visit a grave as I go along hunched over, my cane tapping at every step. Five or six years ago I came across a long, narrow *pickel*, as the Germans call it, and started using it as a cane, but quickly gave it up when a friend grumbled about my poor taste. It wasn't a question of taste, however. Since the typical short cane wouldn't let me walk resolutely, I soon became irritated with it. For one with my physique, a long, sturdy *pickel* was a necessity.

I've also been instructed to hold the cane so it doesn't strike the ground. It gets to be luggage then, and that's something I can't tolerate. When I go on a trip, I figure out how to board the train empty-handed. Life itself is bound to be dreary if you carry a lot of baggage about. The less the better. After spending the thirty-one years of my life more or less weighed down, why should I carry an onerous piece of luggage even while walking?

Whenever I go out with something, I try to stuff the article inside the front opening of my kimono, regardless of how unsightly it looks. I certainly can't do that with a cane, though. A cane's got to rest on the shoulder or hang from the hand, a bother in either case. Besides, a dog might well mistake a cane for some barbaric weapon and begin barking furiously. There's nothing good about carrying a cane. Regardless of how I think about it, I'm just unfit for a silk kimono, felt sandals, white *tabi*, and a cane. Maybe it's just the pauper in me.

While I'm on this subject, I should mention that I haven't worn foreign clothes in the seven or eight years since I quit school. It's not that I dislike them, far from it. Since they're light and convenient, I'm always yearning for such clothes. Mother never sent me any from home, though, and I can hardly wear what I don't own.

Since I'm five feet six and a half inches tall, a suit ready-made in Japan wouldn't fit. And to have a tailor make one would surely cost more than a hundred yen, with the shoes, shirt, and other required accessories. I'm stingy about my needs; I'd rather hurl myself from a cliff into the raging sea than throw away over a hundred yen on a suit of clothes.

On one occasion I had to attend a celebration in honor of a friend's new book. With nothing to wear other than a *tanzen*, I had to borrow from another friend. Clad in a foreign outfit—jacket, shirt, necktie, shoes, and socks—I showed up with a craven smile on my lips. My reputation suffered again, for my friends did not seem impressed with my appearance. I heard all kinds of remarks—So you're wearing a suit for a change . . . Well, it's hardly an improvement . . . Nope, it doesn't agree with you . . . What? Again!

Finally the friend who had lent the clothes whispered to me in the corner. "Thanks to you, that suit of mine's already notorious. I don't think I'll be wearing it to go out anymore."

That's what happened the one time I tried wearing foreign clothes. Since I'm not about to waste a hundred yen on a tailor, it will probably be a long time before I try again.

For now, I have no choice but to go around in the Japanese clothes I have on hand. As I said earlier, I have two lined kimonos, but I don't like the silk one. I prefer my patterned kimono. Anyway I'm comfortable in the poorest kimono, the sort a student might wear, and I would gladly spend the rest of my life living as a student. When I have a meeting scheduled for the next day, I fold my patterned kimono and place it under my mattress for the night. I feel somewhat edgy, as though I were about to take the college entrance exam, but at least the kimono will appear to be pressed. It's a fine garment, one for special occasions. As autumn deepens and I can begin going proudly about in this kimono, I breathe a sigh of relief.

It's the time between seasons that's really troublesome—especially between summer and autumn. Any transition annoys a feckless person like myself, and I can't make up my mind between my unlined summer garment and my lined autumn one. To tell the truth, I want to wear my lined kimono with its flecked pattern right away, but the days are still too warm. So I stick to my unlined garment, and that makes me feel cold and desolate. No wonder that I go about hunched over and shivering in the wind—or that criticisms about "advertising my penury" or "acting from spite" or "menacing people like some beggar" start all over again. In fact, I long to dress properly, without upsetting people by looking like Han Shan and Sheh Teh, those two beggars who appear in the Zen paintings. The trouble is, I don't have a serge kimono, and that's what I need most.

Actually, I do sort of have one. It's a kimono with pale red stripes running both down and across that I bought on the sly during my fashionable days as a high-school student. When I awoke from the spell of fashion, I realized a fellow like me couldn't wear such a garment. It obviously belonged on a woman.

I must have been insane. The kimono was so gaudy that words can hardly describe it. Remembering how I used to put on this garment and stroll aimlessly and languidly about, I can only hide my face and groan. I never should have worn it. I can't stand the sight of that kimono, and I've left it in storage a long time now.

Last autumn I tried to arrange the clothes, blankets, and books I had left in the storehouse. I sold off the useless items and brought the rest back home. My wife was present as I opened the large cloth bundle. Needless to say, I was nervous and embarrassed to reveal before her very eyes how slovenly I had been before our marriage. A filthy *yukata* had been left in the storehouse unlaundered, and a rolled-up *tanzen* with a tear in the backside had not been repaired. Nothing that came out of the bundle was presentable. Dirt, mold, garments with strange, gaudy patterns—that's all there was. This was not the legacy of a solid citizen, and I cringed in self-contempt as I unpacked the bundle.

"Sheer decadence!" I declared. "But I suppose we can sell the stuff to some rag-picker."

"Oh no!" my wife shot back. She inspected each article, ignoring the filth. "Look! This one's pure wool! Let's remake it."

The serge kimono! I almost fled in horror. What was it doing here? It should have remained in storage. I had picked up the wrong article at some point. Blunderer!

"I wore it years ago. Rather flashy, wouldn't you say?"

I hid my embarrassment and spoke calmly.

"What luck! You don't have a single serge kimono,

and now you can wear this."

I couldn't. During the ten years in storage, the kimono fabric had turned a strange color, something on the order of bean jelly, while the red stripes had faded to an unhealthy persimmon color. It was an old woman's kimono, and I turned away from it in disgust.

This past autumn I leaped out of bed early one morning, knowing that I had to finish a story that very day for a certain publisher. An unfamiliar kimono lay neatly folded alongside my pillow. It proved to be the serge kimono itself, just right for the cool weather already in the air. Washed and re-sewn, the garment was more presentable than before, but there was no mistaking the bean-jelly fabric and the persimmon-colored stripes. With work to be done, however, I couldn't bother about my appearance. I dressed in silence and started writing without any breakfast. I finished slightly past noon and was just breathing a sigh of relief when an old friend unexpectedly dropped in.

His timing was perfect. We ate lunch, talked over various matters, and went out for a walk. Only as we were entering the woods at Inokashira Park did I realize how strange I looked. I came to a halt and groaned, "Oh no, I shouldn't be out like this."

My friend stared at me, his brows knit in a worried expression. "What's the trouble?" he asked. "Is it your stomach . . . ?"

"No, nothing like that." I forced a smile. "It's an odd kimono, don't you agree?"

"Well . . ." His tone was somber. "It seems a bit flashy."

"I bought it ten years ago," I mentioned, moving

forward a step or two. "It seems more suitable for a woman, and the color's changed too . . ." I couldn't go any further.

"Calm down," my friend counseled, "It's not so noticeable."

"You think so?" I was already feeling better.

We came out of the woods, descended the stone steps, and strolled around the pond.

But the thing kept bothering me. I was a big, hirsute fellow, thirty-one years old, with some experience of hardship. Yet here I was wandering through the park in a pair of worn-out *geta* and a tasteless kimono. A stranger might take me for some filthy neighborhood bum, and friends would become all the more contemptuous of me. There he goes again, they would exclaim, it's about time he grew up. That's how misunderstood I've been all these years.

"How about going to Shinjuku?" my friend proposed.

"Are you kidding? If someone sees me around Shinjuku in this outfit . . ." I shook my head.

"No one will think the worse of you."

"Count me out," I stubbornly insisted. "Let's stop at the teahouse instead."

"I need a real drink. C'mon, let's get out of here and head for town."

"They serve beer at the teahouse."

I didn't feel like heading for town—not in this kimono. Besides, my story needed revision, and that made me uneasy.

"It's too chilly at the teahouse," my companion countered. "I want to relax with a drink."

I had heard he was having a bad time of it recently.

"Well," I conceded, "Asagaya maybe. But not Shinjuku."

"You've an interesting place in mind?"

It wasn't especially interesting, but the tavern at Asagaya had its advantages. I had been there occasionally, and my credit was good until the next visit whenever I was a bit short. Since they knew me, this strange outfit would not arouse suspicion, either. I needn't worry about how I looked. After all, the tavern didn't employ any hostesses.

Dusk was beginning to settle when we left the train at Asagaya and began to walk down the street. I could hardly bear to see my reflection in the store windows, just like some Han Shan or Sheh Teh in those Zen paintings. Since the kimono was bright red, I remembered how an old man puts on a colorful undergarment to celebrate his eighty-eighth birthday.

These were difficult times, and there was nothing I could do to help. My writing had gone unrecognized. The last ten years seemed to have passed as one day while I loitered about Asagaya in a pair of worn-out *geta*. And I was back again today, decked out in the red kimono as well. Always I seemed to be on the losing end.

"Things don't change no matter how old you get. I've tried my best, and yet . . ." As we walked along, I began to let my grievances against life come tumbling out. "Maybe that's what writing's all about," I went on. "But there's something wrong with me. Imagine, walking about in an outfit like this one."

My friend looked at me sympathetically. "That's right, you've got to dress properly. Now I've suffered plenty of setbacks at the office . . ."

He worked for a company in Fukugawa, but he wasn't the sort to spend money on clothes.

"It's not just how you dress," I tried to argue. "It goes deeper. I didn't get the right sort of education. Now take Verlaine's case,[9] for example . . ."

What did Verlaine have to do with my red kimono? An abrupt shift of thought even for me, and I felt quite sheepish about the remark. Whenever I'm feeling down and out, though, I remember Verlaine's doleful countenance, and it helps. The very weakness of the man gives me the strength to pull myself together and keep going. I firmly believe that true glory can emerge only after the most timid introspection. In any event I want to live on, to have a life bereft of means but filled with pride.

"Was I stretching things with that Verlaine business?" I asked. "Well, regardless of what I say, this kimono is out of the question."

I was at my wits' end, but my friend merely chuckled as the street lights came on. "Forget it," he counseled.

That evening at the tavern I struck my friend in the face—an awful blunder. For this, the kimono was surely to blame. Of late I had disciplined myself to laugh off just about anything, and even violence, up to a certain point at least, did not affect me. But that night I acted. I believe the red kimono was entirely at fault, a good example of the frightening influence clothes can exercise over a man.

I was so depressed when we entered that I took a seat in the darkest corner, abjectly ignoring the tavern keeper as I drank my saké. My friend, for some reason or other, was in very good spirits. He denounced all artists—ancient and modern, Eastern and Western—and ended up lashing out at the tavern keeper. Now the latter, I knew, had a temper. On one occasion a young fellow had gotten out of hand, just like my friend was doing, and begun to shout at the other patrons. The tavern keeper had suddenly looked stern, as if he were a different person. What's the matter with you, he had scolded, don't you realize what the country's going through? He had then ordered the youngster off the premises, with a warning never to return.

Tonight it was my friend who was defying this formidable tavern keeper, and I shuddered to think that both of us might be thrown out at any moment. Normally I would have added my own bombast to his, and to hell with the ignominy of getting tossed out of a tavern. But I cringed over my appearance. Pst! Pst! I quietly hissed, keeping an eye on the tavern keeper. Sharper and sharper became my friend's tongue until we were just one step away from getting kicked out. Then a desperate course of action occurred to me— the precedent of Ataka Barrier and the blow that Benkei delivered to save Yoshitsune's life. Having made this decision, I slapped my friend twice on the cheek—taking care not to hurt him while making the sharpest possible sound.

"Calm down! You don't usually act like this. What's the matter with you tonight? Calm down!" I shouted loud enough for the tavern keeper to hear and was just sighing with relief that we would not be thrown out when Yoshitsune arose and came at Benkei.

"What's the big idea, hitting me like that. You won't get away with it!" he screamed.

The plot had gone awry. Poor Benkei stood up, utterly befuddled as he dodged blows left and right, and hoped that someone would come to his rescue.

Finally the tavern keeper came straight over to where I was and said, "You're bothering the other customers. Would you mind leaving?"

But why was he asking *me* to leave? Come to think of it, I was the one who had started the fracas. And how could someone else realize that I was only playing the role of Benkei and not really chastising anyone? To all appearances I was definitely the aggressor.

Filled with chagrin, I left my friend drunk and raving in the tavern. Once again, my appearance had failed me. If I had been properly dressed, the tavern keeper would have recognized my character to some extent and he would not have humiliated me like that. Thus did Benkei, now expelled from the tavern and trudging with his shoulders hunched through the Asagaya Quarter, reason to himself. I want a serge kimono, he thought, I want something in which I can stroll about without a care. But I'm so stingy about buying clothes that I'll have all sorts of trouble from here on out as well.

Assignment: How about a citizen's uniform?

A Poor Man's Got His Pride

Hin no iji

"A Poor Man's Got His Pride" is the first of two translations in this book from Dazai's retelling of various Japanese tales by the seventeenth-century master of burlesque fiction, Ihara Saikaku. Dazai titled his collection A New Interpretation of "Tales from the Provinces," *in reference to a volume of Saikaku's own stories. However, Dazai did not confine his attention to this one source, preferring instead to select works for refashioning from the entire range of Saikaku's shorter fiction. In fact, the only story that does come from* Tales from the Provinces *is this very one.*

Told with Saikaku's usual conciseness, the original tale highlights a stark fact about the economy of Japan during the Edo period (1603–1868). The samurai may have been the official leaders of society during these years; however, since their code of life required them to disdain money while their fixed stipends lost value as the economy gradually expanded, many of them became impoverished.

While providing Dazai with a plot outline, Saikaku's tale does have a different set of emphases. As in Dazai, Saikaku's principal character, Harada Naisuke, is a fallen samurai living in poverty in the Shinagawa district of Edo, as Tokyo was then called.

As New Year's Eve approaches, Harada writes to his brother-in-law for money, presumably to help him get through the end of the year, when all debts fall due. When the money arrives, Harada invites his cohorts, fallen samurais like himself, to celebrate. In Saikaku's story, the drinking that occurs at the party is given much less emphasis than in Dazai's retelling, the focus in the original tale being on the manipulations that occur with the coins. The guests in Saikaku speak with a collective voice, not one of them being named or singled out in any way. Harada's wife plays an important role, as she does in Dazai too. But Dazai portrays her more fully than Saikaku, allowing her the final comment on samurai virtue, a comment uttered in Saikaku by an impersonal narrative voice.

Dazai's tone throughout the retelling borders on the ironic. The samurai figures in his tale, whether Harada or any of his guests, are initially portrayed as feckless people of ridiculous pretensions. In the end, however, they prove their mettle. Or do they? As happens in certain tales by Saikaku, the samurai characters in Dazai too go to absurd lengths defending their honor. The satire is sometimes quite blunt— for example, the extended passage in which each invited guest is shown patching together an outfit from rags (or from the paper clothing, which was popular at the time) in hopes of living up to his samurai image.

Dazai ends his tale in an anticlimactic but intriguing way—with Harada's wife reflecting on the feat her ex-samurai husband has just performed. Perhaps the author is drawing the wife also into the circle of his satire. Or is he instead affirming through the wife

*that this hard core of samurai discipline remains even
after appearances have long been compromised?*

Long ago in Edo, in a thatched hovel near the
Wisteria Teahouse at Shinagawa, there lived a huge,
middle-aged man named Harada Naisuke. With his
thick, fearsome beard and bloodshot eyes, Harada
seemed quite menacing. But men of his type are
sometimes so intimidated by their own grandeur that
they turn into cowards. Despite a magnificent
countenance—his eyebrows were bushy and his eyes
glaring—Harada was utterly worthless. While fenc-
ing with an opponent, he would shut his eyes and let
out a weird shriek. Then he'd charge in the wrong
direction, shouting "Your match, I concede" as he
slammed into the nearest wall. His reputation as
"The Wall-banger" got a boost every time this happened.

On one occasion a young pedlar beguiled Harada
with a hard-luck story. Harada started to blubber as
the story unfolded, then bought up the fellow's entire
batch of clams. Back home, he got a scolding from
his wife, and for the next three days he ate clams—
nothing but clams—for breakfast, lunch, and supper.
They gave him such painful cramps that he rolled
about on the floor clutching his stomach. Opening
his Confucian *Analects* for consolation, he started
dozing after the first few words, "Learning is . . ."

Harada abhorred caterpillars. One look and he
would let out a scream, his fingers spread apart as he
backed away. Easily swayed by flattery, he seemed
as if possessed by a fox whenever someone paid

him a compliment. After fidgeting for a time, he would race to the pawnshop, trade something for cash, and treat his flatterer to a meal.

Every New Year's Eve Harada would drink from early in the morning and pretend that he was going to disembowel himself, all this just to keep the bill collectors at bay. His thatched hovel, incidentally, did not represent an aesthetic preference. No, the house was merely falling apart from age. Harada was indolent and penniless, his life unadorned by either flowers or fruit; he was a samurai without a master, a man who merely embarrassed his relatives.

Luckily for Harada, two or three of these relatives were rich, and he could turn to them in a pinch. But, since he mostly squandered their largess on drinking, Harada was always in trouble. What were the spring cherry blossoms and the autumn colors to him? Mired in poverty, he was oblivious to such things. After all, one might get by without cherry blossoms or fall foliage, but one surely could not pretend year after year to be unaware of New Year's Eve. Still, as the year's end drew near once more, Harada Naisuke imparted a mad look to his eyes and pretended to be crazy. Fumbling his long, unavailing sword, he let out that eerie chuckle—heh, heh—that made the bill collectors nervous.

It might be New Year's Day tomorrow, but Harada didn't bother to wipe the soot from the ceiling nor to trim his beard. He even left his wafer-thin sleeping quilt lying unfolded on the floor. When he muttered pathetically to the bill collectors—If you want me, come and get me—he seemed feeble and delirious. And afterwards, he again broke into that eerie chuckle.

Having witnessed this nightmare year after year, Harada's wife could bear it no longer. She went out the kitchen door and ran all the way to Kanda, where her older brother, a physician named Nakarai Seian, lived in a lane by the Myōjin Shrine. Rushing into the house, she wept over her plight and begged for help. Though exasperated by these constant troubles, Seian still retained his sense of humor. "Every family," he jested, "has a fool—just to keep it in touch with reality." Then he wrapped up ten coins and wrote on the cover: Poverty Pills. To Be Taken As Often As Needed.

His unfortunate sister took the package and returned home. When she showed the Poverty Pills to Harada, he surprised her by frowning instead of rejoicing. Then, in a rasping voice, he came out with the most ridiculous statement ever—"I can't use this money."

His startled wife wondered whether her husband wasn't truly going mad. But that wasn't really the problem. It was merely that a ne'er-do-well such as Harada will bungle things whenever good fortune smiles upon him. People like him become fidgety and sheepish at the sudden appearance of fortune. They quibble over this and that, then get angry and drive off the luck that has befallen them.

"Good luck brings bad," Harada declared, a somber look on his face. "I might die if I spend this money." Then, glaring at his wife with bloodshot eyes, he asked, "Are you trying to kill me?" Finally he grinned and said, "No, you're not a she-devil, I guess. Well, maybe a drink will help. I'll die if I don't have a drink. Look, it's starting to snow outside. That reminds me—I haven't had my elegant friends in for a while. You go around right this minute and ask them to come over. There's Yamazaki, Kumai, Utsugi, Ōtaké, Iso, Tsukimura—six of them in all. Oh, one more, Tankei the priest. That makes seven. Now hurry up and invite them—and stop at the saké shop on the way back. We'll take whatever snacks they've got."

So the earlier fuss didn't mean anything. Harada was so tickled that he wanted a drink, that was all.

Yamazaki, Kumai, Utsugi, Ōtaké, Iso, Tsukimura, Tankei—all ex-samurai now living in poverty in nearby tenements. When the invitation to the snow-viewing party at Harada's arrived, they felt like sinners in hell blessed by the Buddha's mercy—now each one of them could escape the torment of staying home on New Year's Eve. After smoothing the wrinkles of a garment fashioned from paper, one of the men poked his head into his closet. Wasn't there an umbrella around? Or socks? Pulling together various odds-and-ends, he proceeded to outfit himself in a cotton kimono and a warrior's jacket. Another, with the excuse that he didn't want to catch cold, put on five unlined kimonos and wrapped his neck in an old cotton scarf. Yet another turned his wife's padded silk kimono inside out and rolled up the sleeves to change their shape. Still another donned a riding skirt over a short undergarment, then put on a formal summer jacket with an embroidered crest. Another hitched a quilted cloak about his waist, his hairy shins exposed and fluffy cotton sticking from the torn hem of the garment.

As it turned out, even though none of them were properly dressed, the fact that they were all ex-samurai gave a special touch to their camaraderie.

Thus, when they gathered at Harada's home, there wasn't a single condescending smile to be seen. They greeted one another with dignity, and, after each had taken his proper place, old Yamazaki rose in his warrior's jacket and cotton kimono. Solemnly approaching Harada the host, Yamazaki dwelt at length on how grateful they all were to have been invited.

Though uneasy about the tear in the sleeve of his own paper garment, Harada formally saluted his friends in return. "Welcome, each and every one of you. I thought you would like spending New Year's Eve away from home. Having neglected each of you for such a long time, I am especially pleased that you could all make it to this snow-viewing party even on such short notice. Please make yourselves at home," he added, urging them to eat and drink, humble though the fare might be.

One of the guests started trembling all over as he picked up his saké cup. Asked what the trouble was, he wiped his tears and said, "Oh, it's nothing really. I've been off saké for quite a while—couldn't afford it. I hate to admit it, but I've forgotten how to drink." Then he smiled rather lamely.

"It's the same with me," said the guest in the riding skirt and short undergarment, edging forward on his knees. "I've had just two or three cups in a row and already I'm feeling queer. What should I do next? I don't remember how to get drunk."

Everyone seemed to be thinking the same thing, for the men merely whispered to one another as they passed their cups back and forth. Things went on quietly for a time; but presently everyone seemed to remember how drinking was carried on. As the room grew lively with laughter, Harada Naisuke brought out the paper in which the ten coins were wrapped.

"I've got something unusual to show you," he began. "The rest of you swear off drinking and live a frugal life when your purse is empty. That's why even if you're in a bind on New Year's Eve, you're not likely to be tormented like old Harada. When I'm in a pinch, I want a drink even more. That's the way I am, and so the debts keep piling up. Every time the year comes to an end, I feel like I'm staring right into the Eight Hells.[1] So I'm forced to set aside all this business about samurai honor and run weeping for help to my relatives. It's a disgrace. This year a relative came up with these ten coins—just in time for me to welcome in the New Year like other people. But good luck brings bad—I know that much. So I'd probably die if I kept this bounty for myself. That's why I decided to invite all of you here for some drinking."

Harada was in a good mood, and the entire company breathed a sigh of relief. Several of the men expressed their feelings forthrightly.

"What the hell!" one of them exclaimed. "If I'd known from the start, I wouldn't have held back. I thought Harada would ask for a donation. Wasn't much fun drinking with that on my mind."

"We know better now," another chimed in, "so let's drink up. Maybe Harada's luck will rub off on me. There could be a registered letter at my home— from somewhere unexpected."

Then another cohort spoke up. "You people with the right sort of relatives have it made," he began, "but with me it's the other way around. They all take aim at my purse. Humpf!"

Eventually the company became lively and cheerful, much to Harada's delight. Wiping a drop of saké from the tip of his beard, he came out with a suggestion. "How about holding these coins in your hand for a while. They're quite heavy, but perhaps you'd like me to pass them around. Don't regard them as filthy lucre. Look, it says right here on the paper— Poverty Pills. To Be Taken As Often As Needed. He's quite a wit, that relative of mine. He wrote this and sent it over. Well, go ahead and hand the coins around."

Harada virtually forced the ten coins upon his guests. Each man was surprised by their weight and impressed by the clever inscription. As the money went around, one guest exclaimed that a verse had come to mind. Borrowing a brush and inkstone, he wrote on the blank part of the wrapping: He takes his Poverty Pills as the snow glistens. This made the guests even more merry, and cups of saké were exchanged in a flurry.

When the coins finally came back to Harada, old Yamazaki sat up straight. A discerning look in his eye, he turned to the host and said, "Ah, thanks to you, I've forgotten my years and remained here longer than I expected." But Yamazaki did not stop with this expression of gratitude. Although he had wrapped his throat with an old cotton cloth for fear that he was catching a cold, he now threw out his chest and began singing a ballad entitled "A Thousand Autumns." Not to be left out, the other guests and the host too marked the rhythm by clapping their hands and tapping lightly upon their knees. When the song had ended, the company gathered the warming pans, the tier boxes, the pickle jars, and whatever else happened to be there, took them to the kitchen, and handed everything over to Harada's wife. Whether in olden days or now, samurai breeding will tell; departing birds, as the saying goes, leave no trace.

At the urging of his guests, Harada was casually sweeping together the coins scattered beside his knee when he suddenly turned pale. A coin was missing. Despite his fearsome looks, Harada remained a coward even when he drank. Fretting and fussing as ever about what his guests might think, he decided to act as though nothing had happened and to let even this truly startling discovery pass unnoticed.

"Just a moment," old Yamazaki mentioned, his hand raised. "Isn't there a coin missing?"

"Er . . . no. It's . . . " Harada looked flustered, like a criminal caught in the act. "It's . . . well . . . I spent one of the coins at the saké shop—before any of you arrived. When I passed them around earlier, there were only nine left. There's nothing wrong."

Yamazaki shook his head. "No, that's not true," he insisted, stubborn in his old age. "I held ten coins in my hand before. That's certain. The lamp may be dim, but there's nothing wrong with my eyes."

Once Yamazaki had spoken up, the other six guests all agreed with him. Yes, there certainly had been ten coins. The guests stood up together and, moving the lamp about, searched every corner of the room. The coin, however, did not turn up.

"There's only one thing left to do," Yamazaki said. "I'll strip to my bare skin and prove I'm innocent." He might be emaciated and shriveled, but a shred of samurai spirit still remained in Yamazaki, along with the obstinacy that comes with old age. A poor man's got his pride. To be falsely accused meant undying shame, and Yamazaki was incensed. So he removed his warrior's jacket and shook it out, then proceeded to take off his threadbare cloak. Wearing nothing but a loincloth, he waved the cloak grandly, as though he were casting a net.

"You see for yourselves, don't you?" His face was quite pale.

The other guests could hardly let the matter rest there. Ōtaké stood up next and shook his summer jacket with its embroidered crest. After shaking out his undergarment as well, he removed his riding trousers. That left him without a stitch on, not even a loincloth. Without the least hint of a smile, he turned the trousers upside down and shook them.

The tension in the room was unbearable as Tankei the priest stood up, his kimono tucked about his hips and his hairy shins exposed. Suddenly an angry frown spread over his face, as though he were afflicted with severe stomach pains.

"Aware that my end had come," Tankei began, "I composed a trivial verse to leave behind: He takes his Poverty Pills as snow glistens. My friends, there's a coin in my breast pocket, no doubt about that. No need to even shake out the garment. I never dreamed such a disaster might happen. Only a coward would try to explain. This is it!" he cried, stripping to the waist and fingering the hilt of his sword.

With Harada leading the way, the other guests rushed forward and seized Tankei's hand.

"Nobody suspects you. Even though we're poor and live wretched lives, all of us have had a coin at some time or other. The poor are friends in their poverty. We understand how you feel—you'd take your own life to prove you're innocent. But isn't that foolish when no one suspects you?"

They tried to calm Tankei, but he grew even more bitter over his misfortune. His grief mounted, and he gnashed his teeth.

"How kind of you to say that," he declared. "I'll cherish your generosity beyond the grave. It's so embarrassing to have a coin in my pocket just when this inquiry occurs. Even though you don't suspect me, the humiliation will remain. I'll be the laughing stock, a blunderer for life. As you all know, one can't live without honor. It doesn't matter that I earned this money yesterday when I sold my Tokujō blade to Jūzaemon. He's a foreign goods dealer in Sakashita, and he gave me a coin and two sen for it. A samurai would be humiliated to make such a foolish plea at this point. I won't say anything, just let me die. If you pity your unfortunate friend, go to Sakashita after I'm gone and discover the truth for yourselves. And see to my wretched corpse, I beg you."

Even as Tankei grasped his sword and struggled on once again, Harada suddenly exclaimed, "Look! There it is."

A coin lay glinting directly under the lamp.

"What the devil. How'd it get down there?"

"Well, it *is* dark right alongside the lampstand."

"Lost articles turn up in the most obvious places. But it's important to take the usual precautions." This last remark came from Yamazaki.

"Ah, what a fuss over one coin. Sobered me up completely. Let's have another round," Harada suggested.

The group was talking again and doubling over

with laughter when Harada's wife cried out from the kitchen, "There it is!" In a moment she came bustling into the parlor. "The coin—it's right here," she exclaimed, holding out a tier-box lid. When they saw the glinting coin resting on the lid, the men looked at one another in utter astonishment. Harada's wife pushed a stray hair from her flushed brow and smiled sheepishly. Then she explained what must have happened. When she had brought in the boiled potatoes, her careless husband must have placed the steaming lid of the pot right on the floor mat. She herself had picked up the lid and placed it beneath the tier-box, without noticing the coin was stuck to the underside. After serving the meal, she had returned to the kitchen. Preparing to wash the pots and pans, she heard a tinkling sound—and there was the coin.

She finished her tale, already out of breath. Now that there were eleven coins, the host and the guests could only gaze in suspicion at one other.

After a moment's hesitation, Yamazaki let out a sigh and remarked somewhat pointlessly, "Ah, another stroke of luck. Congratulations. Sometimes ten coins turn into eleven. It happens often. Keep it."

The other guests were amazed at this absurd explanation. Nonetheless, they all realized that urging Harada to keep the coin was the wisest course. Several of them spoke up, endorsing Yamazaki's suggestion.

"You should hang on to it," one of them said. "Your relative must have sent eleven coins in the wrapping."

"That's right. Since he's supposed to be such a wit, he probably showed you ten coins, then played a joke by giving you eleven."

"Yes, of course. It might be an unusual trick, but it was clever of him. You should keep it."

They spoke this drivel in an attempt to force the coin on Harada. Yet, for perhaps the only time in his life, this timid and worthless boozer, Harada Naisuke, revealed an obstinate streak.

"You won't persuade me, no matter what. So don't poke fun at me. You'll pardon me for pointing out that I'm as poor as the rest of you. I was lucky, though, and received the ten coins. I felt guilty before heaven because of that, and toward all of you as well. I couldn't relax—I just had to have a drink. It was so unbearable that I invited all of you here to get rid of this undeserved fortune. Now disaster has struck again. Don't force this extra coin on someone who has too much already. Harada Naisuke may be poor, but there's something of the old samurai in him still. I don't want money or anything. Take the ten coins and go on home, every one of you. And don't forget the extra coin, either."

Truly Harada expressed his anger in a strange manner. When he stands to gain, even if it's only a trifle, the fainthearted man becomes so perplexed that he cringes and sweats. But he seems transformed when threatened with a loss, mustering fine-sounding arguments and striving to deprive himself. He won't listen to reason, either; he just keeps on quibbling. As the saying goes, pull in your belly and your rump sticks out—and it works the same way with self-respect too. Shaking his head, the desperate Harada stammered on about this and that, blindly sticking to his opinion.

"Don't make fun of me. Ten coins turning into eleven—a nasty joke if there ever was one. But it's

not funny anymore. One of you couldn't bear to see
Tankei in distress. Whoever it was happened to have
a coin, so he slipped it under the lamp to solve this
crisis. A cheap trick, really. My coin stuck to the lid
of the tier-box. And the one under the lamp was put
there out of compassion. It doesn't make sense to
force the coin on me. Do you think I want it that
much? A poor man's got his pride. I said it before,
but just when I'm feeling guilty about the ten coins
and disgusted with everything, you try to force
another coin on me. Have the gods deserted me?
When the battle fortunes of a samurai fall this far, he
can't save his honor even by cutting open his belly. I
may be a drunken fool, but I'm not a complacent
dotard. You can't make me believe that coins pro-
duce children. Now, will whoever put the coin there
please take it back.

With his generally fearsome look, Harada became
truly awesome when he sat straight up and spoke in
earnest. The whole company cringed and remained
silent.

"Come, speak up," Harada declared. "A man of
compassion did this, and I would be happy to serve
under him my entire life. On New Year's Eve, when
even a penny means so much, this man dropped a
coin next to the lamp. He did it secretly, to save
Tankei's skin. Poor men are brothers, and he
couldn't bear to watch Tankei suffer. So he slipped
this coin onto the floor. One of you did this fine
deed, and Harada Naisuke admires you for it. Come,
speak up. Tell us who you are."

By this time, the mysterious benefactor was even
less likely to reveal himself. In such a case, Harada
Naisuke was no good at all. The seven guests were

wide awake and sober, despite having drunk so much. They merely sighed and fidgeted at Harada's words, leaving the matter still unresolved. His bloodshot eyes turned on them, Harada urged time after time that the benefactor speak up. However, when the cock's crow announced the coming of dawn, he finally gave up.

"Excuse me for keeping you here so long," he said. "If the owner of the coin won't speak up, there's nothing we can do about it. I'll put the coin on the tier-box lid and leave it in a corner of the entryway. Then, you gentlemen will please leave, one after the other. The owner should quietly take the coin on his way out. Now, how does this idea strike you?"

Relief evident in their faces, the seven guests all looked up and agreed in unison. For the dim-witted Harada the scheme was brilliant—exactly what the fainthearted man will sometimes devise when working against his own interest.

Pleased with himself, Harada placed the coin squarely on the tier-box lid as everyone watched. Then he took the lid to the entryway. "It's on the far right side of the step," he explained upon his return. "That's the darkest part of the entryway, and no one can see if the coin's there or not. The owner should feel around with his hand and take the coin away without making any noise. The rest of you can just go out. Well then, let's begin—we can start with old Yamazaki. No, no, not like that—close the sliding door all the way, please. Now, after Yamazaki is outside and we can't hear his footsteps any more, the next person should leave."

The seven guests all did as they were told, quietly leaving in strict order. And, after they had gone,

Harada's wife went to the entryway with a candle and confirmed that the coin had been removed.

"I wonder who it was?" she uttered, unable herself to understand why a shudder ran up her spine.

"Who knows," Harada replied, looking quite sleepy. "By the way, is the saké all gone?"

Though fallen from his former glory, a samurai is still someone special. With this thought, Harada's wife went proudly to the kitchen and warmed the remaining saké.

(Based on "Tales from the Provinces," vol. 3, no. 1, "New Year's Eve with Debts Unmet.")

The Monkey's Mound

Saruzuka

*In retelling the tales from Saikaku,[1] Dazai usually
followed the general outline of his source while adding numerous details of his own invention. The
source tale for "The Monkey's Mound" is a brief
work with a rather arch title: "Imitating People, the
Monkey Gives a Bath." Eschewing elaborate description and detail, Saikaku again focuses on the main actions of his story—the love of Oran and Jiroemon,
the arranged engagement of Oran to another man
and the subsequent elopement by the lovers, the role
of the monkey-servant, and the tragic death of the
baby Kikunosuke.*

*The opening line of the original tale, one which
Dazai ignored in his reworking, describes a playful
monkey swinging from branch to branch in a tree.
Saikaku explicitly equates the branches with the five
senses, the source of sin in the Buddhist view of
things, thereby investing the monkey with its
sometime connotation of passion on the loose. In his
tale the lovers Oran and Jiroemon disregard the
social code in order to fulfull their own desires. And
so they come to grief, just as the lovers often do in
many of Saikaku's better known works such as* Five
Women Who Loved Love. *Misfortune impels Oran
and Jiroemon to consider seriously the religion the*

164

two of them have casually dismissed in their attachment to one another; in the final line of the tale they are described as chanting the Lotus Sutra[2] without pause.

Dazai turned these religious references into an occasion for comedy. He also blurred the outline of Saikaku's tale by adding incidents and dialogue that make for caricature, especially in the case of Jiroemon. One unnamed and hardly mentioned figure in Saikaku's account is expanded by Dazai into the calculating but foolish figure of Denroku, the intermediary for the two lovers. Again, the beauty of Oran, merely mentioned in Saikaku's story as a fact, becomes in the retelling an imagistic set piece, with a dash of humor thrown in for good measure.

The retelling gains something by its fuller description and dialogue. However, Dazai certainly incurs a loss in omitting the very device that sets the Saikaku narrative in motion—early mention of the monkey's mound as a local feature requiring some historical explanation, a technique common to Noh drama. In another departure from Saikaku, Dazai often has his own narrator abruptly interrupt the action, a regular feature of many of his retold tales.

When the lovers elope, their journey is described in terms that suggest a michiyuki. This type of literary scene, especially notable in the plays of Saikaku's contemporary, Chikamatsu Monzaemon, evokes the beauty and pathos of a pair of lovers as they seek out a place to die. In the final line of "The Monkey's Mound," Dazai departs drastically from Saikaku's original tale by sending his lovers off once more. This time there is no attempt to *render the poetic feeling of the* michiyuki, *the lovers now being past the stage of dying for one another.*

Some years ago Shirasaka Tokuzaemon was the wealthiest man in Dazai Town, the capital of Chikuzen Province. Not only did he have a saké shop that his family had run for generations, he was also blessed with a daughter of unsurpassed beauty. Her name was Oran, and she astonished all who saw her from the time she was six or seven years old. Marveling at her beauty, a man might well recall the sniveling countenance of his own daughter and take to drinking in despair.

In her mid-teens at the time of our story, Oran would drape her delicate figure in a long-sleeved kimono, bestowing her radiance upon the neighborhood. The spring sunlight so enhanced her beauty that the girl's mother merely gazed at her in wonder, forgetting what she was about to say to her own daughter. Oran's beauty lent a sweet fragrance to the region well beyond her own neighborhood. Indeed, many men fell in love without even seeing her.

Let's have a look now at our hero, Kuwamori Jiroemon. The heir to a thriving pawnshop run by his family in the district next to that of Tokuzaemon's business, Jiroemon wasn't terribly bad-looking. True, his face was somewhat plain, what with his large nose, bushy beard, and eyes that seemed to tail downward at the corners. But he seemed an honest person, and he did have fine teeth and a charming smile. Perhaps that's all he needed. Anyway, something got started when he dropped into the saké shop during a rainstorm. Everyone knows that love is blind and foolish and that you don't judge a book by its cover. Nevertheless, Oran fell in love. That's where our story really begins, with Jiroemon winning the affections of this prized jewel.

While the parents on either side were still ignorant of the affair, Jiroemon confided his hopes to Denroku the fishmonger, a regular customer of his family's pawnshop. He urged Denroku to approach Tokuzaemon and propose a marriage between himself and Oran. Denroku was elated over the idea. Deeply in debt to the pawnshop for some time, he was now being asked to do something that Jiroemon could hardly manage by himself. The pawnshop was in this district, the saké shop in the neighboring one. If Denroku could adroitly negotiate the distance between them, he would end up drinking to his heart's content while postponing the interest payment on his debt too. With this in mind, he looked among the unredeemed clothes in the pawnshop for a fancy outfit. Then, all decked out, he marched into Tokuzaemon's place with such a discriminating air that those who saw him might wonder, Now who could *that* be?

"Heh-heh," Denroku chuckled as he snapped his fan open and shut. He then proceeded to praise the rocks in Tokuzaemon's garden. Watching him, Tokuzaemon felt his flesh crawl. But he inquired all the same, "Is there anything I can do for you, Sir?"

"Oh, nothing much," Denroku calmly replied. Eventually, however, he got around to speaking of Jiroemon's hopes. "Sir," he pointed out, "you own a saké shop while the other party runs a pawnshop. Different businesses, but connected all the same—

make for the saké shop, but stop at the pawnshop first; leave a pawnshop and the saké shop's bound to be next." He babbled on in this insolent manner, claiming that the two businesses were related to one another like a doctor and a priest; that their strength was that of a demon armed with a club; that together they could lay the town low.

Denroku strained his wits as never before, and even Tokuzaemon felt tempted by his plea.

"If Mr. Kuwamori is the eldest son and heir, there's no objection on my part. By the way, his religion is . . . ?"

"Well . . . maybe it's . . ." replied Denroku hesitantly. Then he blurted out in desperation, "I'm not positive, but it must be Pure Land."[3]

"Then I refuse," said Tokuzaemon spitefully, his mouth curling with malice. "My family's been in the Lotus Sect for years. During my lifetime we've become especially devoted to St. Nichiren,[4] and everyone recites the Invocation to the Sutra each morning and evening. I've brought up my daughter that way, so I can't have her marrying into another religion. Incidentally," he testily concluded, "If you're going to play the go-between, you shouldn't come around until you've investigated at least that much."

"But, uh . . . I . . ." Denroku felt the cold sweat on his back. "My people have been in the Lotus Sect for years. We recite St. Nichiren's prayer both morning and night. All Hail to the Lotus Sutra—that's how it goes."

"What're you prattling about?" Tokuzaemon retorted. "I'm not marrying my daughter to you. If Mr. Kuwamori is Pure Land, the answer is no. I don't care how much money he has or how good-looking and clever he is. Why, it would be an insult to St. Nichiren. Show me anything worthwhile in that gloomy Pure Land sect. The nerve—asking for my daughter when we've been in the Lotus Sect all these years. Just looking at you makes my stomach turn. Off with you, now."

Having retreated from the fray, Denroku carried the sad news back to Jiroemon. Unperturbed, the latter merely remarked, "Oh, religion's nothing to fret about. My family can switch easily enough. We've been more or less agnostic for generations, anyway. Lotus or Pure Land, it's all the same to us."

Without wasting any time, Jiroemon got hold of a tasseled rosary and began reciting the Invocation both morning and evening. When he suggested to his parents that they do exactly as he bade, neither one had the slightest idea what was going on. And yet, being so indulgent toward their child, they too began chanting, "All Hail to the Lotus Sutra," even as they gawked about and yawned.

Shortly thereafter, Denroku again headed for Tokuzaemon's place. Upon reaching the premises, he proclaimed that Mr. Kuwamori, along with his entire family, had converted to St. Nichiren's sect and had taken up the Invocation.

But Tokuzaemon was a difficult man and his response was blunt. "No," he said, "a faith without root is shallow. Anyone can see that the fellow has converted merely to win Oran." He went on to remark that such conduct was shameful and St. Nichiren himself would hardly approve of it. Why, anyone could see through this scheme in a moment. No, his mind was made up. He was going to marry his daughter into a family of Lotus Sect believers whom he knew.

Upon hearing this news from Denroku, Jiroemon was so horrified that he wrote to Oran immediately. So you're marrying into another Lotus Sect family, his letter began, and Denroku hasn't accomplished a thing. Damn, I recited that disagreeable prayer and blistered my hands pounding a drum just for your sake. Maybe my name's at fault. Jiroemon is quite close to Jirozaemon, and it's bothered me a long time now that Sano no Jirozaemon,⁵ that fellow from the Eastland Province, got jilted right and left. If that happens to me, I'll brandish my sword and take a hundred heads, just like he did. I'm a man, so I can do it. Don't make a fool of me. Having finished the letter, Jiroemon sent it off, tears streaming down his face.

Oran's reply came back by return mail. I can't fathom your letter at all, she began. You mustn't do anything rash, like brandishing a sword or whatever. Before you take a single head, let alone a hundred, you'll be cut down yourself. And what will I do if something happens to you? Please, don't frighten me like that. This is the first time I've ever heard of another proposal. You're always so worried about your nose and your slanted eyes—that's why you lose confidence in yourself and start doubting me. It's terrible to hear the things you say. Who would I marry now? You needn't worry. If Father wants me to marry someone else, I'll run away. I'm a woman, so I'll come to you. Keep that in mind, please.

Upon reading this, Jiroemon smiled a little. Still, he couldn't rest easy yet. Now he truly felt like clinging to St. Nichiren and the Invocation. And so, con-

torting his face into a scowl, he began shouting, All
Hail to the Lotus Sutra, and beating wildly upon the
drum.

The next day Tokuzaemon summoned Oran to his
room and solemnly informed her that, owing to St.
Nichiren's providence, she was going to marry
Hikosaku, a paper merchant from the Honmachi
District. The bond would be forever, he declared,
and she must enter into it gratefully.

Oran was horrified. But she kept her feelings hidden as she bowed circumspectly and took her leave.
Once she was out of the room, however, she rushed
up to the second floor and scribbled a note. I must be
brief, she wrote. It's come, the day of decision is
already here. I'm going to flee. So please, I beg you
to meet me here this evening. Having finished the
note, Oran had one of the clerks take it to the next
district.

As soon as he had scanned the message, Jiroemon
started to tremble. To calm himself, he went to the
kitchen and drank some water. He must make a decision right away, so he returned to the parlor and sat
down in the center with his legs crossed. But he
couldn't figure out what to do. Finally he got up and
changed his garment. He then went to the accounting
room and started ransacking the drawers. Confronted by the watchman, he mumbled, "Oh, just a
trifle," whereupon he threw some coins into the
sleeve of his gown and rushed blindly out of the
shop.

Along the way he realized that his clogs didn't
match. But he was afraid to return, so he went into a
nearby shoe shop and bought a pair of straw, sandals. The money in his pocket was all he had, so he

chose the cheapest pair possible. The soles proved so thin that he seemed to be barefoot. But he walked on to the next district, dejected and weeping. As he reached the back door of Tokuzaemon's house, Oran came rushing out and, without uttering a word, seized his hand and started off. Sobbing as his sandals slapped against the ground, Jiroemon let himself be led off like a blind man.

Well, this tale of a silly, thoughtless couple might seem trivial. It's not over yet, though, for genuine hardship seems to lie ahead.

That night they walked fifteen miles or more. The Sea of Hakata spread out on their left, and they gazed upon its pale, grey waters as if in a dream. They had neither food nor drink; they might be followed, too, and their insides froze in fear whenever they heard a footstep behind them. Tottering on more dead than alive, they reached a place called The Promontory of the Temple Bell, Where Riches are Revoked and Life Comes to an End. Crossing a field at the foot of a mountain, they finally reached the home of an acquaintance of Jiroemon's. The man was rather cold toward them, but Jiroemon realized that this was only to be expected. Wrapping some of his coins in paper, he handed them over while saying, "It's too much to ask, but . . ."

Lodged in a mere shed, Oran and Jiroemon began to suspect that a life of misery lay in store for them. Pale and haggard, they looked at one another and let out a sigh. Oran sniffled over and over, trying to hold back her tears. She also stroked the fur of Kichibei, the monkey she had raised from infancy.

And how did Kichibei get into the story? Well, Kichibei was Oran's pet—and so attached to her that he had instinctively followed along when he saw her hurrying off in the darkness with a man he had never seen. Oran, after noticing that Kichibei had followed them for several miles, scolded, shooed, and even threw stones at the monkey. But Kichibei kept loping along behind until eventually Jiroemon took pity on the animal. Since he's come this far, Jiroemon said, let's take him along. Oran then beckoned, and the monkey scurried up to them. Once he was cradled in her arms, he blinked and gave them both a look of pity.

Eventually Kichibei became their faithful servant. He brought meals to the shed for them and kept the flies away. Wielding a comb, he would even put the stray curls of his mistress back in place. Though a mere animal, he also tried to console the couple, doing one thing after another, even when it wasn't necessary.

Though they had chosen a life of obscurity, one could not expect them to live forever in a cramped shed. Giving most of the leftover money to his cold-hearted acquaintance, Jiroemon asked that a cottage be constructed nearby. When it was finished, the couple moved in with their monkey-servant and started a vegetable garden large enough to supply their table. When he had time, Jiroemon would go off to cut tobacco, leaving Oran at home to spin cotton into skeins. Having betrayed their parents and eloped, now they could hardly eke out a living. Certainly the dreams of youth, whether of love or hate, fade quickly.

So they had ended up as one more hubby and his missis, staring at one another in their poor household. When a clatter arose in the kitchen, each of them would stand up with an angry look. Had a mouse made the noise? They wouldn't tolerate having the beans soiled again. In circumstances such as these, even the autumn leaves and the spring violets failed to interest them.

Sensing that now was the time to repay his debt to Jiroemon, Kichibei would go into the nearby hills to gather decaying oak branches and fallen leaves. Back home, he would squat before the stove, his face turned away from the smoke, and kindle the fire with rapid strokes of his persimmon-dyed fan. After a few minutes had passed, he would serve them each a lukewarm cup of tea—in a manner so comic that the couple found something pathetic in it. Although Kichibei couldn't speak, he was visibly worried about the household's poverty. He would dawdle over his supper, eating just a little before rolling over to sleep as if he were full. Whenever Jiroemon finished his own meal, the monkey would run up to massage his master's back and rub his legs. Then he was off to the kitchen to help Oran clean up. Each time he broke a plate, a look of shame would appear on his face.

Consoled by the monkey, the couple gradually forgot about their wretched fate. After a year had passed and autumn had again come, Oran gave birth to a baby whom they named Kikunosuke. For the first time in months, the sound of laughter came from the simple cottage. Suddenly the couple found life worth living once more. They made a fuss over the child—Look! He's opened his eyes. There! He's yawning—and Kichibei pranced about with delight. The monkey would bring in nuts from the wild and place them in the infant's hand. Though Oran would scold him for this, Kichibei would not leave the baby alone. He seemed beside himself with curiosity. He would gaze in amazement at the sleeping face, only to be startled by the infant's sudden cry. Then he would run over to Oran and tug at her skirt, drawing her over to the cradle. The breast, the breast, he would motion to his mistress. As she proceeded to nurse the child, the monkey would crouch nearby, watching in fascination.

A splendid guardian—that's what Kichibei had become. Yet, no matter how pleased they were over the monkey's attentions, the couple still felt sorry for Kikunosuke. If the child had only been born last year in the Kuwamori house, he would have received heaps of swaddling clothes from the celebrating relatives and slept on silk, too, with several nursemaids in attendance. Not a single flea could have come near him, his skin would have remained like a jewel. For being born a year later, however, the child had to sleep in a thatched cottage exposed to the wind and rain, with nuts and berries for his toys and a monkey as his guardian.

Oran and Jiroemon had themselves brought on Kikunosuke's plight by their rash love. They forgot about that, however, from sheer pity for the child. In spite of their poverty, they were determined to put something aside for when Kikunosuke became aware of such things as wealth. If they could manage that, they would return and set things right with their parents. Impelled by his love for the child, Jiroemon asked a neighbor how he could make some money in business.

Kikunosuke laughed a lot even as he grew plump, imparting to the cottage a sense of life that had been missing a year ago. The child had dazzling looks, resembling his mother in this regard. Since the monkey Kichibei would bring autumn grasses from the field and dangle them playfully over the child's face, husband and wife could go to the garden and dig radishes without having to worry about the child.

As autumn came near once more, the couple felt alive with anticipation. It happened that the neighboring farmer did have some encouraging news for them. So one fine day Oran and Jiroemon went excitedly to see him and inquire more precisely into the matter.

After they had been gone awhile, the monkey Kichibei stood up inside the cottage. From the look on his face, it was evident that he knew it was time for the child's bath. He did exactly what he remembered having seen Oran do. First, he lit a wood fire under the stove and brought the water to a boil. Then, seeing the bubbles rise, he poured the scalding water into the basin up to the rim. Removing the infant's clothes, Kichibei looked into his face just as Oran would do, nodded several times, and then—without testing the temperature—plunged him right into the water.

"Waa!" That very moment the infant Kikunosuke ceased to breathe.

Having heard this shrill cry, the alarmed parents looked at one another and hurried back. Kikunosuke lay submerged in the basin while Kichibei fidgeted.

Oran scooped up her child, but he already looked like a boiled lobster. Unable to bear the sight, she merely fell back and let out a wail. Like one gone mad, Oran said that she would give up her own life to see the child's sweet face one more time. Then she rose and seized this stunned monkey who had murdered her own baby. Though a mere woman, she brandished a piece of firewood over Kichibei's head, intent on clubbing the monkey to death.

Jiroemon too was overcome with grief, and his tears fell without pause. But in spite of his sorrow, he realized that forgiveness would be better than revenge. So he took the firewood from Oran and tried to reason with her. The child had died, he pointed out, because that was his fate. Her wish to kill the monkey was understandable, but vengeance now would only harm Kikunosuke's chances for salvation. The child could not return. Besides, he went on, Kichibei had only wanted to help them. Alas, he was only an animal and didn't know much. It was too late to do anything now. Even as Jiroemon wept and said these things, the monkey shed tears in a corner of the room and brought his palms together in gratitude. Seeing him, the couple became all the more distraught. What sin from an earlier life, they wondered, could have caused this tragedy?

Once Kikunosuke was buried, the couple's will to live on gradually faded, leaving both of them ill and confined to their beds. The monkey Kichibei diligently nursed them, without even sleeping at night. He didn't forget Kikunosuke either. Every seventh day after the death, he visited the grave, adorning it on some occasions with flowers plucked by his own hand. A hundred days later, when the couple were feeling somewhat better, Kichibei went dejectedly to the grave and quietly made a water offering. Then, thrusting the point of a bamboo spear into his throat, he took his own life.

Worried over Kichibei's disappearance, Jiroemon and Oran, each leaning on a cane, hobbled off to the grave. One glance at the pitiful corpse and they understood everything. Their grief was especially poignant, for they now realized how dependent upon the monkey they had become. So they gave him a proper burial in a mound that they built next to the grave of their own child.

And so, Oran and Jiroemon abandoned the world for good . . . But, having written that, I'm not sure whether to have them pray to Amida Buddha of the Pure Land or chant the Invocation to the Lotus Sutra. In the original tale, Saikaku says that they chanted "All hail to the Lotus Sutra" incessantly in their cottage and read the Lotus Sutra without end. Tokuzaemon was a stubborn advocate of the Sutra. But, if his bigotry breaks through now, this tale of woe might well collapse. A real bind, if ever there was one. And so, all I can say is that Oran and Jiroemon, depressed at the thought of staying on in the cottage, set out through the autumn grass, their destination uncertain once more.

The Sound of Hammering

Tokatonton

Dazai wrote this work in the fall of 1946, slightly more than a year after the Japanese surrendered to the Allied forces in World War II. At that time the nation had only begun the task of rebuilding, and extreme physical hardship was a daily fact of life throughout the society. Dazai's story, though referring to material deprivation, focuses on such intangible problems as the collapse of will and the lack of purpose afflicting society in the wake of defeat.

The haunting symbol of these problems, indicated in the title of the story, was not the invention of the author. When a young fan wrote him about the sound he was hearing, Dazai recognized the literary potential of the phenomenon. In his reply he asked the permission of his correspondent to use the notion of this sound as a story motif while pledging not to borrow extensively from the letter. As Dazai went on to say, he was eager to evoke the traumatic effect that the war and the surrender had had upon the younger generation.

Disillusioned with his own age group and with the older generation too, Dazai emphasized in several postwar writings (though not in "The Sound of Hammering") that a New Japan would arise only through the efforts of the young.

"The Sound of Hammering" consists almost exclusively of two letters: the first a long description by a young man addressed to an older writer as a moral authority, the second a brief response from this writer to the youth. The correspondent at first shows how closely he has read the author; in the end, he implicitly asks the writer to live up to his calling by advising him about his dilemma. Whether the writer measures up must be judged in accord with the answer he gives the young man in the coda.

Readers will probably differ as to whether the coda responds to the dilemma or amounts to a confession of failure. The persona of the older author virtually flourishes his biblical quote as a kind of panacea. However, the relevance of the quote is obscure, to say the least, and some readers will probably dismiss it as a mere rhetorical gesture. Given the serious, not to say desperate, tone that the author imparts to the youth's plea, one expects a serious reply from the author within the story. It could well be that Dazai, with his self-mocking tendency, thought it more in keeping to disappoint such an expectation by denying to himself the role of moral arbiter.

Dear Sir,

Please advise me on a certain matter. I'm twenty-six years old and deeply troubled.

I was born in the Teramachi District of Aomori City. You probably don't know the little Tomoya flower shop right next to Seikaji temple, but I'm the Tomoya's second son. I graduated from Aomori High School and went to work in the office of a munitions factory in Yokohama. I worked there three years and then spent four years in the army. When the war ended, I came back home. But our house had been burned down, and my father, along with my older brother and his wife, were living in a shed that had been thrown together on the site. My mother had died during my fourth year of high school.

I might have squeezed into the shed, but that would not have been fair to the others. After talking things over with my father and brother, I took a job at a village post office about five miles up the coast from Aomori City. My mother's family lives there, and her older brother is the postmaster. More than a year has gone by now, and I feel more trivial with each passing day. That's why I'm deeply troubled.

I started reading you when I worked at the munitions factory office in Yokohama. I first read a short story in the journal *Style*, and then I got into the habit of looking around for your books. While reading them, I learned that you had gone to Aomori High School ahead of me and had lived in Mr. Toyota's house during your school days. When I realized that, I was so excited that my heart nearly burst. If that's Mr. Toyota the dry-goods dealer, why he lives in the same neighborhood as my family, and I know him well. Actually there are two Toyotas. Old Mr. Toyota is chubby, and his first name is Tazaemon. That's just right for him, since the first syllable is written with the character for "chubby." His son is also named Tazaemon, except that he's thin and dapper. I'd rather see him named after some lithe Kabuki actor, Uzaemon for example. But all of the Toyotas are fine people, aren't they.

It's a shame that their house was one of those

burned down in the last air raid. It seems that even their storehouse was destroyed. When I learned that you had lived in their home, I really thought of asking the younger Mr. Toyota for a letter of introduction. But I only dreamed of paying you a visit. That's because I'm a coward. When it comes to doing something, I lose my nerve.

Well, after they drafted me, I was sent off to Chiba Prefecture. We were put to work digging fortifications along the coast, and that's how I spent every day until the end of the war. It was only when I got a half day off now and then that I could go into town and look for your books. I took up my pen countless times to write you a letter. But once I wrote, "Dear Sir," I was at a loss. As far as you were concerned, I was an utter stranger. And besides, I didn't have anything particular to write about. I would simply hold the pen in my hand, totally befuddled.

Finally Japan agreed to an unconditional surrender, and I went back home to work in the post office. When I was in Aomori City the other day, I stopped by a bookstore and looked for your works. I found out that the war had uprooted you as well and you were back at your birthplace in Kanagi. When I read that, my heart seemed ready to burst again. All the same I still couldn't work up the courage to pay you a visit. After considering all sorts of things, I decided to send a letter. This time I'm not at a loss after writing, "Dear Sir." That's because this letter has a purpose, a crucial purpose, too.

I would appreciate your advice on a certain matter. To tell the truth, I'm deeply troubled. I'm not the only one, either. Other people seem troubled by the same thing. Advise me for their sake as well. I felt like writing to you over and over—when I worked at the munitions plant, as well as when I served in the army. After waiting all this time, I hardly expected to be writing a letter that sounds so dismal as this one.

We were ordered into formation before the barracks at noon on August 15, 1945, to hear the emperor himself make a statement over the radio. But the static was so bad that hardly a word got through. When the broadcast finally ended, a young lieutenant promptly mounted the reviewing stand.

"You heard it?" he barked. "You see now? Our nation has accepted the Potsdam Declaration and surrendered. But that's politics—it's not our business. We're soldiers, and we'll keep on fighting till the very end. Then we'll take our own lives, every one of us. That's how we'll make up to His Majesty for this defeat. I've been prepared from the beginning, so I want all of you to be ready too. Is that understood? All right, dismissed."

Removing his glasses, the lieutenant stepped down from the platform, tears streaming down his cheeks as he walked away. I wondered if "solemn" was the word to describe the mood of that moment. As I stood at attention, the surroundings grew dark and misty, and a cold wind blew in from somewhere or other. My body seemed to sink of its own weight into the depths of the earth.

Should I take my own life? To die—I thought that alone was real. A hush had fallen upon the woods opposite the grounds, and the trees seemed like dark lacquer. A flock of small birds rose silently from the treetops and flew off like sesame seeds cast into the sky.

Ah, that's when it happened. From the barracks

behind me came the faint sound of someone driving a nail. Perhaps the biblical phrase describes what I felt then—And the scales fell from my eyes. Both the pathos and glory of military life disappeared in an instant. I felt utterly listless and indifferent, as though I had been released from a spell. I gazed across a sandy field in the summer noon without any feeling whatever.

Thereupon I stuffed my duffel bag to the seams and wandered back home.

That faint and distant sound of hammering was like a miracle, stripping me of every militaristic illusion. Never again would I become intoxicated by that nightmare with its so-called pathos and glory. And yet, that tiny sound must have resonated in my brain. For, ever since that day, I have become like one subject to ugly and bizarre epileptic fits.

Not that I ever become violent. Quite the contrary. Whenever I get excited or inspired over something, that faint sound of hammering arises from nowhere in particular, and I grow quite placid. The scene before me suddenly changes, leaving only a blankness in place of whatever images were present. I simply stare straight ahead, with a feeling of utter stupidity and emptiness.

When I first came to the post office, I thought I'd have enough freedom to work at whatever took my fancy. I decided to write a narrative of some kind and send it to you. During my spare moments in the post office, I worked hard at recording my memories of life in the army. By autumn the manuscript totaled almost a hundred pages, and I promised myself one evening that I would finish it the next day. When my shift at the post office ended, I went to the public bathhouse and soaked myself in the warm water. I was trembling with anticipation over getting to the last chapter that very night. Should I write it up as a grand tragedy in the manner of *Eugene Onegin?* Or end in the pessimistic mode of Gogol's *The Quarrel?* While pondering this question, I looked up at the bare lightbulb hanging from the high ceiling of the bathhouse and heard in the distance the faint sound of hammering. At that moment a ripple arose along the surface, and I became merely another bather splashing about in a corner of the dimly lit pool.

Disheartened, I crawled from the bath and washed the soles of my feet. As I listened to the other bathers talk about rationing, Pushkin and Gogol seemed as uninspiring as the names of several foreign-made toothbrushes. I left the bathhouse, crossed the bridge, and went home. After eating my supper in silence, I went to my own room and thumbed through the nearly hundred pages of manuscript on the desk. It was terrible. So absurd, in fact, that I didn't even have the strength to tear up the manuscript paper. I use it for tissue now. And, since that day, I haven't written a line.

My uncle has a small library, and sometimes I would borrow a volume or two of collected stories from the Meiji or Taishō eras. I read purely for pleasure, liking certain stories and not caring for others. On evenings when it snowed, I'd go to bed early. Sometime during these listless days, I looked at a multivolume set on world art. I had once liked the French Impressionists, but this time I was unmoved by their work. Instead I gazed in wonder at the paintings of Ogata Kōrin[1] and Ogata Kenzan,[2] two Japanese artists of the Genroku period. To me, the azaleas of Kōrin seemed better than the work of any other painter, whether Cezanne, Monet, or Gauguin.

Once again my interest in things revived. Of course, I didn't have any bold ambitions. I would simply be a village dilettante, not a master artist like Kōrin or Kenzan. As for a job that I could throw myself into—well, sitting from morning to evening at the post office window and counting people's money was the best I could hope for. And for someone like myself without training or intelligence, this line of work was not degrading. Humility might have its own crown, and devotion to everyday duty could be the noblest life of all.

I was gradually beginning to take pride in my life when the conversion of the yen currency took place. Even in a village post office in the country—indeed, especially in such a place—everyone had to rush about since there were so few of us. We didn't have a moment's rest from early in the morning. No matter how tired we got, we had to receive deposits, stamp old currency, and whatever else besides. Aware that now was the time to repay my uncle for taking me in, I worked especially hard. My hands became numb, as if they were encased in steel gloves; after a time they no longer felt like my own.

Working like this, I would sleep through the night like a dead person. And the next morning I'd leap from bed the moment the alarm clock went off by my pillow, hurry to the office, and begin cleaning up. Cleaning was something the women in the office usually did, but my own working pace had so picked up during the hurly-burly of the yen conversion that I rushed to do any sort of chore, no matter what.

I kept increasing the pace too—more today than yesterday, more tomorrow than today—as though I were half mad.

On the day this uproar over the yen conversion was to end, I rose as usual in the dim, pre-dawn light, frantically cleaned the office, and sat down at my assigned window. As the sun rose, casting its light on my face, I narrowed my sleepy eyes in a mood of utter contentment and recalled the dictum about work being sacred. Then, just as I breathed a sigh of relief, I seemed to hear in the distance the faint sound of hammering. That did it. In an instant everything appeared absurd. I stood up, went back to my room, crawled under the quilt, and fell asleep. When someone called me for breakfast, I refused to get up. I wasn't feeling well—that's all I said.

Evidently the office was busier that day than ever. And, with their best worker lying in bed, the others were sorely tested. Nonetheless, I dozed right on through till evening, an act of self-indulgence that increased the debt to my uncle. I simply had no interest in working and slept late the next day too. After I finally got up and sat down absent-mindedly at my place, I let out one yawn after another, leaving the work to the girl at the next window. The following day, too, and the day after as well, I was sluggish and morose. In other words, I had become your typical post office clerk.

"You're still not feeling well?" my uncle inquired, a faint smile on his face.

"Oh, it's nothing really," I replied. "Perhaps I'm a little worn out."

"Just what I thought!" he exclaimed. "It's because of those books you read. They're too hard for you.

Dumb fellows like you and me shouldn't try to think about things. It's better not to."

He smiled, and I tried to grin back.

My uncle supposedly graduated from some technical school. But he didn't show any interest whatever in matters of the mind.

And then . . . You know, I seem to use that phrase over and over. It's probably another indication of how dumb I am. And then—it just slips out, even though I'm bothered when it does. But I guess there's nothing I can do about it.

And then I fell in love. Now don't laugh about this. Well, I can't help it even if you do laugh. Anyway, I was living in a trance, like an inert minnow near the bottom of a goldfish bowl. Then I felt quite awkward, as the minnow would if it were to find its belly suddenly full of eggs.

When you fall in love, music permeates the soul, doesn't it? I think that's the surest sign of this affliction.

She didn't love me, but I was so crazy about her that I couldn't help myself.

To all appearances she was not yet twenty years old. She worked as a maid at a small inn, the only one in this coastal village. My uncle the postmaster was a real drinker, and, whenever this inn had a party, he would certainly be there. He seemed to get along well with the maid. When she showed up at the post office to take care of her savings or insurance, my uncle always teased her with some stale joke.

"Things must be going well," he would observe. "You're really stashing it away, aren't you? Capital! Capital! Haven't found yourself a nice man, have you?"

"Don't be silly!" she'd retort, looking as bored as a nobleman in a Van Dyck painting.

Hanae Tokita—that was the name written in her savings book. She must have been from Miyagi Prefecture, for there was a Miyagi address in the book with a red line running through it. Her new address had been entered next to the old one. According to the talk among the girl workers at the post office, Hanae's home in Miyagi had been damaged during the war. Apparently she was a distant relative of the mistress of the inn, and that's why she came to this village just before the surrender. She was supposed to be clever beyond her years too, and her behavior was far from ideal.

Still, there wasn't a single refugee here with a good reputation among the local people. That's why I didn't believe a word about her so-called cleverness. On the other hand, her savings weren't all that meager. Postal workers aren't supposed to reveal this sort of thing, but about every week Hanae would deposit a sum, even as the postmaster teased her. The amount would be two or three hundred yen each time, and so her savings grew quite large. I didn't believe she was able to do this because of some nice man. Yet, every time I wrote down the sum of 200 yen or 300 yen and pressed my stamp onto the form, my heartbeat would quicken and my face would turn red.

Gradually I became more and more tormented over Hanae. It wasn't that she was clever. No, every man in the village was after her—that was it. Wouldn't they ruin the girl by giving her all that money? When this thought occurred to me in the middle of the night, I sat straight up in bed.

All the same Hanae calmly came in to make a deposit about once every week. As I said, my heartbeat used to quicken and my face turn red when she first started coming. On later occasions I got even more upset, my face turning deathly pale and my brow oozing sweat. Counting each of the soiled ten-yen notes pasted with stamps which Hanae smugly handed over, I would be assailed time and again by the urge to tear her money to shreds. I also wanted to quote for her the famous words from Kyōka's novel: "Even if you die, don't become his plaything!"[3] But that would be going too far. A peasant like myself couldn't speak such words. Still, being so serious about the matter, I could not help wanting to blurt out, Even if you die, don't become his plaything! What does wealth amount to? Or material goods?

If you love someone, you will be loved in return. Isn't there some truth to that? The middle of May had gone by when Hanae came demurely as ever to the post office window and handed me her savings book and money. With a sigh I took them both and began counting the bills. I was feeling depressed as I entered the amount and silently handed back her book.

"Are you free around five o'clock?"

At first I couldn't believe my ears. She had spoken quickly and softly, and I first thought the spring breeze might have deceived me.

"If you're free then, meet me at the bridge." She smiled lightly and walked away, demure as ever.

I looked at the clock, but it was barely past two. I'm going to seem like a pushover in saying this, but I don't remember how I spent the next three hours. I might well have wandered about the office, barely managing to look serious, and blurted out to one of the girls about how beautiful the day was. I might have glared at her surprised look (the day happened to be cloudy), then headed for the toilet. In short, I must have spent the afternoon like a fool; I left at seven or eight minutes before five. Along the way I noticed that my fingernails were overgrown. Even now I can remember how badly I wanted to cry.

Hanae was standing by the foot of the bridge in a skirt that seemed rather short. Catching a glimpse of her long bare legs, I lowered my eyes to the ground.

"Let's go toward the shore," she calmly suggested.

Hanae set out first, and I slowly followed five or six steps behind. Despite the distance between us, we presently fell into step with one another, much to my embarrassment.

It was a cloudy day with a breeze, and the sand swirled along the beach.

"This will do," Hanae exclaimed. She slipped between two large fishing boats that had been pulled up on the beach and sat down right on the sand. "Come, you'll be warm if you sit here. It's out of the wind."

I sat down some six feet or so from where Hanae had settled with her legs outstretched.

"I'm sorry to bother you, but I had to do this," she began. "There's something I've got to say. It's about my savings account. You're wondering about it, aren't you?"

Here's my chance, I told myself. My voice hoarse, I replied, "Yes, I am."

"That's only natural," she agreed. Then, letting her head fall, she scooped a handful of sand and poured it along her leg. "You see, it's not my money. If it were, I wouldn't put it into an account. It's too much trouble making a deposit every week."

That made sense and I silently nodded.

"Don't you see? The savings book belongs to the mistress at the inn. That's a secret, so don't tell anyone. I can imagine why she handles things this way, but it's so complicated that I don't want to explain right here. You realize how hard it is on me, don't you?" She smiled, and then her eyes glistened strangely. I realized that she was crying.

More than anything, I wanted to kiss her. With Hanae I could undergo any hardship.

"The people from here," she went on, "are all terrible, don't you agree? I thought you might be mistaken about me too, so I wanted to have this talk with you. Today I made up my mind to do it."

At that moment the sound of hammering came from nearby. I wasn't hearing things this time. Someone had indeed begun pounding a nail inside Mr. Sasaki's seaside hut. The sound echoed over and over, and I stood up trembling. "I see. And I won't tell anyone about the account."

A stray dog had left a sizable pile of dung just behind the spot where Hanae was sitting. I debated some moments whether to tell her.

The waves undulated slowly, and a boat with a bedraggled sail tottered through the shallows.

"Well, good-bye then," I uttered.

A vast emptiness lay before me. What did I care about her savings? To me she was a mere stranger. So, what difference did it make if she became a man's plaything or whatever. Stupid! Besides, I was hungry.

Hanae has kept up with her deposits. She makes

one without fail every week or so. Her savings must amount to thousands of yen by now, but I'm not the least interested. Since it doesn't make any difference to me, I don't care whether it's the landlady's money, as Hanae claimed, or simply her own.

So, which one of us got jilted? I suspect it was me rather than Hanae, but I'm not particularly sad about that. It was a strange affair in any event, and, since then, I've gone back to being your typical, idle clerk.

This June I went to Aomori City on an errand and happened to see a workers' demonstration. Far from being interested in social and political movements, I had felt in them something akin to despair. Regardless of the cause, those in charge always seemed to be seeking power and glory for themselves. It's as if one boards a ship only to become the captain's lackey. A leader pompously voices his own views without the least hesitation. Do as I say, he proclaims. Then you, as well as your family and your village and your country and the whole world too will be secure. Gesturing grandly, he roars on about how disaster will come from ignoring him. But then, as has happened time after time, his favorite prostitute gives him the cold shoulder, and this makes him cry out desperately for the abolition of her kind. Sometimes, after attacking his better-looking colleagues in a fit of indignation and raising a general ruckus, he receives his medal of distinction and races home on cloud nine to tell his wife. Mummie! he exults, Look here! Then, he opens the little box and gives her a peek inside. She is not fooled, however. What! Only a Fifth Degree. A Second or nothing, she insists, leaving her husband crestfallen. It's half-crazed men of this kind, unable to tell one thing from

194 THE SOUND OF HAMMERING

another, who throw themselves into political and social movements. And so, when the clamor arose over democracy and whatever else during the general election in April, I wasn't inclined to believe a word. The politicians of the Liberal and the Progressive Parties made plenty of noise, but weren't they simply taking advantage of things? They gave one an indelible impression—of maggots feeding on the corpse of a defeated nation. On April 10, the day of the election, I was told by my uncle to vote for Katō of the Liberal Party. All right, I said, leaving the house. But I only went for a walk along the beach and then came back. I believed that the gloom of our daily lives could not be dispelled, no matter how much one declaimed about society and politics.

However, when I ran into the workers' demonstration that day in Aomori, I realized how wrong I had been. Lively and vibrant—doesn't that describe it? What a joyous event the parade was. I didn't see even a hint of gloom, not one frowning face. There was only bursting energy, with young girls holding flags and singing labor hymns. My breast overflowed with emotion and tears began to fall. How lucky, I mused, that Japan had lost the war. For the first time in my life, I saw the figure of true freedom. If social and political movements gave rise to this, then people should begin by studying the ideas behind such movements.

As I watched the parade, I felt a great joy. It was as if the shining path I should follow had been made unmistakably real to me. Tears flowed pleasantly down my cheeks, and the green surroundings became blurred, just as if I had plunged into a pool and were looking at things underwater. In the middle of this swaying twilight, I saw the flags with their blazing red color . . . Ah, I wept over that color. Even if I were to die, I would not forget this scene. And then, distant and faint, the sound of hammering arose. And that was it.

What does that sound mean? It can't be dismissed simply as nihilism or whatever, for the illusion of hammering obliterates even these things.

When summer arrived, the young fellows around here suddenly got excited about sports. I'm inclined toward the pragmatic view of things that comes with age. Maybe that's why I can't see stripping almost naked and then getting tossed about and badly bruised for no reason at all in a sumo wrestling match, or running a hundred meters with a contorted face just to find out who will win, especially when the sprinters all look as alike as a bunch of acorns. Sports were stupid, and I had never felt like getting involved.

This year there was a long-distance relay in August. The course made its way through every village along the coast, and many youngsters took part. One of the relay points, where the runners from Aomori City were supposed to be relieved by the next group, was right in front of our own post office. Just before ten o'clock, when the runners were due to arrive, the postal workers all went outside to watch, leaving the postmaster and myself alone to clear up some insurance accounts. I heard the crowd shouting, There they are! Over there! So I got up and went to the window. This must have been that "final spurt" one hears about. I saw the lead runner stagger in, clad only in a pair of shorts. His fingers spread out like the webbed foot of a frog, his arms flailing about as if to part the air, his chest thrown out and his head swaying, he collapsed before the post office with his face grimacing in pain. A companion of his ran up and shouted, Hurrah! You've done it! Then, he helped the runner up and brought him toward the window where I was watching. Even after the runner was splashed with a bucket of water, he seemed more dead than alive. But, as I observed him lying there, his body slack and his face terribly pale, I felt a strange thrill.

I would call his deed "touching," but that sounds conceited coming from someone only twenty-six years old like myself. Perhaps a word like "heart-rending" would be better. In any event there was something marvelous about this great waste of energy. Even though no one really cared whether the runner took a first or a second, he nonetheless went all out on that final spurt. He didn't run for some high ideal, either. For example, he wasn't trying to help his country raise its standing among the civilized nations. And he wouldn't mouth any such ideals merely to win the favor of people.

He didn't care about becoming a great marathoner. After all, this was only a country race, and he wasn't going to set any record pace. Realizing that, he certainly wouldn't feel like discussing the event when he returned home. On the contrary, he'd worry that his father might scold him. Despite all this, he had wanted to run, to give the race his utmost without being praised for his effort. He just wanted to run—to do something for nothing. As a boy he had recklessly climbed up persimmon trees to eat the fruit. But he wasn't out to get anything in this grueling marathon. I suppose his passion was almost for Nothing. And that seemed close to my own mood at the time.

Eventually I got into the habit of tossing around a baseball with the other post office employees. I would keep playing until I was dead tired. And just when I felt as though I had shed something of myself, the sound of hammering would arise. That sound demolished even the passion for Nothing.

I hear it more and more frequently of late—when I opened the newspaper to examine each article of the new constitution; when a brilliant solution came to me as my uncle discussed a personnel problem in the office; when I tried reading your novel; when a fire broke out the other night and I leaped from bed to have a look; when I feel like another cup of saké while drinking with my uncle before supper; when I seem to be losing my mind; and, finally, when I think of suicide.

Last evening, while the two of us were drinking, I turned to my uncle and asked in jest, "Define life for me—in just a word or two."

"I don't know about life," he replied, "but the world's nothing but sex and greed."

I hadn't expected so sharp a reply. Should I act upon it and become a black marketeer? When I realized what a bundle I could make, however, the sound of hammering arose forthwith.

Please tell me, what does that sound mean? I'm paralyzed by it at the moment, so how do I escape? Please, answer my letter.

If you'll allow me, I'd like to say one more thing. I began hearing the sound quite distinctly before this letter was half-written. Bored—that's how I felt. Still, I kept going and wrote this much. I wrote in such desperation, though, that I now feel everything was a lie. There wasn't a girl named Hanae and I never saw a demonstration. The rest of it seems to be mostly lies too.

Not the sound of hammering, though. That part alone doesn't seem a lie. I'm sending you exactly what I've written, without even reading it over.

Yours sincerely,

The writer who received this queer letter was piti-fully ignorant. He didn't have a thought in his head either, but he still managed the following reply.

Dear Sir:

Agonizing, isn't it? Well, I don't have much sym-pathy for a hypocrite. You still seem to be avoiding an ugly situation that can't be explained away, a situation others see and point a finger at. Real thought takes courage more than intelligence. As Jesus said, "And fear not them that kill the body, but are not able to kill the soul; but rather fear him that is able to destroy both body and soul in hell." In this passage 'fear' means something like 'to hold in awe.' If you can sense the thunder in these words, you will not be hearing things anymore.

Taking
the Wen Away
Kobutori

Like the preceding two stories, this and the following one are retellings of earlier literature. "Taking the Wen Away" and "Crackling Mountain," are derived from a miscellany of medieval tales known as the Otogi Zōshi. *Dazai retold four tales from the group, "The Split-Tongue Sparrow" and "The Tale of Urashima" being the two additional ones not translated here. Dazai's volume contains a brief preface purporting to explain the genesis of the retellings. A translation of that preface follows immediately after this note.*

Wen is a rather old-fashioned term now, and perhaps a word like boil or cyst would be more appropriate. However, the vagaries of translation have sanctioned the older term to an extent. More to the point, among the available word choices, wen seems to preserve best the air of unreality in much of the tale, especially the scenes involving the demons.

The author intrudes quite directly in the retelling of "Taking the Wen Away," just as he does in other Otogi Zōshi *tales. Some of these intrusions, above all, the rumination on origins and instances related in a monotonous style and delaying the narration of the tale proper, might merely seem pseudo-learned diversions. In these passages Dazai seems to criticize a cer-*

tain strain of humanistic scholarship in Japan for being narrow and bookish, and to contrast this quality with the free play of the creative imagination.

Dazai gives a good illustration in one passage of how to make free use of bookish knowledge. The recital accompanying the second man's dance starts off parodying the style of the Noh drama and ends with an echo of several lines from a famous poem by Shimazaki Tōson.[1]

As with certain other of his stories, including "Crackling Mountain," Dazai ends on a cryptic note. Taken literally, the final lines reflect a common theme of his; that is, the conjunction of the comic and the tragic. But perhaps the long paragraph ending this tale merely leads the reader down a blind alley. Even if it does, the tale itself proves quite engrossing merely for being told.

Preface to "A Collection of Fairy Tales"

"Ah! There they go again."

Setting aside his pen, the father stands up. He wouldn't bother to stop just for the sirens; but when the anti-aircraft guns start firing, he lays his work aside and gets up from his desk. Fastening the air-raid hood on his four-year-old daughter, he picks up the girl and heads for the backyard shelter. His wife is already crouched inside, their one-year-old daughter clinging to her back.

"Sounds pretty near this time," he observes.

"H'mm," his wife replies. "It's still cramped in here too."

"Is it really?" He sounds rather irritated and adds, "If I dug it deeper, we could be buried alive some day. It's just right like it is."

"Couldn't you have made it a little wider?"

"Well, I guess so. But the ground's frozen now and it's hard to dig. I'll get to it sometime." Having put off his wife with this evasive reply, he listens carefully to the radio for information on the air-raid.

Now that one complaint has been set aside for the time being, his four-year-old daughter starts insisting that they leave the air-raid shelter. There's only one way to calm her down, and that's to get out the illustrated book of fairy-tales and read her such stories as "Momotaro," "Crackling Mountain," "The Split-Tongue Sparrow," "Taking the Wen Away," and "Urashima."

Although his clothes are shabby and his looks quite fatuous, this father isn't a nobody. He's an author who knows how to create a tale.

And so, as he starts reading in his queer, dissonant voice, "Long, long ago. . ." he imagines to himself a quite different tale.

Once upon a time there was an old man with a large, cumbersome wen on his right cheek.

This old man lived at the foot of Sword Mountain, located in the Awa district on the island of Shikoku. That's how I remember it, but there's no way to check here in this air-raid shelter. Worst yet, I can't confirm whether this story was first told in *The Tales of Uji*,[2] as seems to be the case. I'm a bit hazy about where the other stories got started, too—Urashima, for instance, which I plan to tell next. I am aware that the true story of Urashima is duly recorded in the *Chronicle of Japan*[3] and that there's even a ballad on him in *The Collection of Ten Thousand Leaves*.[4] And let's see, now—besides that, there's a similar tale in the *Tango Gazetteer*[5] and one in the *Biographies of the Taoist Immortals*[6] as well. Coming down to recent times, didn't Ōgai[7] write a play about Urashima? And didn't Shōyō[8] set the story to music for dancing? In any event, Urashima puts in countless appearances on the stage, whether in Noh, Kabuki, or geisha dancing.

As soon as I've finished reading a book, I either give it away or sell it. Without a library of my own to check things, I'm in a fix right now. I'd have to go around looking for books that I barely remember having read. And that's almost impossible at a time like this. Here I am, squatting in the air-raid shelter with just a picture-book open in my lap. I'd better forget about these inquiries and tell the tale on my own. It will probably turn out more lively that way.

And so, in the corner of his air-raid shelter, this oddball of a father rambles on to himself, as if unwilling to admit defeat. While he reads from the picture-book to his daughter, he ends up concocting his own version of the story.

Once upon a time . . .

. . . there was an old man who really liked to drink saké. Now such a drinker often feels lonely in his own home. Does he drink because he's lonely? Or is he lonely because his family despises him for drinking? That's merely a pedantic question, like trying to decide which hand makes the noise when clapping. Anyway, when the old man was at home, he always looked glum.

This wasn't because his family was malicious, either. Though almost seventy years old, his wife was in fine health, with such a straight back and clear eyes that people still remarked about how attractive she had been as a young woman. She had never talked much, but she did the housework diligently.

Hoping to enliven her, the old man would occasionally say something like, "Spring must be here, the cherry trees have bloomed."

"Is that so," she'd reply unconcernedly. "Move over a bit. I want to clean there."

The old man would look glum.

His only son, almost forty years old at the time, conducted himself in an irreproachable manner. It wasn't merely that he didn't smoke or drink; he didn't even smile, he never got angry nor was he ever happy. He merely worked the fields in silence. Since the people hereabouts could not but revere him, his reputation as "The Saint of Awa" kept growing. He wouldn't take a wife or shave his beard, so one might have mistaken him for a stone or a piece of wood. With such a son and wife, it was no wonder that the old man's house was regarded as exemplary in local circles.

All the same, the old man remained glum. Though hesitant to take a drink at home, he couldn't resist indefinitely, regardless of the consequences. Yet, when he did have a drink, he merely felt worse. Not that his wife or his son, the Saint of Awa, would scold him. No, they merely ate their dinner in silence while the old man sat there sipping from his cup.

"By the way . . ." When he was tipsy, the old man wanted to talk so badly that he would usually come out with some banal remark. "Spring will soon be here," he'd say. "The swallows are back already."

Such a remark was better left unsaid. Both his wife and his son remained silent.

Still, the old man couldn't resist adding, "One moment of spring. Ah, isn't that equal to a fortune in gold?"

He shouldn't have tried that one, either.

"I give thanks for this meal," the Saint of Awa intoned. "If you'll excuse me . . ." Having finished, he paid his respects and left.

"Guess I'll have my meal too." Wearily the old man turned his cup over.

When he drank at home, it usually came to this.

One beautiful morning he went to the mountain to gather firewood.

In good weather the old man liked going up Sword Mountain to gather firewood, a gourd-bottle at his hip. Somewhat weary from gathering wood, he would sit with his legs crossed upon a large rock and clear his throat loudly.

"What a view," he'd exclaim. Then, taking his time, he would drink from the gourd-bottle, a look of perfect contentment on his face.

Away from home, he was a different person. Only one thing remained the same—the large wen on his right cheek. About twenty years ago, the old man passed a milestone in his life by turning fifty. In the autumn of that very year, he noticed that his right cheek was becoming unusually warm and itchy. At the same time, the cheek started to swell. The old man patted and rubbed the growth, and it got larger and larger. Finally, he laughed wistfully and declared, "Now I've got a fine grandchild."

"Children are not born from the cheek," his saintly son responded in a solemn tone.

His wife too, without the least hint of a smile, said to him, "It doesn't look dangerous." Aside from this, she showed no interest whatever in the wen.

The neighbors, on the other hand, were very sympathetic. How did the wen get started? they asked. Did it hurt? Wasn't it a nuisance? But the old man laughed and merely shook his head. A nuisance? Why, he regarded the wen as a darling grandchild, the one companion who would comfort him in his loneliness. Washing his face in the morning, he was especially careful to use clean water on the wen. And when, as happened to be the case now, he was alone on the mountain enjoying his saké, the wen became absolutely essential—it was the one companion he could talk to.

Sitting cross-legged on the rock, the old man drank from the gourd-bottle and patted the wen on his cheek. "What the hell," he muttered, "there's nothing to be scared of. A man should get drunk and not worry about appearances. Even sobriety has its limits. I cringe before that name, Saint of Awa. I didn't realize how great my son really is."

Having confided this bit of invective to the wen, he cleared his throat with a loud cough.

Suddenly the sky grew dark, the wind arose, and the rain began to pour.

A sudden shower seldom comes along in the spring—except for high up on Sword Mountain. Here, one must be alert for changing weather at any time. As the slope turned hazy in the rain, pheasants and quail started up from here and there, flying like arrows toward the shelter of the woods. The old man, however, remained calm. "A little rain might cool off this wen. Nothing wrong with that," he said, smiling.

He continued to sit cross-legged on the rock, gazing upon the scene. But the rain gradually became heavy, until it seemed as though it would never let up.

"This isn't just cooling things off, it's making things downright chilly," the old man complained as he stood up. Sneezing loudly, he hoisted the firewood he had collected onto his shoulder and crept into the woods.

Here he found a great crowd of birds and animals, all of them seeking shelter. "Sorry . . . excuse me," the old man mumbled, picking his way among the animals. He saluted one and all—the wild doves, the rabbits, the monkeys—as he advanced into the woods. Eventually he found a large mountain cherry tree that was hollow at the base of its trunk. "Ah, what a fine parlor," he exclaimed as he crawled in. "How about it?" he called out to the rabbits. "Ain't no saint or grand old lady here. Don't be shy. C'mon in."

Even though your habitual drunkard might spout such nonsense when tipsy, he usually turns out to be quite harmless. The old man was in a merry mood, but within minutes he had fallen asleep and was snoring gently.

As he wearily waited for the evening shower to pass, the old man fell asleep. Eventually the clouds moved on, and the moon shone brightly over the mountain.

A spring moon in its final quarter floated in the

watery sky—perhaps, one might add, a watery sky
of pale green. Moonlight filled the woods like a
shower of pine needles, but the old man slept on
peacefully. When bats started flitting out from the
hollow of the trunk, the old man suddenly awoke,
amazed to see that night had fallen.

"Now I'm in for it," he said, a vision of his somber
wife and austere son floating before his very eyes.
Ah, he had gone too far this time. They had never
scolded him before, but coming home this late would
be very awkward. H'mm, any saké left? he
wondered, giving the gourd-bottle a shake. There
was a faint splashing at the bottom. "A little," he
murmured before quickly summoning his strength
and swilling the saké to the last drop. Slightly drunk,
he muttered another trite thing—"Ah, the moon
is out. A moment of a spring evening"—and then he
crawled from the hollow.

*Oh, what noisy voices! What a strange sight. Was he
dreaming?*

Look! On a grassy clearing in the woods, a
marvelous scene from some other world was un-
folding.

As the author of this story, I must confess here that
I don't really know what a demon is. That's because
I've never seen one. Granted, I've come across
demons in picture-books since my childhood—so
often, in fact, that I'm bored by them. I've never been
privileged to meet a demon in the flesh, though.

Demons come in a variety of types, with names
like "bloodsuckers" or "cutthroats." Since they're
supposed to have a mean nature, we use the word
demon for creatures we despise. But then again, a

phrase like "the masterpiece of Mr. So-and-So, a demonic talent among the literati," will show up in the daily newspaper column on recently published books, and that really confuses things. Surely the paper doesn't intend this shady term as a warning about what a mean talent Mr. So-and-So happens to be. In extreme cases, Mr. So-and-So gets crowned a "literary demon." That's such a crude term you begin to wonder just how indignant Mr. So-and-So might become. But he doesn't seem to mind, and nothing happens. In fact, I'll hear a rumor that he secretly endorses the odd term himself. All this is completely beyond a stupid person like me.

I can't figure out why a red-faced demon who wears a tigerskin loincloth and wields a misshapen club should be our God of the Fine Arts. Perhaps we should go slow in using such difficult terms as "mean talent" and "literary demon." That's what I've been thinking for some time now; but my experience is limited, and I can't help wondering whether I'm just being foolish.

Yes, even among demons there seem to be various types. At this point I might peek into the *Japan Encyclopedia*, which would quickly turn me into a scholar admired by young and old, by women and children. (So-called scholars usually operate in this way.) I'd put on a knowing look and discourse in detail about all sorts of things. Unfortunately I'm crouched here in this air-raid shelter, and all I've got is the child's picture-book lying open in my lap. I'll just have to take it from there.

Look! There where the woods opened out, ten or so deformed—Would you call them "beings"? Or "creatures"? Anyway, these were ten or so large, red figures, and each of them certainly was wearing a loincloth. They were sitting in a circle having a party in the moonlight.

At first the old man was startled. When sober, he may be worthless and lacking in self-respect, just like most other drinkers. But, with a few drinks under the belt, he'll show more pluck than your ordinary fellow. That's why the old man was feeling gay now, even heroic. Why should he worry about his straight-laced old lady or his irreproachable son? While watching the grotesque scene before him, he didn't quail or seem frightened in any way. Crawling from the hollow, he gazed at the strange banquet with a feverish look.

Ah, he could tell they were pleasantly drunk. In fact, he too felt a pleasant glow within his breast, a symptom any drinker feels while watching others carouse. This feeling, by the way, springs from benevolence rather than selfishness, and prompts the drinker to raise a cup to his neighbor's happiness. Somebody wants to get drunk, and so much the better if a neighbor will join in. Even the old man knew this. He saw intuitively that these huge red beings weren't people, nor were they animals. They belonged to that frightful tribe known as demons. Just one look at the tiger-skin loincloths made that clear. The old man would get along with them, however. That's because they were pretty high at the moment, and so was he.

Still on his hands and knees, the old man watched the strange, moonlit banquet yet more closely. Demons they surely were, but not the sort with an awful temperament—not like those "bloodsuckers" or "cutthroats." Although their red faces were actually quite fearsome, the demons seemed friendly and guileless to the old man. He was more or less right about this. These demons, in fact, had such a gentle temperament they might well have been called The Hermits of Sword Mountain. They were an utterly different tribe from the demons of hell. For one thing none of them carried a menacing object such as a steel club. This, one might say, proved they were not bent on doing evil.

At the same time they were hardly like the Seven Sages of the Bamboo Grove, either. Even though we might call them hermits, these demons were hardly akin to these erudite Chinese hermits who took refuge in their grove. No, these Hermits of Sword Mountain were foolish souls, really.

The pictograph for "sage" shows a man and a mountain. That's why, according to a simple theory I've heard, anyone who lives in the depths of a mountain might be called a sage. If we go along with this, then the Hermits of Sword Mountain too deserve the title of "sage," regardless of how foolish they were.

Anyway, I think we should use the right term when referring to these huge red beings now enjoying their moonlight banquet. They're hermits or sages, not demons. Earlier, I spoke of them as foolish souls, and anyone who observed their behavior during the banquet could see why. They let out senseless cries, slapped their knees and howled with laughter, jumped up and pranced about, bent their huge bodies, and rolled from one end of the circle to the other—all of this apparently meant to be some dance or other. Their level of intelligence was more than obvious, their lack of talent simply astonishing. This in itself would show that terms like "demonic talent" and "literary demon" are utterly meaningless. I can't imagine why an ignorant demon without any talent should be a God of All the Fine Arts.

The old man too was flabbergasted by the moronic dance. After snickering to himself, he muttered, "What a clumsy way to dance. Shall I show them one of my supple numbers?"

The old man immediately leaped out and began performing one of the dances he loved so much, and the wen on his cheek flopped back and forth in a strange and amusing manner.

The saké he had drunk gave the old man courage. Besides that, he was beginning to feel easy about the demons. And so, he broke into the circle, not the least afraid, and began the Dance of Awa[9] which he took pride in doing so well.

> *Girls in Shimada coiffures*
> *And old women in wigs;*
> *How tempting are their red sashes.*
> *Won't you go, wife, in your straw hat?*
> *Come . . . come . . .*

The words were in the Awa dialect, and the old man sang them beautifully. The demons were delighted! They gave forth a strange staccato shout, then rolled on the ground laughing, weeping, and slobbering.

> *Across the great valley filled with stones,*
> *Over the high mountain of bamboo grass . . .*

The old man had lost all restraint. His voice ascending another octave, he danced on and on to his heart's content.

The demons were immensely pleased. "Come every moonlit night and dance for us. But we'll need something valuable as a pledge."

The demons talked over the matter, whispering to one another. Didn't the wen glimmering on the old man's cheek seem to them like some unusual jewel? If they kept it, he would surely return. And so, having made this silly conjecture, they immediately tore the wen off without any trouble. A stupid thing to do, but after living so long in the depths of the mountain, they probably took it for a magical charm.

The old man was horrified. "No! Not my grandchild!" he exclaimed.

The demons gave a joyful shout of triumph.

Morning. Listlessly stroking his cheek where the wen had been, the old man descended the mountain road which glistened with dew.

With his wen gone, the old man felt somewhat lonely. After all, there was no one else he could talk to. Still, the cheek felt lighter, and the morning breeze on his skin seemed quite agreeable. Both gain and loss, both good and bad had come from this episode then, and perhaps the two sides simply canceled out one another. It had been good for the old man to sing and dance to his heart's content after these many years, wasn't that so? As he was going down the mountainside musing on these questions, he nearly bumped into his saintly son who was heading for work in the field.

The saint removed his hood and intoned, "Good morning, Father."

"Oh," the old man replied, somewhat at a loss.

Nothing more was said as they passed by one another.

Realizing that the old man's wen had disappeared overnight, even the saint was slightly taken aback. But he believed that quibbling over the features of a parent went against the Saintly Way. So he pretended not to notice and went on in silence.

When the old man got home, his wife calmly said, "So you're back."

She didn't ask about what had happened the night before. "The soup's gotten cold," she grumbled as she set about preparing the old man's breakfast.

"Oh, that's all right. Don't bother warming it up," the old man countered. He felt small and sheepish as he sat down to eat. Yet, the urge to describe his wondrous adventure of last night was very strong, and he almost began to relate what had happened. The words stuck in his throat, though, so cowed was he by the old lady's stern manner. Bowing his head, he ate his meal dejectedly.

"The wen looks like it shriveled up," his wife remarked offhandedly.

"H'mm," the old man mumbled, the urge to talk having passed.

"It broke, then, and the water just squirted out from inside?" She did not seem particularly impressed.

"H'mm."

"It'll swell up again if more water collects, then."

"That's true."

In his own home this business of the old man's wen didn't much matter.

One of the neighbors, though, a second old man with his own wen, was quite curious about what had happened. This man's wen was on the left cheek, and he found it quite annoying. Believing it had kept him from advancing in the world, he hated his wen with a passion. Every day he looked repeatedly in the mirror and sighed. How much scorn and derision, the old man wondered, had been heaped on him because of it. He had let his sideburns grow long, hoping to conceal the wen; but, alas, the tip glowed on his flowing white beard like the New Year's Day sun rising gloriously from the sea. Rather then hide the wen, the beard set it off like one of the wonders of the world.

With his sturdy physique, large nose, and glaring eyes, this oldster looked every inch a man. He spoke and acted with dignity, too, and he dressed with a certain splendor. His learning was impressive, his mind discerning. Rumor had it that his wealth far surpassed that of the other old man, the drinker. All the neighbors knew this second old man was special, so they addressed him as "Master" or "Sir" without fail. He was a fine man, a perfect man—except for that annoyance on his left cheek. His wen depressed him day and night, and he never could relax.

Though just thirty-seven years old, the man's wife was not particularly attractive. She was fair and plump, however, and she laughed as merrily and as often as a coquette. Her daughter, who was thirteen or so, was very pretty. The girl could also be quite saucy, but this gave her something in common with her mother. The two of them were constantly in stitches over one thing or another, and this made the home lively in spite of the master's scowling face.

"Mother, I wonder why Father's wen is so red? It's like the head of an octopus." The saucy girl would come out unhesitatingly with such a remark. Her mother would laugh rather than scold her, and then she would reply, "Well, maybe you're right. But, to me, it's more like one of those wooden drums that hang from the eaves of a temple."

"Shut up!" the old man would thunder. Glaring at his wife and daughter, he would spring to his feet and head for one of the darker rooms well within the house. There he would peek into a mirror and give way to despair. "It's hopeless," he would mutter.

Should he apply the knife, even at the risk of killing himself? It had come to this when the old man heard the rumor that the other man's wen had suddenly disappeared. Under cover of night he slipped over to the old man's hut and heard from him the marvelous tale of the moonlit banquet.

When he heard the story the old man was overjoyed. "Well, well, then I too can surely have this wen removed."

Fortunately the moon was out again that very night. Excited by what he had heard, this esteemed man ventured forth like a warrior heading into battle, his mouth set in a grimace and his eyes glaring. Come what may, he would impress those demons this very night by dancing with gusto. And, if by some slight chance he didn't impress them, why then he'd lay them low with his iron-ribbed fan. He figured that a bunch of foolish, drunken demons couldn't amount to much.

And so, to dance for the demons or else to quell them, he marched into the depths of Sword Mountain, his shoulders thrown back and his right hand grasping the iron-ribbed fan. But a performance meant to impress the audience will often turn out poorly. In his very eagerness the old man was almost bound to fail.

He began with a stately move right into the circle of reveling demons. "Your humble servant," he proclaimed, flipping open his iron-ribbed fan and gazing at the moon overhead. After pausing momentarily as if he were a giant tree, he shuffled his feet lightly and began a slow, groaning chant.

A priest am I
Performing my late spring meditation
By the Straits of Naruto.
It pains me to realize
That in this locale
The entire Heike Clan met its end,
And every evening
I come to this shore
To read the holy sutra.
As I wait among the rocks of the dune,
As I wait among the rocks,
A boat—whose I do not know—
Goes rowing with a splash of oars
Amid the white-capped waves.
How still the inlet this evening!
How still the inlet this evening!
But yesterday has passed,
Today draws to an end,
And so too will tomorrow.

Moving ever so deliberately, he again looked up at the moon and struck a rigid pose.

The demons were dumbfounded. They rose one after another and fled into the depths of the mountain.

"No! Wait!" The old man cried out in a pathetic voice and ran after the demons. "You can't forsake me now."

"Run! Run! He must be Shōki, the demon-queller."[10]

"No, I'm not Shōki!" the old man exclaimed. Then, catching hold of a demon, he pleaded in desperation, "Please, I want you to take off another wen."

"What's that?" replied the confused demon. "You won't stop until we place on another wen? Oh, but we're keeping that one for the old man. It's splendid, but if you want it so bad, you can have it. Just stop your dancing! We'd just gotten nice and drunk, and then you came butting in. We've had enough of you, so just let me go. We'll have to go somewhere else now and get drunk all over—that's enough. Let me go, now. Hey! Somebody! Give this fool that wen we got the other night. He says he wants it."

So the demons attached the wen they had been keeping to his right cheek. There! The old man now had two flopping wens and they were heavy. He returned to his village in shame.

Truly a pathetic ending. In these old tales someone who does wrong usually ends up getting punished for it. However, in this case, the second old man didn't do anything especially wrong. It's true that he became overly tense at one point, and so the dance he performed got out-of-hand. But that hardly counts. Come to think of it, there weren't any bad people in his family, either. And the old tippler too, as well as his family, and even the demons on Sword Mountain, didn't do anything wrong, either. Even though there's not a single episode of wrongdoing in this tale, one of the characters comes to grief. Try drawing a moral from this story and you're in real trouble. So why did I bother telling the tale? If the anxious reader presses me on this question, I'd have to answer that there's always something both tragic and comical in people's very nature. It's a problem at the very core of our lives, and that's really all I can say.

Crackling Mountain

Kachikachiyama

The traditional tale of "Crackling Mountain" describes a vendetta that a rabbit carries out against a badger. The badger had been captured by an old man and was going to be made into a stew. While his captor was away, however, the badger killed the old man's wife and, assuming her form, served her as the stew to the old man upon his return. The rabbit, as a friend of the old couple, took vengeance by performing the deeds elaborated by Dazai in his reworking of the tale.

As with "Taking the Wen Away," Dazai begins "Crackling Mountain" with a preface, this one meandering for several pages before the story itself gets underway. Among other things, he describes a problem that arises from a recent change in the old tale, a change that tones down some of the cruelty for the sake of young readers. Dazai sees this change as giving rise to a new problem. For when the badger is himself killed after merely wounding the old woman in self-defense, then justice is ill served.

Perhaps this commentary is not meant to be taken seriously. Dazai writes at least partly in jest, and the surest note that he plays in these opening paragraphs is one of self-caricature. Indeed, as the story unfolds, the suggestion that the author is poking fun at himself through his portrayal of the badger becomes almost irresistible.

Certainly Dazai transforms the traditional tale radically, even as he retells its main episodes. Satirical to a heavy-handed degree perhaps, "Crackling Mountain" can be read all the same for its humor, energy, and inventive play. As with the previous selection, "Taking the Wen Away," the principal puzzle crops up in the epilogue.

Given the total context of the tale, this episode could amount to the author's playing a joke on himself. For, after raising in his preface the problem of the unjust treatment of the badger in the newer editions of the traditional tale, Dazai claims to provide a solution with his revolutionary interpretation of the identity of the two principal characters. But, rather than make the tale more understandable, this ploy creates its own problems, and intractable ones at that.

One certainty about "Crackling Mountain" is the author's pose of personal involvement. Dazai was thirty-seven when he wrote "Crackling Mountain," the same age as his badger. Indeed, the association between author and badger is hinted at throughout the tale. This makes the epilogue doubly perplexing. For, in addition to wondering whether to dismiss the foolish badger or sympathize with him, one also must question if the author sees himself in this badger to the very end.

In spite of appearances, the rabbit in "Crackling Mountain" is actually a teenage girl, while the badger who undergoes a heartrending defeat is an ugly man in love with her. That's how things look to me, no doubt about it.

The setting of the tale is supposed to have been around Lake Kawaguchi, close to Mount Fuji in the Kōshū region. The exact spot is now called The Inner Mountain of Funazu. People in the Kōshū region are—well, brusque is the word. Maybe that's why "Crackling Mountain" is rougher than the other *Otogi Zōshi* tales. First of all, the story begins on a cruel note, with the old woman being turned into a stew. Now *that* was hardly a prank! No, it was downright wicked. The badger committed other atrocities too—like that terrible business of scattering the old woman's bones under the veranda. It's a shame, but the tale had to be banned for children.

In the illustrated version now on sale, the badger only wounds the old woman before running away. In my opinion no one should object to this change as a means of getting around the ban. But, in taking vengeance for this mischief, the rabbit goes much too far. A valiant avenger should dispatch the enemy with one blow. Not in this case, though. Our rabbit taunts her victim, mocks and almost hounds him to death before luring him into the clay boat that, as it crumbles, leaves the poor creature gurgling helplessly in the water. Yes, a cunning scheme from beginning to end, but hardly in accord with the Way of the Japanese Warrior. If the badger had followed through on his vicious intention to serve up the old woman as stew, no one would think twice at the well-deserved punishment he receives. But in the new version that protects innocent children and circumvents the ban, the badger merely wounds the old woman and flees. In all fairness the rabbit shouldn't be allowed to torture and humiliate the badger so relentlessly, drowning him at last in that disgraceful manner.

The badger was merely frolicking in the hills when he got caught by the old man. With his captor planning to make him into stew, the situation seemed hopeless. Desperate for a way to escape, he finally succeeded in tricking the old woman and saving his own skin. Now, the scheme to make her into stew was wrong. But the badger's only crime in the recent illustrated version is to claw the old woman while making his escape. One can hardly call reasonable self-defense a terrible deed, even if unintended injury is inflicted.

My five-year-old daughter is very homely—just like her father. Unfortunately she thinks in the same eccentric way too. We were in the family air-raid shelter together, and I was reading the illustrated "Crackling Mountain" to her when she blurted out, "The badger . . . what a pity." "What a pity"—that's a phrase she's picked up recently, and she repeats it over and over regardless of what she sees. Since she's obviously trying to play up to her softhearted mother, her behavior is hardly surprising. Of course, in this case it could well be that she likes badgers. She once saw a group of them nervously trotting about in their cage when her father took her to the neighborhood zoo in Inokashira Park. Maybe that's why she's instinctively drawn to the badger in "Crackling Mountain." Whatever the grounds, though, this little tenderheart of mine is mistaken. Her notions are flimsy, the origins of her compassion obscure. Actually, I shouldn't be making this much fuss over her.

Still, that chance phrase—"What a pity"—seemed to have something suggestive about it, even when mumbled by a mere child. Reflecting on the matter, the girl's father began to realize that, yes, the avenging rabbit had indeed gone too far. With this toddler of his, he might gloss over the matter; but wouldn't older children, having been taught about The Warrior's Way and Forthrightness, find the methods of the rabbit underhanded? Now that he had reached the heart of the matter, the dim-witted man started frowning.

When things happen as in the recent illustrated books—the badger terribly mistreated by the rabbit for merely clawing the old woman; his back burned and then smeared with red pepper; and his death assured by the ride in the clay boat—well, then it's only natural that any child smart enough to attend our public schools might begin to wonder. Even if the badger had tried to make the old lady into stew, why couldn't the rabbit have acted like a true warrior by solemnly proclaiming its pedigree and dispatching the enemy with a single blow? A rabbit may be frail, but that's no excuse for deviousness. God favors the righteous, and revenge must be carried out openly. Even in the face of heavy odds the avenger must cry out, Heaven wills it! and leap directly upon the foe. When his skills aren't equal to the task, he must discipline himself like that vanquished Chinese king of Yueh who slept every night on a woodpile to remind himself of the bitter taste of defeat.

Or else he might wholly devote himself to practicing the martial arts at Mount Kurama. For ages the Japanese hero has generally acted in this manner—in fact, there don't seem to be any other vendetta tales in which the avenger, regardless of how extreme the provocation, uses wily tricks and torments his opponent to death. Only in "Crackling Mountain" is revenge accomplished by disgraceful means. Hardly the way a man would act, is it? Child or adult, anyone with even a slight concern for justice would feel something was wrong.

But don't worry, I've thought this problem over. And I've figured out why the rabbit took this unmanly approach to vengeance. The rabbit's not a man, but a pretty girl. No doubt about that. She's fifteen years old—not quite ready to flirt and meaner than ever for just that reason.

Everyone knows that lovely goddesses often appear in the Greek myths. Even in their company Artemis is alluring beyond compare—after Aphrodite at least. Artemis is well known as Goddess of the Moon, and her brow displays the pale glimmer of a new, crescent moon. Like Apollo, she is shrewd and determined, and all of the wild animals are subject to her. That doesn't mean she's a sturdy Amazon, though; she has a small, slender figure, and her limbs are delicate. Her face is so uncommonly beautiful as to give one a shudder. In spite of this, she lacks the femininity of Aphrodite. Her breasts are small, and she is callous toward those whom she dislikes. By splashing the hunter who peeked at her while she was bathing, Artemis instantly turned him into a stag. If that's what happened to someone who saw her bathing, I can't imagine how she would punish a man who tried holding her hand. Such a woman will humiliate any suitor. It's too bad that stupid men easily give into temptation and thereby seal their own fate.

Those who doubt what I say should observe our poor badger as he yearns for his Artemis-like teenager. If I'm correct, the malicious and unmanly chastisement of the badger is perfectly understandable. Whichever crime he committed, stewing the old woman or clawing her, makes no difference to the girl—this we must grant as fact, even as we sigh over it. Moreover, our so-called badger is just the sort who would woo an Artemis-like teenager. That is, he's a roly-poly glutton both stupid and uncouth who cuts a sorry figure even among his cohorts. One can surmise already the wretched end awaiting for him.

In the story itself, then, the old man had captured the badger and decided to make him into stew. But, desperate to see his rabbit-maid once more, the badger fretted and struggled until he finally escaped into the hills. Restlessly he searched all over for her, mumbling something or other all the while.

"Cheer up!" he exclaimed upon finding her. "I got away in the nick of time. I waited till the old man was gone; then I let out a shriek, went right for the old woman, gave her a mighty blow and escaped. Was luck ever with me." Thus did the badger speak of his brush with death, his face beaming and spit flying from his mouth.

As the rabbit listened, she sprang back to avoid the spray. Humbug!—that's what her look said. "What's there to cheer about?" she retorted. "You're a filthy . . . Imagine, spitting like that. And besides, the old man and lady are friends of mine. Didn't you realize that?"

"Oh?" the badger exclaimed, taken aback. "No, I didn't. I'm so sorry, if only I had known . . . Even if they were going to make stew of me or whatever . . ." He was obviously disheartened.

"It's too late for excuses now! You must have known about their garden, and how I'd help myself to their luscious beans ever so often. If *only* you'd known . . . Liar! You've got a grudge against me."

Even as she berated him, the rabbit was already thinking ahead to revenge. A maiden's ire can be scathing and merciless, especially when her victim is both ugly and dumb.

"C'mon, forgive me—I didn't realize. I'm no liar. Honest, I'm not." Even as he entreated her in his sweetest manner, the badger stretched his neck and gave the rabbit a bow. He also noticed a fallen berry and instantly gobbled it up, his eyes darting hither and thither in search of more. "I'd rather die than see you so angry," he said. "Really, I mean it."

"Nonsense! All you think of is eating." She turned away primly as though she felt nothing but contempt for him. "Besides being a lecher, you're the filthiest glutton I can imagine."

"Please, don't make a fuss about that. I'm so hungry . . ." Having confessed to this weakness, the badger anxiously scoured the nearby area even as he lamented, "If you only knew how I suffer . . ."

"Didn't I tell you to keep away from me? Phew! Move over there. You want to know what I heard? I heard you eat lizard, that's what. And scat, too!"

"Oh, surely . . ." The badger smiled lamely, but he didn't seem able to deny the charge. His mouth twisting as he smiled once again, the badger meekly repeated, "Oh surely . . ."

"You needn't bother pretending. I can tell because you smell even worse than usual."

Even as she dismissed him, the rabbit seemed taken with a brilliant scheme. Suddenly her eyes glittered and she turned to the badger. Suppressing the cruel smile that seemed ready to cross her face, she said, "Well, I'll forgive you this once. Hey! I told you to keep your distance. You need watching every moment. And how about wiping that slobber from your face. You're dripping under the chin. Now listen closely. I'll forgive you just this once, but there's a catch. The old man's feeling dejected now, so he won't be up to gathering firewood in the hills. Let's go ahead and do it for him."

"Together? Both you and me?" The badger's small, turbid eyes lit up with pleasure.

"That doesn't suit you?"

"What do you mean—doesn't suit me? C'mon, let's go right now." The badger was so happy that his voice turned hoarse.

"Let's go tomorrow instead," the rabbit countered. "Is early in the morning okay? You're probably worn out today—and hungry too," she added, her generosity beyond belief.

"How good of you!" the badger responded. "I'll gather plenty of things for a meal. When we get to the hill, I'll work with all my might and cut a whole cord of firewood. I'll deliver it to the old man's place, and then you'll forgive me, won't you? And we'll be friends again?"

"You do carry on, don't you? Really, it depends on how well you do. I guess we'll be friends."

"Heh-heh," the badger snickered. "What a provocative tongue. So you're putting me on the spot. Damn! I'm already . . ." The badger paused, then snatched a spider crawling nearby and devoured it.

"I'm so happy I could cry."
He sniffled and pretended to weep.

The summer morning was cool, and a white mist enveloped the waters of Lake Kawaguchi. Though drenched in dew, the badger and the rabbit busily gathered brushwood on the mountain top.

To all appearances the badger was utterly absorbed in the task. He had worked himself into a near frenzy—flailing his sickle about, groaning excessively, and making his travail known by crying "Ouch!" now and then. He rushed about without pause, anxious that the rabbit notice how hard he was working. This rampage had gone on awhile when he suddenly flung away his sickle, his look proclaiming that he was through.

"There!" he exclaimed. "You see these blisters? Ah, my hands really sting. I'm thirsty too—and hungry. Well, hard work'll do that to you. Shall we have a break? And get to the lunch, maybe. Heh-heh."

Having let out this sheepish chuckle, the badger opened the lunchbox. It was as huge as a utility gasoline can, and he stuck his nose right in. Thereupon the box echoed with sounds of snatching, munching, and swallowing, the badger losing himself in the task of eating. The rabbit stopped cutting brushwood, a stunned look on her face, then peeked into the lunchbox. Whatever was inside must have been awful, for a tiny squeal escaped her lips and she immediately covered her face with both hands.

All that morning the rabbit had refrained from abusing the badger as she usually did. Perhaps she already had another scheme in mind; for, even as she ignored the capering rascal and concentrated on quickly cutting the brushwood, an artful smile had played about her lips. Though astonished by the inside of the great lunchbox, she merely cringed and went on cutting the brushwood in silence.

So lenient was the rabbit that the badger almost hugged himself with glee. Even this impudent girl had finally given in. Hadn't his brushwood-cutting act done the trick? Well, this masculinity of his—what woman could resist it?

Ah, he had eaten his fill. And was he ever weary. Yes, he'd have just a quick nap. Putting on his carefree manner, the badger became so relaxed that he was soon fast asleep and snoring heavily. Even as he dreamt, he mumbled about love potions—they weren't worth a damn, they didn't do any good . . . And when he awoke from his lewd dreams, it was almost noon.

"You really had a good sleep," the rabbit said, still indulgent. "I've got my wood bundled up too," she went on, "so let's hoist the load on our backs and take it to the old man."

"Oh," the badger answered, "let's be off then." He yawned prodigiously and scratched his arms. "Am I ever hungry. How could anyone sleep on an empty stomach like this? Too sensitive—that's my problem." Having said these things—without the least hint of a smile, either—he went on. "Well, I'll hurry up and collect my brushwood, and then we'll head down, I guess. Since the lunch is gone, I'll have to finish this chore quickly so I can look for more food."

They set off, each one carrying a load of brushwood.

"You go first," the rabbit urged. "There are snakes around here and I'm scared of them."

"Snakes? Who's afraid of snakes? When I spot one, I'll grab him and . . ." About to say "eat him," the badger caught himself just in time. "I'll grab him and kill him," he said, correcting himself. "You just stay behind me."

"At times like this you can really depend upon a man."

"Oh, please, no flattery," the badger answered sweetly. "You're certainly nice today, aren't you? It almost makes me edgy. Surely you're not taking me along so the old man can make badger stew. Hah-hah, you can count me out of that."

"Well! That's a queer thing to suspect. If that's how you feel, maybe we should part company right here. I'm perfectly capable of going alone."

"No, no, I didn't mean it that way. We'll go together, all right? I'm not afraid of snakes or anything else in this world—except for that old man. He talked about making badger stew, and I didn't like that. Downright disgusting, isn't it? And hardly in good taste, if you ask me. Anyway, I'll take the brushwood to the hackberry tree in the old man's garden, but no further. I'm turning back there, so you'll have to carry it the rest of the way. All I can say is, a queasy feeling comes over me when I see the old man's face . . . Hey! What's that? That strange noise—what could it be? Don't you hear it too? It's sort of a crackling noise . . ."

"What did you expect?" said the rabbit. "That's why they call this place Crackling Mountain."

"Crackling Mountain? Here?"

"Sure. You didn't know that?"

"No, I didn't. It's the first time I've heard this mountain even had a name. It's such a strange name too—you're not making it up, are you?"

"Oh, really! But every mountain's got a name. There's Mount Fuji and Mount Nagao and Mount Ōmuro . . . They all have names, don't they? So this one's called Crackling Mountain. Listen, don't you hear that crackling sound?"

"Yeah, I hear it. Strange, though. I've never heard that sound before on this mountain. I was born here, and for thirty-some years this . . ."

"Wha-a-at! You don't mean to say you're *that* old? Why, just the other day you told me you were seventeen. Oh, this is too much. Your face is all wrinkled and you stoop a bit too, so I didn't take you for seventeen. But I hardly thought you'd hide your age by twenty years. So you're almost forty—the nerve!"

"No, seventeen, I'm only seventeen. Seventeen, I tell you. The stoop comes from hunger, and it doesn't have anything to do with age. My older brother—he's the one in his thirties. You see, he's always talking about it, and I mimicked him, that's all. It's only a habit I've picked up, my dear." Calling her "my dear!"—*that* certainly showed how flustered the badger was.

"Only a habit?" the rabbit replied curtly. "This is the first I've heard of an older brother. You once told me how lonely you were—no parents, no brothers or sisters. How did you put it then? I didn't know how forsaken you felt—wasn't that what you said? Now what did you mean by that?"

"Yes, yes . . ." the badger replied, losing track of what he wanted to say. "Things are certainly involved, you know, and it's not so simple. I've got an older brother, and yet I don't . . ."

"Nonsense!" interjected the rabbit, now totally fed up. "You're talking through your hat!"

"Well, to tell the truth, yes, I've got an older brother. It hurts to say this, but he's just a drunken scoundrel. I'm ashamed, embarrassed really, because for thirty-some years—no, that's my brother—you see, for thirty-some years he's been giving me trouble . . ."

"That's odd. A seventeen year old . . . trouble . . . for thirty-some years?"

The badger ignored this remark.

"There are plenty of things you can't sum up in a word. Right now, he doesn't exist, not for me, anyway. I disowned him and . . . Hey, that's odd. Smells like smoke . . . Don't you notice it?"

"Not at all."

"H'mm." The badger was always eating smelly food, so he couldn't trust his own nose. Twisting about with a suspicious look on his face, he said, "Could I be imagining this? There! There! That noise—isn't that roaring and snapping like something on fire?"

"Well, what did you expect? That's why this place is called Mount Roaring-and-Snapping."

"Liar! You just said it was called Crackling Mountain."

"That's right. The same mountain's got different names, depending on the spot. Halfway up Mount Fuji there's Smaller Fuji, and Ōmuro and Nagao are lesser peaks of Mount Fuji too. Didn't you know that?"

"I'm afraid not. So that's it—we're on Mount Roaring-and-Snapping. Well, for thirty-some years I've been—my brother, I mean—he's been calling it The Mountain Out Back. Oh, is it ever getting warm. Is there an earthquake brewing? Something's really wrong today. Yaa! Oh, is it ever hot! I can't stand it! Help! Help! My brushwood's on fire! Ouch! . . ."

The next day the badger remained secluded in his lair. "Oh," he moaned, "how painful. Too much even for me. I'm done for. Come to think of it, I've got the worst luck. The women shy away just because I was born good-looking—a respectable man always loses out. They all take me for a woman-hater. Hell, I'm no saint. I like women. They must think I'm noble-minded, so they never play up to me. But, when it comes right down to it, I want to run around screaming, I'M CRAZY ABOUT WOMEN! Ouch! Ouch! Oh, why can't I do anything about this nasty burn? It just keeps throbbing. After I'd barely escaped becoming badger stew, I had to stumble onto this unheard-of place—Roaring Mountain, wasn't that it? And did my luck ever run out there. What a good-for-nothing mountain! Brushwood going up in flames—was it ever horrible. In thirty-odd years . . ."

The badger paused, his eyes darting about.

"So why hide it?" he went on. "Magic, I'm thirty-seven. Heh-heh, what's wrong with that? Be forty in three more years. It's so obvious anyone could figure it out. All it takes is one look. Ooh, that hurts! I've been playing on The Mountain Out Back ever since I was born, and not once in my thirty-seven years did I run into anything so weird. Crackling Mountain, or Roaring Mountain—even the names are odd. How strange," the badger concluded, knocking himself on the head and then lapsing into a reverie.

Presently a pedlar called out at the front entrance, "Magic Ointment for sale. Anyone here suffering from burns, cuts, or a dark complexion?"

Dark complexion—that really woke up the badger. "Hey, ointment pedlar!" he called out.

"Oh, where are you, sir?"

"Here! In this hole! So it'll really cure a dark complexion?"

"In one day."

"Ho-ho." Elated, the badger crawled from his lair. "Whaa! You're a rabbit."

"Yes, I'm certainly a rabbit—and a medicine man, besides. Been peddling in this area for thirty-odd years."

"Whew," the badger wheezed, tilting his head. "There's another rabbit just like you. Thirty-odd years . . . Ah yes, so you must be the same . . . Look here, let's just forget about my age. Damned silly, anyway. Enough is enough. Well, that's that." Having confused the issue, the badger went on. "Anyway, could you spare a bit of that medicine? To tell the truth, I've got a little affliction."

"Oh dear, you've got a terrible burn! This will never do. Ignore it, and you're dead."

"Damn, I'd rather be dead—I don't care about the burn. Right now, it's my looks that . . ."

"What are you saying! This burn could be fatal—don't you realize that? Oh, your back's even worse . . . How did this happen?"

"Well, you see . . ." The badger twisted his mouth about. "You see, I'd just gotten to this place with the fancy name—Mount Roaring, Snapping or whatever, and the craziest thing . . . It was amazing."

The badger looked puzzled as the rabbit began snickering helplessly. But he too joined in and started laughing. "Absolutely," he went on. "It was the craziest thing ever. I'm telling you, don't go near that mountain. First it's Crackling, then it's Snapping, and then it's Roaring—and that's the worst kind ever. Things are bound to go wrong. When you get to Crackling Mountain, you'd better just beg off. If you stray onto Mount Roaring, you'll end up like me. Ooh, the pain! You follow me? I'm telling you for your own good, now. You're still young, so when an oldtimer like myself says—well, I'm not *that* old. Anyway, you just take what I say as friendly advice and don't poke fun at me. You see, I speak from experience. Ooh, that hurts . . . ouch!"

"Thank you, sir, I'll certainly be careful. Now, what about the ointment? In return for your kind advice, I won't charge anything. Shall I put some on your back? Lucky I came just now, otherwise you'd be good as dead. Something must have brought me here. I guess it was fate, wouldn't you agree?"

"I suppose so," the badger moaned. "If the ointment's free, rub it on. I'm pretty broke nowadays— fall in love and it's bound to cost you. By the way, would you mind putting some of that medicine on my palm."

With an anxious look, the rabbit asked, "And what will you do with it?"

"Oh, nothing at all. I just want a look—so I can tell the color."

"It's the same color as any ointment. Here, have a little." The rabbit dabbed a speck on the badger's outstretched hand.

When the badger suddenly tried to rub it on his face, the startled rabbit seized his hand—the badger mustn't learn about this ointment just yet. "Aa! Don't do that!" the rabbit cautioned. "This medicine's slightly strong for your face. It won't do."

"No, let go!" the badger pleaded desperately. "I beg you, let go of my hand. You don't know how I feel! Or how wretched I've been for thirty-odd years—and all because of this dark complexion. Let go. Just let go of my hand so I can use this ointment. I'm begging you, just let me rub it on."

Finally the badger lifted his foot and kicked the rabbit away. Then, quicker than the eye could see, he smeared the medicine on his face.

"I'm ashamed of my face," he exclaimed. "The features are fine, but this dark complexion—well, this'll fix it. Wow! That's awful. Does it ever sting. If the medicine wasn't strong, though, it wouldn't cure my complexion. Ah, this is terrible. I'll bear it, though. Damn! Next time we meet, she'll really be taken with this face of mine. Heh-heh, so what if she hankers for me. Won't be my fault. Ah, does that ever sting. This medicine'll do the trick for sure. Well, I've come this far, so you might as well smear it all over—on my back or wherever. I don't care if I die, not if it lightens my complexion. Go ahead, smear the stuff on. Don't hesitate, just start splashing."

Already the badger was a pathetic sight. But a proud, beautiful teen is a virtual demon who is utterly ruthless. The rabbit calmly picked herself up and applied a thick layer of the pepper paste to the badger's burnt back.

The badger writhed in pain. "Oh, nothing to it.

This medicine'll work for sure. Wow! That's awful. Gimme water! Where am I! In hell! Hey, you've got to forgive me—I don't remember falling into hell! I didn't want to become badger stew, that's why I went after the old woman. I haven't done anything wrong. In my thirty-odd years—and all because of this dark complexion—not one lady friend! Then, there's that appetite of mine—ah, what an embarrassment! But nobody's concerned about me, I'm entirely on my own. Yet I'm a good man and not so bad-looking, either." Racked with pain, the badger kept on with his pathetic ranting before fainting to the ground in a heap.

Even so, the badger's ordeal wasn't over yet. So terrible was his plight that your author, even as he writes these words, can feel a sigh welling up inside. In all of Japanese history, there are scarcely any instances of so depressing an end. No sooner had he rejoiced over escaping the ordeal with the badger stew than he sustained that queer burn on Mount Roaring and barely escaped alive once again. He just managed to crawl back to his lair where he lay groaning through twisted lips—only to have so much hot pepper smeared over his burn that he fainted in agony. Next he'll launch his clay boat on Lake Kawaguchi and sink to the bottom. What an utter mess! Yes, there's something to be said for a broken affair. Unfortunately, a sleazy instance like this one hasn't got any romance to it.

Hardly able to breathe, the badger remained in his lair for three days, his spirit wandering forth, but only along that dim border between life and death. When the hunger pangs started up on the fourth day, he was more miserable than words can describe.

Nevertheless, he hobbled forth on his cane, mumbling to himself as he searched here and there for food.

Thereafter he quickly recovered, thanks to the large, sturdy body with which he was endowed. Within ten days he was back to normal, his appetite flourishing as of old, his lust also beginning to stir. He should have known better by now, but eventually he found himself heading once more toward the rabbit's nest.

"Here I am," the badger sheepishly announced. "Just thought I'd drop by for a visit, heh-heh."

"Oh!" the startled rabbit exclaimed, the malice in her look conveying a good deal more. So it's you?!! Or something even stronger, like, What's the big idea! Here! Again? The nerve . . . No, it was even stronger than that. Oh, I can't stand it! The plague's arrived! Or even worse. Filthy! Stinking! Rot in hell! Yes, her look was one of utter hatred. But our uninvited guest doesn't seem to notice the host's mood—a strange phenomenon which the reader should take note of. You set out grudgingly for a boring, irksome visit and end up being most heartily welcomed. On the other hand, you fondly imagine, ah, what a comfortable place . . . it's almost like my own . . . no, more cozy than home even . . . a refuge . . . Yet, in spite of your high spirits, the host is usually upset, frightened, repelled—and the broom behind the sliding door is turned upside down to bring about your early departure. One who looks for refuge in the home of another proves himself a fool. A mere visit can lead to amazing blunders, so one should keep away even from close relatives unless there's a special reason for the visit. If you doubt my advice, observe the badger as he becomes entangled in this very folly.

The rabbit exclaimed, "Oh!" and gave the badger a malicious look, but he did not catch on. To him that "Oh!" seemed a maiden's impulsive cry of surprise and delight—and her look conveyed sympathy because of his recent accident on Mount Roaring. The badger shuddered with pleasure and said, "I'm fine, thank you," even though he had not been asked how he felt.

"Don't worry," he continued. "I've already recovered. The gods were with me. And I'm lucky. Mount Roaring wasn't much—just a farting *kappa*.[1] A *kappa*'s supposed to be tasty, too. I've thought about getting hold of one and having myself a meal. Well, that's another matter. That was some surprise the other day. A real blaze. How'd you make out? Don't seem to have any burns. You got away quick, then, did you?"

"Got away quick, my foot!" the rabbit objected, looking quite peeved. "You're the one. You ran away and left me alone with that fire. The smoke was so stifling I almost choked to death. Was I ever furious. I realized then how little I meant to you. Now I can see what you're really like."

"I'm sorry, please forgive me. I got a bad burn too. Maybe the gods weren't with me. I ran up against it there. It's not that I forgot about you. You see, my back got scorched right away and I didn't have time for a rescue. Can't you see that? I'm no traitor— anyone would be helpless with a burn like that one. And then there's that elementary—I mean, alimentary salve or whatever it was. The worst thing—just terrible stuff. Doesn't help a dark complexion at all."

"A dark complexion?"

"No . . . I meant to say a dark, syrupy concoction. That was really strong. There was this odd runt—he looked a lot like you—and he said he wouldn't charge, either. Nothing ventured, nothing gained. And so I asked him to put some of it on. Good lord! I tell you, be careful when the medicine's free. You can't be too cautious. I felt this whirlwind swirl right through my head and then I toppled over."

"H'mm," the rabbit murmured disdainfully. "Serves you right. That's the price for being stingy. Trying out a medicine because it was free—and not the least ashamed to tell about it, either."

"Damn your tongue," the badger muttered, although he didn't appear upset. Indeed, he seemed to bask in the warm presence of his sweetheart. He plopped down, his turbid, dead-fish eyes roaming about for something he could snatch up. "Guess I'm just lucky," he uttered, gobbling an insect. "I keep ticking no matter what happens. The gods must be with me. You made it through, and this burn of mine got better without any trouble. So now we can just take it easy and have a chat. Ah, this is just like a dream."

The rabbit had been hoping he would leave, and now she could tolerate him no longer. He was so awful she felt like dying. Desperate to be rid of him, she again came up with a devilish scheme.

"By the way," she asked, "have you heard that Lake Kawaguchi is swarming with carp? They're supposed to be delicious."

"Nope, I haven't heard that," the badger replied, his eyes now sparkling. "When I was three years old, my old lady caught me a carp. That was some meal. But I can't even catch any sort of fish, let alone a carp. Not that I'm clumsy—no, not at all. I know how delicious carp is, but for some thirty-odd years now—hah-hah, there I go again, mimicking my older brother. He likes carp, too."

"Is that so?" the rabbit remarked offhandedly. "I don't care for them myself. But if you like them that much, I can take you fishing."

"Yeah?!" The badger was elated. "Those carp are slippery fellows, though. I tried catching one and almost went under for good." Having confessed to his own ineptitude, the badger came right out and asked, "But how do you catch them?"

"It's easy with a net. Some really big carp have been coming near the shore at Ugashima. Well? Shall we give it a try? How about a boat? Do you know how to row?"

The badger sighed. "I wouldn't say I can't row. Not," he anxiously insisted, "if I put my mind to it."

"Then you do row?" The rabbit knew the badger was only putting on, but she pretended to believe him. "Ah, that's perfect. I've got a boat, but it's so small we can't get in it together. It's not well made, and the flimsy boards always leak. I don't care about myself, but nothing must happen to you. Why don't we both pitch in and build you a boat. A wooden one's dangerous, so let's build something sturdy out of clay."

"Sorry to be such trouble. I'm about to weep—you won't mind if I have myself a good cry. Oh, why do I break down so easily?" But even as he pretended to weep, the badger came out with a brazen proposal. "Could you go ahead and build a sturdy boat, then?

Huh, would you do that? I'll do something for you in return. Maybe I could put together a small meal while you're working. I do think I'd make a fine chef."

"Oh yes," the rabbit nodded, as if she agreed with this conceited opinion. The badger, musing about how indulgent people were, smiled gleefully—and thereby sealed his fate right then and there. The rabbit was nurturing a horrible scheme even as she pretended to indulge his silliness. But the simpering badger didn't notice. He merely thought that all was well.

When they arrived at Lake Kawaguchi, the surface was clear and utterly calm. The rabbit went quickly to work, kneading the clay for a fine, sturdy boat. For his part the badger scampered about diligently gathering a meal and mumbling over and over, Sorry to be such trouble. Eventually an evening breeze came up, and tiny waves rose all over the lake. In due course the small clay boat, gleaming like a piece of steel, slid into the water.

"Yep, not bad," the badger jested as he placed on board the large gasoline utility can that held the lunch. "You're good with your hands too—building such a nice boat in a twinkling. Now that's real talent," he concluded, a piece of flattery so transparent as to set your teeth on edge.

Greed, as well as lust, now held the badger in thrall. He imagined himself taking this clever, industrious girl for his wife, then living a life of ease and luxury on her labor. Regardless of what happened, he would cling to her forever. And, with this thought in mind, he clambered aboard.

"I guess you're pretty good at rowing too, then?

When it comes to rowing a boat, even I . . . certainly . . . Well, it's not that I don't know how. But just for today I'd like to observe my wife's skill." It was utter impudence, and it didn't stop there. "I used to row in the old days," he went on. "They called me an expert, a champ, and all that. But I'll just lie here today and watch. Since it's all right with me, you go ahead and fasten my boat to yours. If our boats hug one another, we can only perish together. Don't abandon me now." After this odious and affected speech, the badger sprawled out on the bottom of his clay boat.

Did the fool suspect? Fasten my boat to yours—that remark had caught the rabbit off guard. One glimpse, though, and she knew that nothing was amiss. The badger was already dreaming, blissful love written all over his smiling face. The rabbit grinned scornfully as the badger began to mumble in his sleep—Wake me up when the carp's ready. I can taste 'em now. Thirty-seven, that's me. Presently the rabbit tied the clay boat to her own and dipped her oar in the water. With a splash, the two boats slid away from the shore.

The Ugashima pines seemed to flare up, bathed as they were in the light of the setting sun. Now this next part will make me seem a know-it-all, but that description of a pine grove comes from a pack of Shikishima cigarettes. I've checked this out with a dependable person, and readers won't be any worse off taking my word for it. But then again, Shikishimas aren't around any longer, so younger readers won't care anyway. To them, I'll just be showing off about nothing. Pretend to know something, and you end up with this sort of foolishness. Oh, *those* pines! Perhaps readers thirty years or older—no one else—will faintly remember the pines, along with their geisha friends and parties. Maybe such readers can't do anything other than look bored.

"Ah, how lovely," the rabbit murmured, entranced by the sunset over Ugashima.

This is strange indeed. It seems that not even the worst villain could be taken with natural beauty the moment before carrying out some cruel deed. Yet, our fifteen-year-old charmer squints her eyes and contemplates the scenery, an indication that innocence is truly a hairbreadth from villainy. Certain men will sigh—Ah, the Innocence of Youth—and drool over the nauseating affectations of a selfish, carefree teen. They had better watch out, though. She remains as composed as this rabbit, even while Murder and Intoxication dwell together in her breast. A wild and sensuous dance goes on, and no one notices. It's like the foam on beer—nothing more perilous.

Idiotic, demonic—such words come to mind when mere skin-deep feeling takes precedence over ethics. Sometime ago popular American movies portrayed boys and girls who were full of innocence. Highly endowed with this skin-deep feeling, they fidgeted around and darted about as if on springs. I don't mean to stretch things, but this "Youthful Innocence" I'm talking of might well be traced to America or thereabouts. It's just a Merrily-We-Ski-Along sort of thing.

On the other hand these innocents commit silly crimes without the least concern. That's the demonic, rather than idiotic, side of this. Or, maybe sometime in the past, the demonic was idiotic. Once comparable to Artemis the Moon Goddess—she of the graceful limbs and small, delicate figure—our fifteen-year-old rabbit has suddenly become dull and dreary. Idiotic, you say? Well, that's the way things go.

"Hyaa!" cries a strange voice from down below. It's that dear badger of mine, a thirty-seven-year-old male who's not the least bit innocent. "Water!" he cried, "it's water! This is awful!"

"What a nuisance you are! A clay boat's bound to sink. You didn't know that?"

"I don't get it. This is much too much. And not proper at all. Unreasonable—that's the word for it. Surely you wouldn't—not to me, anyway—surely not such a dastardly thing as . . . No, I don't get it at all. Aren't you my wife? Ya! I'm sinking! That's all I can tell—I'm sinking! The joke's gone too far—it's almost a crime. Ya! I'm sinking! Hey, what're you do-ing to me? Won't the meal go to waste? There's earthworm macaroni and skunk droppings in the box. Isn't that a shame? Gulp! Ah, I just swallowed water. Look here, this bad joke's gone far enough. I'm begging you. Hey there, don't cut that rope! If we perish, it'll be together. Husband and wife for two lives—that's a bond you can't sever. No! Don't! Oh, now you've done it. Help! I can't swim! I'll be honest with you. In the old days I could swim a little, but the muscles stiffen here and there on a thirty-seven-year-old badger. I can't swim at all. I'll be honest. I'm thirty-seven—too old for you, really. But you mustn't forget the old maxims—Respect your Elders! Help the Aged! Gulp! Ah, you're a nice girl. So act like you should now and stretch your oar over here. I'll get a grip on . . . Ouch! What're you doing?

Don't you know that hurts—banging an oar on someone's head really hurts! So *that's* it. I get it. You mean to kill me. Now I know." Faced with his own death, the badger finally saw into the rabbit's scheme. But it was too late.

The oar banged mercilessly against his skull time after time. The water glistened in the sunset as the badger sank into the lake and rose to the surface over and over again.

"Ouch! Ouch! Aren't you going too far? What did I do to you? What's wrong with falling in love?" he exclaimed before going under for good.

Wiping her brow, the rabbit declared, "Whew, I'm drenched with sweat."

So, what have we here? A cautionary tale on lust? A comedy scented with advice on avoiding pretty teenagers? Or perhaps an ethics lesson that bids the suitor to moderate his delight in the beloved? After all, persistent visits provoke such contempt that one's life is endangered.

But maybe the tale is mostly humorous, merely hinting that people don't revile and chastise one another because of morality. (Actually, they do these things simply out of hatred, just as they praise others or submit to them out of affection.)

But no, let's not fret over what conclusions a social critic might reach. Sighing, we allow instead the last word to our badger—"What's wrong with falling in love?"

That sums up, briefly and without any exaggeration, all of the world's woeful tales from the days of old. In every woman dwells this cruel rabbit, while in every man a good badger always struggles against drowning. In the mere thirty-odd years of your author's life, uneventful though they be, this has been made utterly clear. And probably, dear reader, it's the same with you. I'll just skip the rest of it, however.

Notes

Introduction

1. Masuji Ibuse is known outside of Japan primarily as the author of *Black Rain*, a novel describing the atomic bombing of Hiroshima and some of its aftereffects. Besides *Black Rain*, Ibuse has written of everyday life in Japan in a variety of settings. Born in 1898, he became Dazai's mentor, advising the younger writer on problems of style and helping him find outlets for his early stories.

Memories

1. Requiem posts are pointed slats of wood propped against railings and gravestones in a Japanese cemetery. The writing on the posts consists of Sanskrit letters, sutra passages, and religious admonitions.

2. The Festival of the Dead is a traditional Buddhist feast observed in July or August. Akin to All Soul's Day, various rituals are conducted as a way of welcoming back the spirits of one's ancestors and then seeing them off.

3. The Girls' Festival, held on March 3, is marked by a display of dolls on a tiered platform. The dolls are thought to originate from paper figures used in an ancient Chinese rite of purification. The Girls' Festival is also known as the Peach Festival.

4. "Earthquake, Lightning, Fire, and Father" constitutes a humorous aphorism pinpointing the four most frighten-

ing things, in descending order, to the Japanese people.

5. The Full Moon Festival is held on the fifteenth night of the eighth month according to the lunar calendar. Occurring as it does in late summer, the occasion essentially is regarded as a "Harvest Moon" festival, with various vegetables and fruits selected as offerings to the moon.

6. "River bums" is a reference to the origins of Kabuki in a dance performed in the dry bed of the Kamo River in Kyoto in 1603. The performers were a troupe made up mostly of women who danced under the direction of a female attendant of Izumo Shrine name Okuni.

7. During the Insect-Expulsion Festival, bells and drums are used to frighten away the insects that damage the rice plants.

8. The theme of the ballad of Ranchō is a common one in Edo literature—a husband's love for a prostitute and his wife's attempt to persuade her rival to give up her claim.

9. *Hakama* are formal Japanese trousers for men; they are sometimes called a "divided skirt" due to their shape.

10. The period when the narrator of *Memories* is first exposed to "democratic ideas" would be shortly after the end of World War I in 1918. Japan underwent severe economic problems following the war, allowing liberal and Marxist doctrines to find fertile ground.

11. The "well-known novel by a Russian author" is Tolstoy's *Resurrection*.

12. A tatami mat, a kind of rush mat serving as a floor covering in a traditional Japanese house, measures about three by six feet.

Undine

1. See note 2 of *Memories*.

2. A *tengu* is a demon of grotesque appearance, especially conspicuous for its long nose or beak. The *tengu* derives from a mountain god associated with large trees, and its evil doings include the abduction of children.

3. The adzuki bean was introduced early to Japan from China. The red color of the beans is considered auspicious, and they are often served on happy occasions.

Monkey Island

1. With respect to this paragraph, it should be pointed out that Dazai's own father was a landlord who employed tenant farmers to work his lands. With its reference to "white gloves," the paragraph seems to pick up on the portrayal of Victorian society suggested in the previous use of such language as "heavy snakeskin canes" and "gaudy feathers." It must be admitted that "belly-button" remains a cryptic usage in the passage; perhaps it is meant to suggest somewhat comically just how uncertain the monkey's grasp of human society actually is.

On the Question of Apparel

1. For a lively description of the incident at Ataka Barrier, see Ivan Morris, *The Nobility of Failure* (New York: New American Library, 1975), pp. 89–94.

2. An *odenya* is a rather plebeian sort of establishment specializing in *oden*, a kind of stew, and serving saké and beer as well.

3. *Tabi* are socks, usually of white cotton, made with a division between the big toe and the other four toes to accommodate the thong of the sandals or wooden clogs with which *tabi* are generally worn.

4. A *haori* is a loosely fitting jacket.

5. *Geta* are wooden clogs either worn barefoot or with *tabi*.

6. Kurume refers to cloth dyed according to the ikat method. This method is used principally in Chikugo and Kurume, towns on the southern island of Kyushu.

7. A *yukata* is a light summer kimono, and a *tanzen* is a large, padded kimono worn in cold weather.

8. According to Japan's mythology, Ninigi was the grandson of the Sun Goddess Amaterasu and was sent down from heaven to rule the Japanese islands in 660 B.C. The Fire Festival commemorates the fact that Kono-hanasakuya set fire to her parturition hut while giving birth to Ninigi's children as a means of proving they were indeed his. For a fuller account of the circumstances of this event, see Donald Philippi, trans. *The Kojiki* (Tokyo: University of Tokyo Press, 1968), pp. 144–47.

9. Paul Verlaine (1844–96) was a French symbolist poet whose "Chanson d'automne" became one of the most celebrated of the verse translations by Bin Ueda (1874–1916) in his epochal volume, *The Sound of the Tide* (1905).

A Poor Man's Got His Pride

1. The Eight Hells are those in which the sinner is subjected to the punishment of flames and heat. There is also a contrasting set of hells in which cold is the medium of chastisement.

The Monkey's Mound

1. Ihara Saikaku (1642–93) was a writer of popular fiction, especially noted for his *koshokubon*, or amorous works. *Five Women Who Loved Love* is a well-known example of this genre.

2. The Lotus Sutra is a Buddhist scripture that emphasizes devotion as the principal means of salvation.

3. The Pure Land sect represents a devotional strain in Japanese Buddhism from the tenth to the thirteenth centuries. It advocates faith in Amida, the Buddha of Unlimited Light, as the way to salvation.

4. Founder of the Nichiren sect of Buddhism, Nichiren (1222–82) entertained doubts early in life about the validity of Pure Land forms of Buddhism. His own religion em-

phasizes the superiority of the Lotus Sutra expressed in a chant commonly recited by his followers.

5. Sano Jirozaemon, as dictionaries usually render the name, was a farmer in what is now Tochigi Prefecture. Certain events of his life during the late seventeenth century, especially the slaying of the Yoshiwara courtesan Yatsuhashi, became the basis for a Kabuki play formally titled *Kagotsurube Sato no Eizame*, but more often referred to by the hero's name.

The Sound of Hammering

1. Ogata Kōrin (1658–1716) was a highly versatile artist who painted both portraits and natural scenes and who also designed textile patterns and utilitarian objects. Among his screen paintings, his depiction of irises is especially admired.

2. Ogata Kenzan (1663–1743), the younger brother of Kōrin, worked both as a potter and a painter. Despite a difference in temperament—Kōrin was a flamboyant romantic, Kenzan a scholarly recluse—Kenzan created a number of ceramic objects that his older brother helped to design and decorate.

3. Kyōka Izumi (1873–1939) is noted for his portrayal of the supernatural and the grotesque in a literary style that harked back to the Edo period.

Taking the Wen Away

1. Tōson Shimazaki (1872–1943) is probably better known as a novelist than as a poet. However, before he published his first novel, *The Broken Commandment* (1906), he had already established his reputation as a fine lyric poet, especially with the publication of *Seedlings* (1897).

2. *The Tales of Uji* is an anonymous collection of 197 tales, most likely compiled between 1180 and 1220. The

range of works is from simple folktales to stories of religion and the supernatural.

3. *The Chronicles of Japan*, or the *Nihon Shoki*, to give the work its well-known Japanese title, is the first officially sponsored account of the mythic origins and early history of Japan. The chronicle runs from the Age of the Gods to the reign of the Empress Jitō (686–97).

4. *The Collection of Ten Thousand Leaves (Man'yōshū)* is the first anthology of Japanese poetry, containing approximately 4,500 works in three distinct forms. The tale of how Urashima passed three years in an underwater realm only to return to his village and find everything changed and himself presently transformed into an old man is detailed in a *chōka*, or "long poem," in Book Three of the anthology.

5. A *fudoki*, or "gazetteer," was a compilation of reports in the eighth century on various natural features of a given region in Japan. The *Tango Gazetteer* survives only in fragmentary form.

6. The *Biographies of the Taoist Immortals* is a collection of marvelous tales compiled at the end of the eleventh century by Ōe no Masafusa (1041–1111).

7. Ōgai Mori (1862–1922) was one of Japan's greatest men of letters during the latter part of the Meiji period (1868–1912). He also pursued a career in the army medical corps, ultimately rising to the position of surgeon general.

8. Shōyō Tsubouchi (1859–1935) is best remembered as the first Japanese translator of Shakespeare's plays and as an advocate of reform of the novel and drama in Japan.

9. The Dance of Awa is performed as part of the Festival of the Dead in the town of Tokushima, the capital of a province in Shikoku, formerly known as Awa. The dance is said to have originated in the seventeenth century, when the local lord provided his subjects with too much saké on one occasion.

10. Shōki is a mythic being of Chinese origin whose principal function is the expulsion of demons. With his bulging

eyes, abundant red beard, and large frame, Shōki makes a frightening appearance.

Crackling Mountain

1. A figure of popular folk belief, the *Kappa* is a grotesque, adolescent-like creature that lives in water. When out of its element, the *kappa* must keep water in a saucer-shaped depression on top of its head in order to maintain its superhuman strength. The creature attacks both animals and people.

Printed in Poland
by Amazon Fulfillment
Poland Sp. z o.o., Wrocław